Seven Graves of Evil

By: Mary Reason Theriot

Dedication

Without the love and support of my family and friends, I would not have pursued this new path in life. I would especially like to thank those that have proofread copy after copy, to give me their honest opinion of the books.

Theresa, thank you so much for your continued encouragement. Without you, some of the characters would not have "come to life."

To my wonderful husband, Mat, your continued love and support mean the world to me.   I don't know what I would do without you in my life.   One of these nights I'm sure you will be able to sleep with both eyes closed. Eventually, I should run out of ideas... or maybe not. These books wouldn't be what they are without you pushing me forward.

To my fans, I would like to offer a special thank you for your continued support.

ISBN-10: 1-945393-62-9
ISBN-13: 978-1-945393-62-4

Also Available by Mary Reason Theriot:

The Hideaway
The Traveler
Dr. Frankenstein
Above Suspicion
Horror in the Night
Echoes on the Bayou
Seven Deadly Sins
A Kiss So Deadly
A Deadly Combination
Seduced by Voodoo
CarnEvil of Souls
Redemption
Haunted Visions
Love's Embrace
Secrets

www.maryreasontheriot.com

Prologue

Paul Fontaine walked into his son's room, "Come on, son. It's time."

Gerald rubbed his eyes, groggy from being woken so early, "Time? Time for what dad?"

Smiling, "I have a surprise for you. It's in my workshop."

Paul grinned when his son immediately perked up. Until now, his workshop had been forbidden to his son, and especially his wife. But Gerald was turning ten this year, and it was time for him to learn what made the Fontaine family so special – and why this plantation must stay in the Fontaine family.

While they walked under the moonlight to the workshop, Paul explained, "Harold Fontaine, III started this tradition generations ago. But, you must remember, everything we do and say can never be talked about to ANYONE. This is a tradition that must never be revealed."

"What is it dad?"

"You will soon find out."

Once they were safely in the workshop, Paul handed Gerald a knife, "It is time for you to become a man, son."

Gerald looked at the knife bewildered. "What is this for dad?"

Paul led his son to the table he had previously prepared for this special day, and removed the sheet covering their 'guest'. "It is time for you to learn what makes us so special."

Chapter 1
August 29, 1864

It was a hot and muggy summer night. The plantation was quiet as darkness enveloped the grounds. Aurora Fontaine feigned sleep next to her husband, Harold Fontaine, III. Soon she would meet her lover in the garden. She had a special gift for him. Something she bought in New Orleans, something she had managed to keep hidden from her prying husband's eyes.

As she slipped out from under the covers, her husband grabbed her arm in a firm grasp, "Where do you think you are going, my wife?"

Aurora had not expected her husband to wake up. She assumed she had given him more than enough of the potion the traiteur had sold her, "I can't sleep, my love." Kissing his forehead, she stated, "Go back to sleep."

He stared at her with a red, angry face, "No, cher, I know where you are going. How dare you dishonor my name by spreading your legs for that man! It is a disgrace!" Spittle landed on her face as he spoke with venomous rage. She had never seen him this angry.

"I will see you and your lover burn in hell before I allow you to leave this room once more." With a sinister sneer, he pinned Aurora underneath him, "Instead you will give *me* what you so freely give another man."

***

Harold Fontaine watched the tears flow down his wife's cheeks. A burning fury overwhelmed him. Raising his right hand, he slapped her hard across the left side of her face. How had his life come to this? He had been born the son of a French immigrant father and a genteel Englishwoman with a hefty dowry. When Harold was five, his parents had mapped out his future by arranging a marriage to the daughter of one of his mother's best friends. A family who held the same standing in this community as the Fontaines.

As a wedding present to the couple, his parents had ordered the construction of this impressive house on the bayou of the Mississippi River here in central Louisiana. Wooded swamps, sugar cane fields, cypress and gum trees surrounded the picturesque southern plantation, along with large live oak trees dripping with Spanish moss. Duck and deer were plentiful in this particular area. The most reliable source of transportation was a flatboat that could travel along the waterways and bayous that snaked through the area.

While Harold had been pleased with the arranged marriage and the new house, he had not known that his beloved wife had already given her heart to another man. As the years passed and Harold Fontaine accumulated more wealth and expanded his properties, he failed to notice his wife's indiscretions.

With each passing year, she had managed to keep her love affair secret while Harold became even more prominent in the community. Harold became obsessed with flaunting his wealth and started hosting parties after Sunday mass. The men gathered in the parlor after dinner to discuss crops, weather, and politics. The impending war with the North was on everyone's tongues. The men drank their bourbon whiskey and smoked cigars, while the women sat in the smaller parlor sipping their brandy and gossiping about the latest news around town.

If invited to a dinner party hosted by Harold Fontaine, word soon spread that it would be wise not to decline the invitation. Harold was a man not to be disrespected or trifled with.

It had been by pure misfortune that Harold had learned about his wife's affair. A slave had run away and Harold had stumbled upon the lovers tryst by chance. They were so caught up in the throes of passion that they never heard Harold approaching. At first, Harold wanted to murder both adulterers immediately, but soon thought better of it. He would punish his wife first, before handing out his own brand of justice to her secret lover.

Chapter 2

Aurora could not live one more day without seeing her lover. When she spiked Harold's drink at supper, she gave him double what the old traiteur woman had told her. This time, he should sleep until morning.

Shimmering waves of soft moonlight shined down on the bayou as she made her way to their secret rendezvous spot. The humid air had her clothes clinging to her.

The swamp was alive with nocturnal creatures. She cringed in fear as a snake slithered up the tree and curled itself around a thick limb as it searched for prey. Up ahead, a nutria rat hastily scurried into its home, not wanting to be the snake's supper. The crickets mating song filled the night as they called out for their mates.

It was dangerous to meet her lover, but she needed to see him. If Harold did discover them, it would be the end of both of their lives.

Aurora could barely contain her excitement as she slipped deeper into the night. Her heart pounded in her ears. She bit down on her bottom lip, trying to calm her nerves. Her eyes were sharp and alert, watching in case Harold had feigned sleep and was tracking her. An eternity had passed since she last saw her lover. She prayed he received the message and was waiting for her.

Beads of perspiration slowly made their way down her body. The stress of what she was doing would not dampen her mood. They may be forced to keep their love hidden, but their brief time together was pure heaven to her. Yes, their interactions were forbidden, but she would do anything for Grayson Manning.

She quickened her steps as she rushed to see her one true love. A chorus of night sounds urged her on. The discordant voices of frogs croaking confirmed the bayou was nearby. A splash sounded in the distance as an alligator slipped into the murky water. She was close to her destination.

The full moon hanging high overhead helped to light her way. Its silvery light danced across the water.

As soon as she saw Grayson, she leapt into his waiting arms. His calloused hands felt exquisite against her smooth skin. She looked deeply into his eyes and felt his love for her flow like a current into her soul.

Aurora whispered to her secret lover, "Grayson…"

"No. Don't say it."

Her eyes glittered with unspent tears, "I had to see you. My husband has been incorrigible."

Silencing her with a finger to her lips, "Hush now. You and I will run away together. You are the only woman for me. I am a slave to your love."

Trying to stay strong, she informed him, "No, we mustn't run away together. Harold would come after us and he would most certainly kill you. I cannot bear the thought of you dying, my love."

"I am nothing without you cher. We will find a place for us to love each other freely, far away from your husband."

Aurora looked deep into his eyes and shook her head, "You are too much of a romantic. We can never be together as long as Harold is alive." Holding back a shudder of fear, "Besides, his actions lately have given me cause for concern."

"You cannot live in that house any longer, we must leave."

"No, not yet. It is too dangerous."

Chapter 3

1990

Vivian clasped her hand over her mouth and scurried backwards, trying not to make a noise. She found it hard to believe the repulsive sight in front of her. This could not be the man she loved, the man whose children she wanted to bear, doing this horrid act. *Mon dieu. Please tell me that this isn't so.*

When she had followed him down here, she had feared she would catch him with another woman – but not like this. This was something no one would ever fathom a loved one capable of doing.

Frantic, she rushed up the stairs. Her heart felt as though it was pounding its way out of her chest. Fear pulsated through her bloodstream. *Was this his first victim? Or worse, has this been a pastime of his, and if so for how long?* Regardless of the answer, she must stop him. She cannot let this happen to another woman. *But how?* She had to find a way.

As she entered the house, the grandfather clock's ticking seemed to reverberate off the walls, as if it were counting down the seconds of her life. For now, she must remain calm – until she had a plan. She rushed up the stairs, holding onto the banner for support. Looking down the stairs behind her, she grimaced. She no longer saw the home she had loved, but instead she saw a house of horrors. The flickering light of the lamps gave off an eerie glow to the downstairs. For a moment, she swore she saw images of dismembered women walking out of the shadows and coming towards her. Their images plagued her thoughts.

"Help us! Please help us." they called out.

Tears pooled in her eyes. Her throat closed as an overwhelming sadness consumed her. Shaking her head, she told herself that now was not the time to give in to self-pity – nor fear. No, she must stay calm and outwit him. She would put an end to this.

Once in her bedroom, she quickly dressed for bed and climbed under the covers. The sound of his heavy footsteps on the stairs made her skin crawl. Her heart thudded loudly as she feigned sleep. There was no way she could pretend she did not know forever. No, she would have to end his life and soon.

Chapter 4
Present Day

Weeks had passed since Nicki Brady had discovered the old plantation. Now, she had to wait for the closing date. She had purchased Rosewood Plantation. Merely saying the word plantation summoned up images of oak lined drives, women drinking mint juleps on vast front porches, and massive homes framed with white columns.

Her mom, or her friends for that matter, could not believe that she had bought the old plantation. But she did. The house was hers, for better or worse.

When the realtor called, joy and panic had overwhelmed her all at once. She never thought the offer would be accepted. But it had! She had actually bought a piece of history, and was about to go down a new path, one that would be a veritable journey through time. Perhaps this would be the perfect tonic that she needed to soothe her dispirited soul. When she saw the ad, it had beckoned her and she became swept away by the home's underlying beauty.

She could not believe that she had done something like this. This was something Tom would do, not her. Yet she did it. She was really going to renovate an old plantation. She would see that one of Tom's dreams would be fulfilled.

Besides, it was time to move forward and living here was a continuous reminder of Tom. Everywhere she looked, all she saw was Tom. When she saw young couples smiling at each other, their happiness and energy, Nicki felt a gut-wrenching pain in her heart. But, perhaps that was better than feeling numb.

Even though she had prepared herself mentally for Tom's death, emotionally it had taken a toll on her. These last few years she had been living in a whirlpool, spinning round, and round but not going anywhere.

After his death, she had a difficult time deciding what to do with her life. She kept waiting for him to walk through the front door, as if these last few years had never happened. She could no longer live in the house that they had shared; it was time to move on. A part of her ached at the thought of leaving, though. She thought she had married the man she would grow old with, have his children, but instead she buried the one man who had made her feel alive and loved.

Cancer was a cruel disease, one that she had been helpless to fight against.

Chapter 5

Jake Mayon busied himself around the old plantation. There was still so much to do before the new owner would arrive. The chores tended to be endless here. The house was quickly deteriorating. The old hardwood floors creaked as he worked.

Stepping out onto the back porch, he stared out into the vast expanse of grounds that made up Rosewood Plantation. A part of him would miss working here. Hell, he had practically grown up here. Although these last few years had been more to keep Mrs. Fontaine company rather than to work. In all honesty, he had not minded spending time with Mrs. Fontaine. She had passed on interesting bits and pieces of local history and even talked about the history of her plantation. It was a shame that she did not have any children to pass this legacy on to; she would have made a great mother. Mrs. Fontaine was a true sweetheart and a loving person.

After listening to her stories, he understood more about the woman, and the struggles the family had gone through to keep the house. Through it all, the Fontaine family had managed to hang on to the plantation.

As he walked towards the bayou, he could smell the murky waters. The sound of birds chirping created a peaceful setting today. Yet ever since he was a child, he had feared venturing into these woods unarmed. Not only was there the countless number of snakes hiding and waiting for the perfect time to slither up your leg and bite you, but there were other creatures rumored to live in this part of the bayou as well.

The hairs on the back of his neck rose. He thought he heard something moving, but the woods were too dense to make anything out.

A breeze blew through the trees and he thought he heard a moan. Perhaps it could be from the ghosts of those long since passed. There had been rumors that Harold Fontaine III had killed his wife and hid her body somewhere on the property. The story went that she was leaving him for a lover. Could it be that Aurora Fontaine's spirit inhabited these woods?

Turning back toward the plantation, the sound of a branch being broken caught his attention. It was as if someone had stepped on it. But, then again, it could have been an animal moving about. Whatever it was, he had no intention of finding out what had made the noise.

His grandfather used to tell him stories about a rougarou that roamed these woods. A while back, several men fishing in the bayou swore something threw large rocks at their boat. Then a loud piercing shriek echoed through the air. It did not take the men long to leave and vow never to return.

Recently, a few had claimed to have seen a large, hairy creature lurking about. As a kid, he had sworn that something lived in the swamp.

When the noise sounded again, he glanced over his shoulder to see if someone was following him. As he entered the house, the quietness surrounded him. The sound of his footsteps bounced off the walls.

While he finished his chores, he noticed something seemed different about the house. He could not quite place it, but something was off. Perhaps it was his imagination playing tricks on him. Or was the house threatening to reveal its secrets – secrets that were best left untold.

Chapter 6

He eased the bateau through the murky water, observing the area before guiding the old boat to land. He hastily hid the boat underneath an ancient, moss covered, oak tree limb.

Before continuing any further, he listened for any tell tale signs of visitors. After being satisfied that the only creatures nearby were of the woodland variety, he silently moved down the leaf hidden path that would bring him to his destination.

Upon reaching the hidden doorway, he again checked to ensure he was alone. Once certain, he opened the door and quickly climbed down the rickety ladder. While it would have been easier to enter through the house, he couldn't risk someone being there. Silently, he cursed his misfortune once more.

His first stroke of bad luck had been when Mr. Fontaine had died. Mr. Fontaine had taken him on as an apprentice while he was a young boy. Neither of them had known that Mr. Fontaine's time here on this earth would be short lived. While he had been a good student and learned from his mentor, he had been too young at the time to take over his actual work. But thankfully he had found the journals, which explained in detail their joyous work.

So until he had reached an age where he could take over where Mr. Fontaine had abruptly stopped, he had studied – and dreamed. Oh, how he had dreamed and fantasized!

He would always be grateful that Mr. Fontaine had seen that potential in him, and brought him on as an apprentice. Mr. Fontaine had given him a reason for living – and for visiting Rosewood Plantation. If it had not been for Mr. Fontaine, his frequent trips over here would have been pure misery.

According to Mr. Fontaine, when Harold Fontaine, III had started this profession, he had sought out those who were new to the city. He invited them in and gave them a place to stay, especially those who didn't have the money for a decent place. They sought out those who would not be missed.

It was while experimenting with one particular "guest" that he had discovered watching her bleed to death had been particularly stimulating. But, he soon had realized he needed a way to easily dispose of what had remained of the body. This is when he began dismemberment.

But it was Harold Fontaine, IV, that had discovered the pleasurable experiences of dismembering a "guest" while they were alive. He was the true visionary and had passed on that legacy.

Once on firm ground in the hidden chamber, he took out his flashlight, turned it on and surveyed the room. He desperately missed the time spent in this room. If only that old biddy had done as he had requested and given him the house. But she had said that she didn't want to burden him with such a curse. She actually thought she was doing him a favor by selling this beloved place.

In the corners of the room, shadows began to take shape. *Perfect.* "I know you are here. I can feel your presence in the air."

He waited as each shadow took the shape of a man. "I need your help. I have failed. The house has been sold. I will no longer be able to continue our work here."

A low growling resonated from the apparitions, "Enough. I had no way of knowing that she would sell the house. But we managed to scare away Mrs. Fontaine, so we should be able to scare away this new owner."

The growling transformed into more of a low mumbling. He walked over to where the tools were hanging on a wall and picked up one of his favorite pieces. He turned around and faced the spirits, "Besides, if we can't scare them away – then perhaps they will meet an unfortunate end."

Chapter 7

Rosewood Plantation loomed in front of her. It was as if the house was hoarding a dark and mysterious secret, only to be shared with a select few. She took a deep breath and tried to calm her nerves. *You can do this. This is your future. No more past, no more death. It's time to move forward.*

The exterior of the house needed more work than she had anticipated. It was dingy and needed a good cleaning. Yet she could see the grandeur of the home behind the tattered façade. The property surrounding the home oozed with southern charm, from the weeping willows to the ancient oak trees dripping with Spanish moss.

The current caretaker obviously did the bare minimum to maintain the grounds. She could see that at one time there had indeed been a splendid and spacious garden in the front of the home. Now all that remained were several overgrown shrubs that begged to be trimmed.

The flowerbed would be the perfect project for her, physically and psychologically. She would clear away the old debris, prune the dead branches, rejuvenate the soil, and plant new flowers. This would represent resurrection, rebirth, and a fresh start.

Graceful twin arches of a double staircase lead to the second floor. Tall arched windows and ornate white columns framed the porch. Gothic turrets crowned the corner bay windows. The wide, front door had large windows on either side. There were more rooms and alcoves in this sprawling mansion than she would ever use.

Towards the back of the house, several slave quarters remained standing. Even the overseer's cottage, while uninhabitable, still stood. After some renovation, they could be turned into small cottages that could be rented out.

There was also an old barn, a stable, and various workshops on the property. Chimneys flanked opposite ends of the house. She wondered what it would have been like back when the plantation was built. It must have been bustling with activity, brimming with life.

Instead, a cloud of gloom hung overhead. As Nicole Brady pulled the moving truck in front of the plantation, she vowed to change the depressing appearance of the house. While looking at the property she imagined the grand parties that had been held here on sultry summer nights. She could envision how dashing the men looked in their three piece suits and how beautiful the women were in their elegant gowns.

She was full of giddy optimism and hopefulness as she opened the truck door. The land, the house, and the outbuildings were all hers. Every penny she had was tied up in this venture. A secret part of her hoped the house was haunted.

She hadn't decided what she wanted to do when the property was restored, but she had plenty of time for that. Oscar, her labradoodle, was eager to get out of the moving truck as well. Currently he was peering out the window with his tail wagging, waiting to see his new home. No sooner than she opened the door, he rushed outside.

A man's voice greeted her as she closed her door, "Ms. Brady, welcome. I trust you had a pleasant drive."

The man appeared to be perhaps mid forties, wearing a pair of jeans that had seen better days, a well-worn pair of work boots and a t-shirt that molded his body. Smiling broadly, he extended his hand, "I'm Jake Mayon, the caretaker. We spoke several times on the phone. It is a pleasure to finally meet you."

Shaking his hand warmly, "Mr. Mayon, I'm pleased to meet you as well." Smiling up at him, "I guess we have a lot to talk about, don't we?"

"Please, call me Jake. When I hear Mr. Mayon I look for my dad."

Laughing, "Please call me Nicki."

"I did manage to get a good bit of the house cleaned once I found out you would be moving down here. The water is working, for now at least, and the electricity was never turned off. Poor Mrs. Vivian could no longer live out here by herself, and she never had any children of her own. I tried to do what I could, but one person can't keep up with everything that a house like this requires. Unless, of course, they live here."

For a moment, Nicki thought she heard an undertone of resentment in his response. Brushing it off, she responded, "Well, I guess I will need you to show me around. I plan on hiring locals as much as I can for any repairs needed to restore the house."

"You definitely need to hire an electrician. The wiring in the house is ancient, but the bones of the house are good. It is a solid house."

When Nicki stepped onto the front porch, she noticed that the hardwood boards underneath her sneakers had lost their shine and were developing cracks, and the white paint on the pillars was peeling. The floorboards creaked as she walked inside.

When Nicki walked in the front door, her breath was taken away. A gorgeous oak staircase was the focal point of the foyer, leading straight up to the second floor. Its curved balcony railings dominated the foyer. Near the front door, a large, vintage grandfather clock with a massive pendulum grabbed her attention.

"What about the items she left behind?"

"As far as I know, it goes with the house. The only surviving family she has left is on her side, and she believed everything should stay with the house. You see, the house was her husband's legacy and not hers. I sometimes felt that she hated living here, but never pressed her on the matter when we talked."

The huge entryway was simply breathtaking. The chandelier, although in need of a serious cleaning, cast glorious prisms of light around the room. It amazed her that something this beautiful had survived all of this time. People have a tendency to destroy older fixtures to make way for new, more modern ones.

Beyond the grandfather clock was the doorway leading to the dining room. On the other side of the hallway was the doorway to a large parlor. There was also a smaller sitting room and a library off the parlor. Off of the dining room was the expansive kitchen. Nicki looked around and noticed the peeling paint on several of the walls. The hardwood floors were scuffed, but still beautiful. Surveying her surroundings, she stated, "There are some nice pieces of furniture here."

As they walked through the dining room into the butler's pantry, which led into the kitchen, Oscar let out a low growl and refused to walk into the tiny thruway. "I don't know what has gotten into him." Nicki tried to coax Oscar into the room, but even she had to admit there was a dampness in here that she couldn't explain. There was also an odor that she couldn't pinpoint. Picking Oscar up, she carried him into the kitchen so they could continue the tour of the house.

The second floor consisted of bedrooms, with not only private sitting rooms but also private restrooms. "Isn't it unusual for plantations from this era to have so many bathrooms?"

Nodding his head, "The family that built the house was well off. They enjoyed flaunting their wealth. He knew that when people stayed, they would go back and tell everyone that not only did the house have indoor plumbing, but each guest had their own 'facilities' as well."

Nicki was taken aback to see that most of the rooms had sparse furnishings. She also learned the small, cramped rooms were actually nurseries or sewing rooms. Nicki had a ton of questions she wanted to ask, but she also didn't want to scare Jake away with her endless questions.

Once back downstairs, Jake asked her, "Do you plan on staying the night or did you plan on going into town?"

With a chuckle, she confessed, "I have been so anxious to get started on the house, that I made sure to pack bedding and all the necessities. I packed my mattress and box spring last so it would be the first thing unloaded.”

“That may not have been a bad idea. I’m not sure how old the beds are, but the mattresses are rather lumpy.”

“Do you live out here?”

Shaking his head, “Mais non. I will help you out as long as you need me, but I go home each night. Mrs. Fontaine hired me to help her keep the place up, but it really does need a live-in owner.”

Looking at his watch, he stated, “Well, if you want to get that moving truck unpacked before dark, we best get to it.”

With the two of them working together, it didn’t take long to make a dent in the overstuffed moving truck. “What happened to your hand?”

Jake shrugged his shoulders, “I wasn’t paying attention the other day and cut it.”

She thought to herself that it must have been a pretty bad cut for him to use such thick bandages.

Jake asked her, “Which room did you want to sleep in? Perhaps the parlor for the night?”

“No, I will sleep in the room that overlooks the bayou.”

Jake hesitated briefly, "Are you sure that you don't want to spend the night in the parlor for your first night?"

"No. I'm going to jump in this feet first all the way."

Shrugging his shoulders, he helped her get the box spring and mattress set up in the room. "We can store the old set in one of the spare rooms for now."

As the day came to an end, Jake became eager to leave, "Would you care to walk down to the bayou before I leave?"

The question took Nicki by surprise, but she had to admit that it would be a pleasant respite from unloading boxes. "That would be nice."

It was a lovely stroll to the bayou. The older trees had to be some of the largest she had ever seen. Their tips stretched to the top of the house and patches of bushes and vines crowded the spaces around their trunks. She inhaled deeply and savored the smell. The air felt cleaner and crisper here. She could even pick up faint animal noises from the woods.

As they made their way down the trail, Nicki looked back at the house. She marveled at how majestic the house looked from where she stood. Countless hours of hard labor had to have gone into the building of this house. She could almost envision the pathway they were walking on being used as a wagon road at one time.

Tall grass, wildflowers, and an occasional weed grew at will. She relished the fragrant aroma, sweeter than any perfume she could purchase. She could even smell the tantalizing scent of the pine straw that lined the surface of the trail. Up above the branches of the oak trees, heavily laden with dripping spanish moss, reminded her of a lover's embrace. Their dense outstretched branches had seamlessly grown together over time.

Nearing the bayou, she noticed how the air became cooler. She could hear the water lapping against the bank. At one time this might have been considered the main entrance, since most visitors would have arrived by water.

Once at the bayou, she noticed how the oak trees offered a protective cover over certain areas and how the weeping willow limbs draped elegantly over the water and danced as the wind gently blew. She imagined what this area would look like when the dogwoods were in full bloom. She stood awestruck at the beautiful sight in front of her, and it was all hers.

She could already feel the stress of the day melting away. She watched as frogs hopped along the bank and the fish jumped and made ripples in the water.

She could see herself spending countless hours down here taking in nature's true beauty.

When they arrived back at the house, he asked "Are you sure you will be okay? It can get spooky if you aren't used to it."

"I will be fine. Besides, I will be so busy unpacking boxes that I won't notice I am alone."

Laughing, he said his goodbyes and drove off. As she watched Jake's vehicle drive away, a feeling of being watched overcame her. Glancing towards the woods, she saw the outline of a man standing there. Then in the blink of an eye, he was gone. Perhaps her eyes were playing tricks on her. Shaking her head, she went back inside.

As she passed by the mirror hanging in the entryway, she caught a glimpse of her disheveled state. Her auburn hair had come free from its confines; several unruly wisps curled and framed her face while others were off in various directions. She removed the hair band from her hair and pulled her hair up into another tight ponytail. The smeared makeup beneath her bright, hazel eyes added to her fatigued appearance. Sighing at her reflection, she wondered what kind of impression she had given Jake Mayon. Although, truthfully, it didn't matter. She hadn't set out the impress the man with her looks anyway.

With Jake gone, Nicki felt a little more at ease exploring her new house. She marveled at its size. Truth be told, it felt more like a small hotel than a home. It held far more space than she could ever imagine. Downstairs, past the laundry room, she had discovered a large empty room that may have been used as a ballroom at one time.

Walking upstairs, she started inspecting the bedrooms. When she entered one of the bedrooms, the smell astounded her. *Phew. It reeks in here.* She made a mental note that this was one of the first rooms that would need to be scrubbed clean and repainted.

She looked around to see if she could find what caused the horrid smell. Not finding anything, she closed the door and continued to explore the rest of the house. The room across from hers was decorated in varying shades of maroon. Gold leafy designs adorned the wallpaper, which was peeling in several places. Nicki inspected the damage and was pleased to see that the tears in the wallpaper revealed the original plaster walls. The bedspread and curtains looked decades old, as did the limp pillows that were haphazardly stacked on the bed.

Returning to the staircase, she swore she saw a shadow dart across the hallway. A shiver of fear snaked down her spine as she followed the dark mass's movements. Without warning, it disappeared into thin air. *What happened? Where did it go?* It had to be a trick of light.

She glanced around once more before descending the stairs. Her cell rang. Her mother's voice bellowed from the other end of the line as she answered it, "Honey, why didn't you call me this morning? You did say that you would call me when you arrived."

"I'm sorry. As soon as I made it to the plantation, the caretaker was ready to show me around. We have been steady working."

"Well, I was worried about you and all. I just knew since I didn't hear from you that something bad had happened."

Nicki cringed at the disappointment she heard in her mother's voice, "I'm really sorry to worry you mom. I didn't mean to do that. I was just so excited when I arrived."

"Is the plantation what you were expecting? Sometimes real estate companies swap out photos to lure in potential buyers."

"No, it is absolutely gorgeous here. I can't wait for you to come see it in person."

"Well, does it need a lot of renovations? I hate to see you throw your money away on an old house when you could have built one a lot cheaper."

"Oh, but mom, you could never build a house like this today. You should see the artisanship in the woodwork. It is like nothing I have ever seen. Whoever built this house took pride in their work."

With doubt in her voice, "I don't know. Those old houses can be drafty. You may end up spending more than you want on electricity every month."

Biting back a sigh, "I'm sure it will be fine. I want to do this for Tom. This is something he dreamed of doing."

"Honey, I know that you miss Tom, but could it be that purchasing this old plantation is another way to keep him alive in your memories?"

Nicki held back the tears building up inside of her, "No, this is a way for me to show that his life did have meaning to me. I am doing something that he couldn't accomplish before his death."

Huffing, "Well, if you say so, honey. I just don't want you to throw away the rest of your life on a husband who has left this earth. I know Tom wouldn't want you pining away for him, either. He would want you to get on with your life."

"I am getting on with my life. I had to do this, not only for Tom, but for me. I need my life to have some meaning. Maybe by restoring this old house I can find the passion for life I once had with Tom."

"Well, if you need anything, anything at all, you give me a call."

"I will, I promise. Listen, it is getting late and if I want to sleep in an actual bed tonight I need to get back to work."

"Well, I love you."

"I love you too."

Nicki didn't give her mother a chance to continue with the conversation. She hung up. Besides, her mother would call again first thing in the morning, trying to convince her that this had been a bad idea. Her mother wanted her to move back home with her, but that was the last thing that Nicki wanted to do.

Now that it was dark outside, the moonlight danced across the bayou in shimmering waves. If it weren't so muggy, it would be a perfect night to watch the fireflies. She was astonished at how peaceful it was. She felt as if she was in her own little corner of the world, cut off from everyone else.

Her mother's conversation flitted through her mind. Would she be able to handle this house? She had never done anything like this before. She has no experience in renovating a house.

Now, more than before, she missed Tom. She missed their time together and talking about their day over a glass of wine. Mostly, she missed being wrapped in his arms, letting his embrace wash her troubles away.

Even while he had been dying of cancer, Tom had been her rock. He had died in her arms at home, instead of in the hospital. She had felt helpless as the cancer spread and ravaged Tom's body. But in the end, he had lost his fight to live and cancer had won. Tom had finally found peace and was no longer in pain.

Nicki tried to stop her thoughts from wandering back to Tom and his death. She tried not to think about how much she missed him. Thinking about Tom would break her resolve and open the wound again.

Nicki walked into the kitchen and started unpacking several of the boxes. While putting away the dishes, the lights began to flicker. Unexpectedly, total darkness surrounded her as the lights went off. Her heart pounded wildly against her chest. She thought she heard footsteps behind her. She paused to listen. There it was again, a creaking noise. *So what*, she asked herself. Old houses creak.

There was an ominous feeling in the air. Even though she couldn't see anything or smell anything, she sensed something. She was certain that there was someone in the room with her. Someone ready to pounce on her. Which was ridiculous, ghosts didn't pounce. They weren't supposed to have physical power, and they most definitely weren't supposed to hurt people – or did they?

She had to swallow back a scream when a raspy voice called out, "Nicki…"

Calling out, she asked, "Jake is that you? Did you forget something?"

Her stomach clenched when no one answered back. Feeling her way around the kitchen, she found the light switch and flipped it up and down several times in hopes of turning the lights back on. After the third time she realized that she would have to go check the breaker. However, the lights unexpectedly flickered and turned back on. Relief washed over her. Everything had remained the same as before the lights went out. She walked around the house to find whoever had called out her name, but instead only confirmed that she was indeed alone. Shaking her head, she told herself that it must have been the wind. And as far as the lights going out, Jake had warned her that the wiring needed to be upgraded.

By ten o'clock Nicki was exhausted. She started to turn off the lights downstairs and stopped herself, recalling Jake's statement earlier about leaving the lights on at night. Perhaps since she was unfamiliar with the house, it wasn't a bad idea. Still, a part of her wondered why he had made that comment.

Making her way around the boxes and other obstacles, she noticed how, despite the summer heat, the house had a chill to it.

As she headed upstairs, she watched as the shadows settled around the house. She had to admit that this house had a poignant hint of elegance about it even in the shape it was currently in. While she walked up the stairs, a faint breeze blew through her hair and a whisper, "Nicki." When she looked around, though, she didn't see anything. Shrugging her shoulders, she must be more exhausted than she realized.

Once upstairs, she went into the bathroom and prepared her a hot bath in the old claw foot tub. Her body ached in places she had long since forgotten.

While she waited for the tub to fill, she brushed her teeth. Staring at the reflection in the mirror, she made a mental note that the walls in here needed to be painted. It didn't help that the lights were all dim in the house. More than likely the light fixtures had years of dust coated on them. A good cleaning should bring some much needed light into the dreary rooms.

Pulling her hair up, she stepped into the freshly cleaned tub and luxuriated in the hot, cherry almond scented bubble bath.

Oscar came in and curled up comfortably on the bath mat beside the tub. While Oscar napped, Nicki enjoyed her bath. Only when the water became lukewarm did she get out of the tub. It had been a long, tiring day and she would have no problem falling asleep.

As Nicki brushed her hair, Oscar's ears pricked high and he let out a low, yet menacing, growl. Nicki jumped at his sudden behavior. Placing the brush down on the bathroom counter, she bent down to comfort Oscar. "It's okay boy. There is nothing to be scared of." Opening the bathroom door, "Come on, let's go to bed."

Oscar stared at the open door briefly before following his master. Inside the bedroom, dim, pale moonlight filtered in through the curtains. Shadows danced around the room. She let out a groan as she climbed into bed. Her overextended muscles ached and throbbed from the exhaustive work. Settling into bed, she listened to the sounds that echoed around her. No sooner than her head hit the pillow, she drifted to sleep.

Around four o'clock in the morning sounds from the bayou merged with the groaning of the house, causing Nicki to stir in her sleep. The faint sound of footsteps woke her. She listened intently, making sure that it wasn't a dream. All that greeted her was the sound of a few crickets chirping. With a mental shrug, she turned on her side, wrapped the comforter around her and tried to go back to sleep.

As she drifted off, she could hear the ticking of the grandfather clock. She let the tick tock rhythm lull her to sleep.

The footsteps were back. This time they sounded as if they were right outside her room. The faint smell of pipe tobacco teased her nostrils. The air around her turned cold. She had to be dreaming. If there was someone walking the halls of the house, Oscar would be barking. Yet he was asleep at the foot of the bed. She pulled the covers tightly around her body and surveyed her surroundings. Hugging a pillow close to her, she drifted off to sleep once more.

The next morning, after letting Oscar out for his morning rituals, Nicki grabbed her purse and keys and headed into town for some much needed supplies.

It took her most of the morning to get familiar with the town she would be calling home. While there, she treated herself to a quick breakfast of beignets and café au lait. Afterwards, she headed to the hardware store for sanding supplies and a variety of other items she would need to work on the plantation.

At the grocery store, she stocked up on coffee, quick meals, dry cereal, and plenty of dog food for Oscar. As much as she would enjoy exploring the quaint town, she needed to return home and get to work. Although she had to admit, it was difficult to avoid the temptation of the antique shops. It was as if they were luring her inside.

Chapter 8

The bayou water was as still as the night sky. And as dark as his heart – that was if he had one. No light dared to shine here. Only a sliver of moonlight made its way through the dense canopy of branches overhead.

This part of the swamp had a life of its own. The tall, bald cypress trees stood guard as the weeping willows bowed their limbs as if in fear of him. The live oaks with their twisted trunks and gnarled branches looked as if they would reach out and grab him at any moment, as if they could swallow him whole – erasing him from the face of this earth.

As he made his way to his destination, glowing red eyes of an alligator peered out from the reeds of the water's surface. After all, night is the time for the hunter and the hunted. A thick mist moved in over the murky bayou water, hovering between the trunks of the tupelos and sweet gum trees.

Of all the predators out tonight, he was the most cunning and vicious. His motivation was not for survival but for the thrill of the kill. There was an overwhelming rush in holding another's life in your hands and savoring the power to snuff it out.

Somewhere in the distance, a panther screamed and broke the silence of the night. A sly smile formed on his face as he recalled his latest kill. He could still smell the blood as it mingled with the murky aroma of the bayou. To him it wasn't just another kill, another rush, another dizzying high. No, it was something much more. It was pure, raw power. Nothing could beat the exhilaration of witnessing unadulterated fear pulse through a victim's body. The frantic pounding of her heart beat, and then the slow ebbing as it faded into nothingness. The feel of warm blood on his skin was even more seductive than sex.

Once he arrived at his destination, he watched the house. He felt his blood begin to boil, as if he would actually char from the inside out. All he saw was red.

Anger flowed over him, every muscle tense, nerves strung tight as piano wire. She wasn't supposed to be here, no one was ever supposed to be here. He had finally scared the old woman enough to where she wanted to move out of her family home. For a while, he had feared that she would die in the house without ever moving out. He had grown tired of curbing his appetite and sneaking around at night to indulge in his one true passion. His plan had eventually worked and she had become too afraid to keep living there in the end. However, he had hoped that she would leave the house to him; after all, she owed him for keeping her company over the years. Instead, she had moved into a nursing home and put the house up for sale, leaving him nothing in return. And, worse, even the banks refused to loan him the money.

He must fight the anger. Anger drove a man to lose control. Anger made a man behave foolishly, irrationally. He refused to give in to the anger; he was a genius after all. A person as brilliant as him was always in control. He did NOT make mistakes. But the monster lurking inside him had grown insatiable. He could feel the hunger growing to unbearable dimensions. He must satisfy this hunger, and soon.

He shut his eyes and breathed in the heady scent of the fragrant magnolia and sweet olive trees, mingled with the insidious aroma of the bayou. The scents, the gentle caress of the warm breeze against his face, the chorus of frogs calling out to their mates, calmed him, and brought a rush of memories.

He had been a gangly child, unsure of himself. Until he met Mr. Fontaine. He taught him that there was more to life than simply existing. He quickly became his mentor. Now the apprentice had surpassed the master.

A movement from the upstairs window shook him out of his reverie. He watched as she removed her hair free from its confines. Long and wavy, the strands gleamed a tempting auburn in the light. He swallowed as he felt the stirrings of desire between his legs and forced down the lump caught in his throat. He actually wanted her, no ached for her with a need like none other.

Looking at her stirred something deep inside of him, something he thought he was incapable of feeling. He could actually hear his heart beat, felt his blood course through his veins. As he peered at her through the window, he began to wonder if perhaps she was the one he had been waiting for.

Driving away from the house, he checked the rearview mirror. Eyes the color of warm honey stared back at him. "Bedroom eyes" is what several women had told him. He let out a soft chuckle. Those foolish women had thought he could be seduced. It was only when they had looked deep into his eyes that they caught the glimmer of the man he truly was, and by then it was too late.

Chapter 9

A soft wind blew while Paige Sommers walked down the narrow street toward home. It had been a long night, but she preferred working as a waitress at the bar rather than working the streets of New Orleans. One thing for certain was the night life around the small town of Lost Bayou was a lot quieter. By midnight in New Orleans, the town was coming to life, where here everything was winding down.

The breeze was a welcome reprieve to the oppressive heat. The heat of the day had merged with the dampness of the bayou and created a rolling fog across the land. As she walked, she listened to the wind as it rustled the leaves on the trees. It was almost peaceful walking home. Even the moon helped to create a romantic setting, if only she had someone to enjoy it with.

A noise behind her caught her attention. Laughing nervously, "You scared me."

The man gave her a shy smile but made no attempt to move towards her. Instead, he continued to stare at her. Although slightly overweight, he was still a handsome man. She had seen him in the bar several times, but he was always alone, as if he was overly shy.

The way he kept staring at her tonight put her on edge. Out of instinct, she reached into her purse, fumbling for the pepper spray. Not wanting to waste any more time, she continued walking toward home, her pace a little faster now.

She never felt him strike her. Her face slammed against the sidewalk. She tried to scream, but a burning deep in her back took her breath away.

***

He carried her back to her house with complete ease. He promptly secured her to the bed, making sure the gag was tight enough to prevent any noise from escaping. He ran his finger across the skin of her arms, the upper swell of her breasts. Her dark hair pooled in shimmering waves at her shoulders. *Oh, how he had missed this.* It had been far too long since he released that monster living inside him. But that would soon change.

While he stared down at her, her body tensed as her subconscious began to sense the danger that her conscious mind wasn't ready to accept.

He watched her take a hard swallow. One that was so loud he could swear that he actually heard it. Like a frightened animal, she stared into the eyes of the predator that was about to strike.

She laid there, paralyzed in fear. He inhaled deeply, briefly closing his eyes and reveling in the scent of fear that oozed out of her pores. Fear had such a distinct aroma. It was sharp and tangy, with a biting edge.

Oh, yes, he was going to enjoy this one. Very much.

She began panting when he caressed the cold steel of the blade along her body. Her breaths came out in short bursts. The knife repeatedly plunging into her. He felt so alive. The warmth of her blood gave him a renewed strength. Looking down at her body brought an elated feeling of raw power in him. The pale face looked clownish with the rouged cheeks, smeared lipstick, slack mouth, and open eyes staring up unseeing. Perhaps she was looking up to the heavens, pleading for mercy and begging for deliverance. But it was too late for either.

She would be found, eventually, but no one would find him.

He was too clever, too cunning. No one would ever suspect him.

Chapter 10

Detective James Cook appeared to be an easy-going, low-key type person. A trait that served him well when interrogating suspects. His voice lulled and he was soft-spoken. Everything about him seemed mild-mannered – except looks could be deceiving. He had a sharp gaze and moved with the agility of a large cat.

He had also earned the respect and friendship of his brothers in blue. He had come to love the town of Lost Bayou and was proud to serve with his fellow officers here. He had grown tired of living in larger cities where there was an abundance of crime, and no matter how many criminals he put away, there was another one right behind him, ready to take the person's place. He wanted to live in a place where he felt like he was making a difference.

He thought he was dreaming when the phone rang. As he went to answer the phone, he glanced over at the alarm clock and groaned when he saw that it was barely three a.m. A call this early in the morning meant a homicide. "Cook speaking."

He listened while the dispatcher relayed all the information. "I'm on my way."

He jumped out of bed and called his partner, Detective Adam Veret, "We have a homicide. The roommate came home and found the body."

Detective Veret simply stated, "I'll be waiting outside for you."

James didn't bother with a shower. He grabbed the outfit he removed a few short hours ago and headed out the door. It was going to be one of those days.

After he picked up Adam, they drove straight to the crime scene. When they arrived, the scene was in complete chaos. The media had already caught wind of the murder and was on scene as well as more than a dozen police cruisers. Several police officers were attempting to keep everyone a good distance from the scene.

As he walked to the house, one of the younger officers working the perimeters informed him, "Sir, Dr. Metcalf called to say he is almost here."

Adam yelled, "Get these media vans out of the way so the crime scene vans can get in here. Let's not keep Dr. Metcalf waiting."

It took ten minutes to get the media to move further away from the scene so Dr. Metcalf and the crime scene techs could get in with their vans.

When James spoke to the responding officer, he could tell this was his first homicide. The poor guy had never been exposed to such carnage before. Even from this distance, the scent of blood and death hung heavy in the air.

"Sir, how could someone do that? The killer literally dismembered her."

James knew this case would leave a permanent mark on the young rookie's mind. Once inside the house, he instructed one of the crime scene techs, "I want you to photograph the crime scene from every angle. We need accurate measurements on the position of the body. I want plenty of pictures. Don't worry about how many rolls of film you use, just get it done."

To the responding officer, he instructed, "Make sure you take plenty of notes regarding everything you saw, not just when you arrived, but also during and after the discovery of the body. Don't leave anything out. No matter how unimportant it seems to you, it may turn out to be vital evidence afterward."

Another crime scene tech was combing the house for evidence. James instructed him, "I want you to catalog everything you take. Mark down everything in the immediate vicinity. Write down what you removed and the location it was removed from."

To everyone, he announced, "I want to be overly thorough with this crime scene. Take your time and be careful. I don't want anything missed. Understood?"

They chimed in unison, "Yes, sir."

He had a feeling they were going to be dealing with a serial killer before long, although he did not want to breathe a word of that possibility to anyone yet. What may be worse though was that it looked like they may be searching for a highly organized killer.

Organized killers tended to have a mission or plan in mind when they began. These killers never acted on the opportunity or impulse. The only thing that bothered him, however, was they stalked their victims beforehand and never left the scenes in a frenzy.

This type of killer took their time with the body and scene to make sure that he left no evidence behind. This killer displayed an extreme amount of rage on the victim.

It had taken her a long time to die. While he stared down at the carnage left behind by the killer, he noted the series of shallow cuts that plagued her body. This killer meant to torture this woman, and cruelly. Death had not come to her easily.

Her arms and legs had been restrained and her mouth gagged to keep her from screaming out in raw pain.

He watched the flurry of activity around him as Dr. Metcalf walked towards the body. He looked over at James, "What have we got?"

"DOA. The body hasn't been moved. We wanted you to have a look at it first."

Dr. Metcalf grimaced when he saw the body. After directing his assistants to remove the body, he informed the detectives. "I will have the autopsy reports for you as soon as possible." He continued to bark orders to his personnel before leaving the scene.

* * *

Dr. Metcalf whistled softly while he prepared to work on his latest patient. He lifted the sheet that covered what remained of her mutilated body. His gaze observed her wounds. It bothered him how precise the wounds were. This killer knew what he was doing.

"I'm sorry you had to cross my slab, my dear," he whispered.

He was always sorry to see what horrors another human being could inflict on their own. But gruesome murder was the worst. It was because these poor people never died easy. Especially this latest victim.

Of all the deaths he had witnessed, hers made him shudder. "Let's get you cleaned up before your loved ones come pay you a visit."

His main focus when loved ones came was to show the body, be kind to the grieving party, and help them leave as soon as possible. The morgue was no place for the living – or at least most of them. He had felt at home here, and had wanted to give the dying a voice. He wanted to help those who needed justice.

***

When James and Adam made it to the coroner's office that afternoon, he found the young woman's parents waiting for them. Mr. Sommers looked down at his wife, "Why don't you stay here? I can do this by myself."

She shook her head, "No, I want to do this with you."

James tried to reason with her, "Mrs. Sommers, trust me, you don't want to remember your daughter like this."

She shook her head, "No, I must see her. I have to know that it is her."

Dr. Metcalf met them in the reception area of the coroner's office. "Dr. Metcalf, this is Mr. and Mrs. Sommers. Mr. and Mrs. Sommers, this is the medical examiner, Dr. Metcalf."

Dr. Metcalf shook each of their hands, "I'm sorry we have to meet under such a somber occasion. If you will sign in, I will wait for you in the back. Detective Cook will bring you back when you are ready." Dr. Metcalf had said those words more times than he cared to admit - but he meant them. He hated seeing people in pain as they viewed their loved ones.

Before entering the morgue, James knocked on the door to let Dr. Metcalf know that they were there. He opened the door, "You can come in. She is ready."

James led the distraught parents into the room. Inside the room stood a steel table with a sheet covering a prone figure. An involuntary shiver ran through James's body. This was one aspect of the job that he despised. The morgue was cold and impersonal. The air smelled of chemicals and death. There was no possible way to bring comfort or to ease the pain of those left behind as they came to identify the body.

Mrs. Sommers moved towards the table in slow motion. Dr. Metcalf pulled down the sheet. The good doctor had spent a considerable amount of time cleaning the victim's face. She actually looked as if she might be sleeping.

The doctor only revealed her face, leaving the rest of the body covered. There was no reason for the parents to have those images imprinted in their minds.

Mr. Sommers wrapped his arms around his wife. She took in a sudden breath and went pale; her eyes rolled back and her knees buckled.

Thankfully, Mr. Sommers still had his arms around her as she fainted. Dr. Metcalf rolled the wheelchair he kept handy for these occasions over to her. James helped Mr. Sommers settle her into the chair.

Once back in his office, Dr. Metcalf reached into his pocket and broke out the smelling salts. He waved it under her nose. She came to with a start and pushed his hand away from her. She stuttered, "I… I… I'm fine now."

Dr. Metcalf asked, "Are you sure?"

She nodded her head, "Really, I am fine. I never expected that reaction, but it was more than I could take." She wiped the tears from her eyes. "I don't know what I am going to do without my baby. I never even got the opportunity to apologize to her or reconcile our differences." Great, heaving sobs began to shake her body. Dr. Metcalf handed her a box of tissue from his desk as her husband took her in his arms.

This was the part of the notification James hated, the tears, and the emotions. He was not good at providing comfort and he feared this killer was just getting started.

Mr. Sommers applied a firm grasp to James's shoulder, "Please find the monster that did this to my daughter. We may have become estranged, but she didn't deserve to die and especially in this manner."

James patted Mr. Sommers' back, "I promise I will do everything in my power to find the person responsible for your daughter's death."

The next morning James picked up a copy of The Harold to see exactly what Frank Ingalls had reported in the paper. He didn't like to admit the man's writing was captivating. Now he understood why the paper had hired him. His writing seemed to draw readers in.

While he read the article, he wondered how he managed to report about some of the details of the case. He stated several facts that he knew the public was not privy to. That may be something they needed to follow up on. He didn't see someone at the sheriff's office releasing information to the press, but there was a chance that someone had a big mouth.

Chapter 11

Feeling restless, Nicki decided to venture out for the day. On the outskirts of town, she found what she was looking for, an antique store. When she walked in the doors to the shop, she felt at home. Tom and she used to love walking through antique stores and flea markets in search of hidden treasures. They would even stop at out of the way pawn shops and thrift stores. They never knew what they would find.

The inside of this particular antique store had shelves and shelves full of knick-knacks, glassware, and various items.

As Nicki looked around, the shop owner came to check on her, "Good morning miss. Is there anything in particular you need?"

Shaking her head, "No, sir. I am new to the area and wanted to do a little sight seeing."

"Ah, you must be the one who purchased the old Rosewood Plantation?"

Laughing, she extended her hand, "I did indeed. I'm Nicki Brady."

"Well, Ms. Brady, welcome to Lost Bayou. If there is anything I can help you with please let me know."

Looking at Nicki with interest, he asked, "Pardon me miss, but do you mind if I ask a question?"

"No, what is it?"

"Mrs. Fontaine swore the place was evil. She had hoped that by selling it, she would break the curse that it had. Have you seen any ghosts?"

Nicki shook her head at the question, "If the house is haunted, the ghosts have yet to make their presence known to me."

Leaning towards her, "Do you know the history behind Rosewood Plantation?"

"No, I was only told that the plantation and property had been in Mr. Fontaine's family for some time now."

"Mais, it is sad that there were no heirs to pass the home down to, but I can see that you will love the house perhaps more than Mrs. Fontaine ever did."

"That is a shame. It is a beautiful home."

Nodding his head in agreement, "Mais, it is. They don't build homes like that one anymore."

"No, they don't."

"I envy you. You have a gorgeous home, and one with a story to tell. It is rumored that when Harold Fontaine married his wife, Aurora, he didn't know that she had loved another man."

"If she loved another man, why did she marry someone else?"

"Ah, back then, cher, many marriages were arranged. Aurora's father had promised her hand in marriage to Mr. Fontaine years before. I don't even think that at the time, Aurora's father knew she was seeing another man."

Mr. Trahan leaned against the counter as he continued his tale. Nicki found herself mesmerized by the man's storytelling. "What happened to the two lovers?"

"Ah, that is what is so sad, cher. No one knows. There are rumors that the mistress and her lover decided to run away. They disappeared in the middle of the night, and no one heard from them again. Mr. Fontaine simply said that his wife had embarked on a journey, and when she didn't return, he said he had received the news she had passed away. He remarried a few years later, and continued on with his legacy."

Before Nicki could ask the man anything more, another customer walked in the door. Nicki looked down at her watch, shocked to see that it was way past noon, "Oh my, I have kept you far too long."

"Please come visit again. I would be more than happy to tell you more about the town's history."

Smiling, "I would love that."

Nicki truly meant what she had said. She would love to find out as much about the plantation and this small town as possible. *Oh how exciting it would be to have a house that had a story of romance and intrigue to it.*

On the drive back to her new home, Nicki thought about the story that she had been told. She wondered about the lost lovers and the footsteps she had heard. Could they belong to a ghost searching for its long lost lover?

Once home, Nicki unlocked the door and was greeted by an overly excited Oscar. "Did you miss me that much boy?" She carried the pizza into the kitchen and placed it on the counter.

Low rumbling…. Squeak…. Thump….. Thump….. Thump…… Noises came from upstairs. It sounded as if someone was moving furniture.

She peered up at the ceiling, trying to make sure that she had indeed heard a noise coming from upstairs. Not hearing anything else, she decided she had better make certain. She searched the bedrooms, one at a time, confirming nothing was amiss. She laughed, assuring herself that it had to have been the wind whistling through the eaves. Besides, this old home does have a tendency to make a great deal of noise at night. She hadn't had a quiet night since she moved in.

Once back in the kitchen, she leaned against the counter and listened to the house with new ears, looked around with new eyes. Perhaps living a solitary life was playing tricks with her mind.

After eating the pizza, she worked well into the night dusting and putting away items from several boxes. When the grandfather clock chimed that it was midnight, Nicki found herself suddenly exhausted. She hadn't realized it was that late.

Upstairs, in her bed, Nicki listened to the settling of the house groan and creak while she fell into a deep sleep. In the early morning hours, a low moaning brought Nicki to a drowsy consciousness. The low moaning soon began to sound as if someone was crying out in distress. Before Nicki was fully awake, the moaning stopped. Still groggy, she shook her head, "Perhaps it was the wind blowing through the house. Guess I had better get that checked."

Once asleep, she started dreaming. She was outside and it was dark. The moon was high in the sky, but the glow it cast was eerie and teemed with dancing shadows. A storm brewed in the distance. She could hear the distinct sound of rumbling thunder. Observing her surroundings, she realized that she was on the plantation grounds. She could see the house, stark white against the darkness. The windows resembled eyes glowing in the dark.

Movement from a window on the second floor caught her attention. It appeared to be someone moving around in one of the bedrooms, only the person didn't have a true form, more of a misty haze.

Rain was released from the sky and fell around her – but not on her. The night sky became filled with an intense moaning and was quickly replaced with maniacal laughter. She fought against the wind and pushed towards the house. Then the rain began to fall on her, only when she looked at her hands, she realized that it was blood and not water. Ghostly apparitions, torn and tattered, rose from the ground, their moaning growing incessantly louder.

She woke up screaming and staring into a pair of glowing, white eyes hovering over her. A startled Oscar woke and moved closer to her, nudging her arm for comfort. "It's okay boy. I must have had a nightmare."

Chapter 12

Darren Fontenot pulled into one of the only free parking spots in front of The Gumbo Pot and slowly climbed out of his truck. When Jake Mayon had mentioned the possibility of a new job, Darren jumped on the chance.

Darren couldn't understand why Jake didn't want the job of renovating Rosewood Plantation all for himself. He had mentioned something about potentially losing some customers. Personally, Darren believed that was a load of crap, but being that there were several handymen after this particular job, Darren was eager to see what needed to be done. Perhaps he would make enough to catch up on his bills and put a little money in the bank. When he started this business, he knew he wouldn't make it rich, but he enjoyed the work.

Opening the door to the small restaurant, the smell of boiled seafood and gumbo greeted him. The familiar aromas reminded him of Friday nights at the hunting camp. Growing up, his dad would go out fishing, crabbing or crawfishing on Fridays. When he came back, they would cook whatever he caught and enjoy the night. They never knew what they were having until his dad returned. It didn't matter to Darren though, he loved it all.

The place was crowded. Waitresses wound their way through the mob with large trays chock-full with plates of food and beer. Booths were overfilled with patrons laughing, talking, and enjoying the good food that was being served.

Darren found Jake sitting in a booth towards the back. "Mon ami, you don't know how much I appreciate the job opportunity. I feel bad about taking this from you."

Before they could continue their conversation, the waitress came over to take their orders. Jake ordered his usual shrimp and crab gumbo with a side of potato salad. Darren ordered the shrimp po'boy, fries, and a pitcher of cold beer.

After the waitress left, Jake told Darren, "Mais non, mon ami. Don't you fret about taking the renovation job. There is more than enough work there to share."

"Does the old place really need that much work?" The waitress returned and set cold mugs and beer on the table before taking off again.

Jake took a swig of beer, letting it roll easily down his throat before replying, "There is enough there. The Fontaines were good people to work for but I don't think either one cared enough about the place to worry about the upkeep. For a while, Mrs. Fontaine's nephew would visit her quite often and I had thought she would leave him the place, but then she put it up for sale. To be honest with you, I think that surprised him."

Darren shook his head, "I have seen him around town. He acted like he was too good for this place."

Jake nodded his head, "The only reason Charles Guilliot came around was because he had hoped he could sweet talk his aunt into leaving him everything. He was her only living relative."

"That's right. The Fontaines didn't have any kids, did they?"

"Nope, they didn't and as far as I know Mr. Fontaine didn't have anyone left on his side of the family either." Looking at his friend, he stated, "Mrs. Fontaine wasn't a fool though. She had mentioned the only reason Charles hung around there was for a free handout."

Shrugging his shoulders, "Maybe he realized she had no intentions of giving him anything because I haven't seen him around in a while."

"I don't know what happened. All of a sudden, he stopped coming over. Perhaps you are right and he realized it was a lost cause visiting his aunt."

Darren took a swig of beer, "So tell me about this new owner. I hear a single woman bought the house."

Jake shrugged his shoulders, "She seems to be alright. She keeps to herself. I haven't figured her out. Sometimes when she talks, there is a sadness about her that I can't pinpoint."

"Hmm, she good looking?"

"She's not a bad looking woman. But I don't know if I would get mixed up with her."

"Is that your way of telling me you want her all to yourself, mon ami?"

Shaking his head, Jake chortled, "Mais non. She just sends out very clear body signals that she wants to be left alone."

"Hmm, if you say so. Tell me something. Do you believe the house is cursed?"

"I haven't run into any ghosts, but there is something rather unsettling about being in that home by yourself. I was surprised when Ms. Brady had said she would be staying out there."

"Hm, funny. I was bored when I was over there as a child, but never scared."

Chapter 13

He watched from the shadows as Nicki slept. She had kicked the covers off in her sleep and he wondered what dream tormented her enough to cause her to thrash about.

This beautiful creature would be perfect for his apprentice. If only he were still alive and could feel her warm blood on his hands as he dismembered her. But alas, that was never to be. He had learned from listening to her conversations that she had no nearby relatives, and perhaps it would be a while before she was missed. It would be so refreshing to watch another body be dismembered in this very house. He had missed that so much, and he was certain that his ancestors had missed that as well.

***

Sleeping fitfully, Nicki extended a leg out of the covers. She felt an icy hand caress her foot. Fear snaked up her spine while the tiny hairs on her arm stood up in alarm. Nicki bolted upright in bed.

She looked around the room. She couldn't explain it, but she swore someone was watching her sleep.

She heard the sound of an object clattering near her dresser. Her eyes darted to that area, but saw nothing. No one was there.

Then she heard the sound of footsteps outside her room. They were monstrously loud in the quietness of the night. Her hands clutched the blankets in terror. *Was she about to find out if there were ghosts haunting this house?*

Her ears strained to hear another noise, anything that may give her an idea as to who, or what, was outside her bedroom door. The only problem was all that she could hear was the pounding of her own heart.

She tried to talk herself into getting out of bed, but her limbs were slow to respond. She couldn't seem to make herself leave the cocoon of warmth she had found in the bed.

A low moan in the darkness made her blood freeze. Something was out there. Slowly she eased herself out of bed. As she went to open the door, she began to doubt her actions.

The pokers by the fireplace caught her attention. She quietly drew one out and wrapped her fingers tightly around its handle as she eased her way back to the door.

She knew that she had left the lights on in the hallway, yet there were no lights burning when she opened the door. No illumination came through the windows. In front of her was a dark abyss.

She took a deep breath and crept forward. The silence of the house menacingly taunted her. "Nicki…"

Icy terror snaked down her spine. She snapped her head from side to side. From the end of the hall, a woman materialized, surrounded by a hazy white glow, "Leave her alone." As the figure moved closer to Nicki, the woman appeared to be in her early twenties. She had shiny brown hair that cascaded down her shoulders in ringlets. By the look of her nightgown, Nicki suspected that she probably died in the 1800's. Another figure emerged behind the young woman. The man was dressed in an outdated suit from the same era.

A black figure moved between Nicki and the two ghosts. Instinctively, they all took a step back. Nicki stifled a scream when the shadow began to take shape. When he turned his malevolent eyes on her, it was as if he could see right into her very soul. He reached out a hand. His icy cold breath sent a chill down her spine, "Nicki…"

Nicki was frozen in terror as the apparition moved closer to her. "Leave this house, or you will become a permanent guest!" His gaze intensified.

The air around her changed and became thick with evil. Nicki swore the man sneered at her.

Oscar bounded from the room and lunged at the ghost. As the ghosts faded back into the shadows,

Nicki petted Oscar's head. "Good boy. Now, let's try to get some sleep."

Chapter 14

James woke up with a heavy sense of foreboding. They still didn't have any good leads concerning the current murder case. He had a bad feeling about it and wanted to review the file again. He refused to let the case grow cold! He took a quick shower and dressed, then headed to work.

He grabbed the file and told the receptionist, "I am going to get coffee and find a quiet spot to look over this case. Call me on my cell phone if you need me."

The local coffee shop should be quiet for another hour. When he entered, he confirmed his assumption. He placed his order and found a booth in the back corner to spread out in.

Flipping open the manila folder, pictures of the young woman greeted him. He shook his head in disgust. This poor young girl's life was cut too short by some maniac. If only her death had come quickly, but instead most of the dismemberment had been performed while she was alive.

The blade was about six or seven inches long and very sharp, with a smooth edge. The wounds were neat with no hesitation marks.

So far, she had no known enemies or a jealous boyfriend. What twist of fate made this poor girl intersect with such evil? Was this written in the stars or just plain bad luck?

James took a bite of his breakfast sandwich before taking a sip of coffee. He studied the information in front of him. The same questions kept plaguing him. Who did this and why? When would the killer strike again? James's gut told him this killer had no plans of stopping. This case was big and it was going to get bigger. They needed to nail this guy before he struck again.

Although they tried to keep the grisly details of any murders from the public, the story had still been sensationalized to the point of exhaustion. Many of the "facts" reported were not even being verified. The masses didn't care about that. The only "fact" the public could wrap their heads and their hearts around was that a young woman's life was cut short by a monster. At least the fact that she had been dismembered while alive was not released to the public.

No, instead rumors circulated about how the officers and detectives of The Lost Bayou Police Department were incompetent. They even went as far as stating that they were incapable of keeping the citizens of this town safe. It did not matter to rumormongers that the officers and detectives were all well trained in investigative procedures.

James massaged his temples. He could feel the beginning of a headache coming on. He had stared at these files for too long. Every page was memorized now, but he still kept looking over them, hoping he had missed something.

He despised being at the mercy of some whack job. His stomach turned with the knowledge that they must wait for him to kill again.

Chapter 15

Nicki's mind raced with everything that needed to be done. The house seemed to reach out to her, begging her to make it whole again. She could already envision how beautiful the place could be with a little tender loving care. It merely needed someone to give it the love it so richly deserved.

As she walked downstairs, a dark blur bolted across the living room. A startled shriek escaped her when the dark shadow disappeared. She put her hand over her heart, struggling to catch her breath. It had to be a trick of light, perhaps a shadow moving across the room.

As she regained her composure, there was a knock at the door. She had to hold back a startled gasp when she opened the door. Just the sheer size of the man was intimidating. There was a raw power that seemed to pulsate from him. He appeared to be in his late thirties, with a deep tan complexion, wide cheekbones, and the most mesmerizing brown eyes.

She extended her hand, "You must be Darren Fontenot. Jake Mayon had told me you would be coming this morning."

Darren accepted her outstretched hand, "I hope you don't mind that he told me about the job."

Nicki opened the door wide for him, "I must say I was surprised when Mr. Mayon had mentioned that he had a friend who did renovation work. I'm not sure if he didn't like the idea of working for someone other than Mrs. Fontaine or what, but I really do want to get started."

"Jake was afraid that the work here would take time away from the clients he did landscaping work for." Looking directly into her eyes, he asked, "Before we get started, I have heard rumors that this house is cursed. I am curious if you believe that."

Laughing, "I don't think the house is cursed. It just needs some tender loving care."

Inside the foyer, Darren looked around. "This house is a work of art. I can't wait to uncover the beauty hidden beneath the years of neglect."

After Darren completed his inspection of the house, he found Nicki cleaning the kitchen cabinets. "The foundation and framework of the house are in good condition. Still, this place does need some work. Most of it is cosmetic though."

Nicki let out a sigh of relief, "That is good to know. For a moment I was afraid you were going to tell me there was some major structural problems."

"If you don't mind me asking, why did you buy this particular plantation? Are you planning on opening a bed and breakfast out here?"

Nicki shrugged her shoulders, "To be honest, I haven't made up my mind yet. I have considered opening it up for tours and possibly a bed and breakfast. As time goes by, I am sure that it will come to me. But, before I can do anything, it will need to be renovated."

"When I was walking around I noticed that a few of the window latches are broken. Before I leave, I will wedge some pieces of wood in between the frame until I can repair it. This will at least prevent anyone from opening the windows from the outside."

"I appreciate that, but I don't think that I have to worry about too many break ins out here."

Shaking his head, "One never knows. It is better to be safe now, rather than sorry later on."

While Darren made a list of the things he needed, Nicki contemplated which project she wanted to tackle next. When Nicki walked past the front parlor, the oil painting hanging over the mantel caught her attention. She swore the person in the painting had moved. Which was absurd, it had to be her imagination.

While upstairs she went from room to room, opening windows to allow the fresh air to wash away the musty smell that had accumulated. Sunlight streamed in through the curtains and weaved into dancing phantom shadows around the rooms.

The sound of plodding footsteps caught Nicki's attention. Darren must be eager to start working on the floor above her. She listened intently, trying to ascertain exactly where he was working. Unfortunately, the footsteps ceased.

As she continued working, the noises from the bayou seemed to fill the small room. She couldn't wait to bring happiness to this house once more. It could be such a beautiful home, and she wanted to dispel the rumors that the house was cursed.

The view from the back bedrooms was gorgeous. She had never imagined living on the water could be this peaceful. She stepped out onto the balcony and breathed in the fresh air.

Moving into another room, she heard the branches of the oak tree brush up against the window. Perhaps this was the root cause of the mysterious scratching noises at night. She jotted down a note to have Jake cut back the limbs. This particular room was cold and unsettling. She couldn't explain it, but it was not as cheery as the previous room.

The air around her became thick and oppressive. Heavy footsteps sounded through the house again. The room turned frigid and the smell of cigar smoke permeated the air. The footsteps came closer and closer as they echoed throughout the house. Her heart pounded hard in her chest. Then, as suddenly as it had begun, it stopped and the room fell deathly quiet. All she heard was the sound of her breathing.

The bedroom door slammed shut. BOOM! The small room shook from the force. The air in the room turned frigid. She walked over to the door, noticing even the doorknob was freezing cold. The door creaked loudly when she opened it. She peered down the hall. There was nothing there but dust particles floating in the air. A part of her wondered if perhaps it was a ghost, but then remembered she had opened all the windows. There was probably enough of a cross wind to blow the door shut.

Needing some fresh air, Nicki walked outside. While she thought about all she had to do, she began to feel overwhelmed. Perhaps her family and friends were right and she had made a rash decision to move down here. She had no clue how to renovate a house and she was far away from all of her loved ones.

Deep in thought, she made her way to the bayou. A shadow moved in behind her that caught her attention. She stopped and let the atmosphere of the place seep into her.

This was what she needed. For a moment, she could see how majestic this plantation had looked at one time. That very image gave her the desire to restore this old place once again to its elegant status. If she closed her eyes, she could imagine the lush gardens that had existed here.

A movement beside one of the oak trees caught her attention. She thought she saw a man watching her, but just as quickly, he disappeared. She really wished her mind would stop playing tricks on her.

***

A rasping, scratching noise permeated her dreams. Dreams where she was walking down a dark pathway with trees flanking each side. The rasping noise followed close behind her. The woods reminded her of a maze, never leading anywhere.

When she turned a corner, she found herself in a graveyard. Broken headstones stuck out of the ground like crooked teeth. When she tried to back away, she found herself blocked by a giant mausoleum. A cold wind blew through the area as skeletal hands began to break free from the dirt.

Nicki woke with a jolt. While the dream hadn't been a nightmare, it had been disturbing. It had her heart racing.

She pushed her hair out of her face and with a shaky hand, reached over and turned on the bedside lamp.

Then she heard it, a soft scraping sound – barely audible over her ragged breathing. She sat up straight and held her breath, listening intently. It sounded like metal being raked across the wood. Rattle…. Rattle…. Rattle. The doorknob slowly began to move, as an unknown source attempted to open the door. Her blood ran cold as pure terror took hold of her. Then, just as suddenly, the doorknob stopped moving.

A shiver ran through her as she stumbled out of bed and slipped on her shoes. She slowly opened her bedroom door and slunk into the hallway.

The moonlight cast eerie shadows along the long corridor. She walked slowly and carefully towards the stairs while she searched for the intruder.

A multitude of noises crept into her awareness with each step she took. The sound of the floorboards creaking, doorknobs rattling, and a low moaning as the wind blew. There was also the grinding noise of the old plumbing as it settled for the night.

She had been warned that some older houses snored while they slept, and this house certainly did. It resembled a living creature, resting after a long and tiring day. Perhaps whiling away its days here on this earth. The windows were its eyes as it watched time go by.

Her foot landed on the first step and it whined in protest. It astonished her how different the house looked at night. What was dim and dingy during the day held almost a luminous effect under the moon and starlight. The wood seemed a deeper color and the secrets hidden in the walls became alluring. The shadows didn't seem as sinister as they danced across the floor and bloomed out of every corner of the house.

Once downstairs, she began turning on lights – one by one. Not seeing anything, she walked back upstairs and returned to her room. Once settled in bed, Nicki reached over to turn the bedside lamp off and hesitated. Shaking her head, she decided to leave it on for the remainder of the night. The sound of rain falling helped lull her back to sleep.

An impatient Oscar was her alarm clock in the morning. Needing to go relieve himself, he continued to nudge her arm until she was awake. "Okay, boy. Let's get you outside."

They rushed downstairs and she let Oscar outside while she went into the kitchen and brewed a cup of coffee. After the coffee was done, she took her cup of the aromatic brew onto the front porch and waited for Oscar. As she looked over the grounds, she was in awe. Last night's rain had transformed her surroundings. Leaves dripped with rain in steady, musical plops. The air shimmered with the mist left behind from the storm. A low lying mist crept along the ground with smoky tendrils curling around the trees. When the sun broke free from the dark clouds, it created a romantic and mysterious aura.

***

Watching the plantation and its new owner from his hiding spot in the woods, he let out a silent curse. She was going to be a problem. He would make her realize the house was haunted. He couldn't afford for this woman to stay out there for too long, and he sure as hell couldn't have someone snooping around.

Chapter 16

Sheriff Ryan Thompson sat at his desk in his office and stared out the window. From here, he could see the boathouse and the boats that belonged to the sheriff's office.

Being a sheriff for a close-knit community was usually fairly easy. The best way to make his job successful was to know what went on around town and know the residents. With that being said, he made it his business to know what everybody was up to, whether it was illegal or not.

This case, though, had him stumped. He thought he knew what skeletons everyone had hidden in their closets and he was finding out that was not true. He had a hard time picturing anyone in this town capable of committing these heinous murders.

Sheriff Thompson groaned when he heard the intercom go off. He hated the blasted thing most of the time. This time, however, he was glad to have a warning. The buzz of the intercom could only mean one thing, "Sorry to bother you, sir, but the mayor is here to see you." Mais oui, he knew it. His day deteriorated in the matter of minutes. He did NOT need this man telling him how to do his job.

"Send him back." Getting up from his desk, he opened the door to greet Mayor Andrew Jenkins.

After shaking hands, they headed back into Sheriff Thompson's office and he shut the door. Mayor Jenkins stated, "Morning, Sheriff. I wish it was under different circumstance that I had to come see you today."

Sheriff Thompson nodded his head in agreement, "Same here, sir."

"I understand you have Detectives Cook and Veret working on the case."

"Yes, sir, they are. They are more than capable of handling things."

Mayor Jenkins replied, "Do we need to approve overtime or hire extra officers to help patrol the town?"

"That would be nice, but do we have the funds for that?"

"I won't have any problems getting the town council to agree right now."

Sheriff Thompson would like to increase their personnel. A few more officers would help a lot. "If we can get this pushed through then I say let's do it."

"Now what about this case? Do we have any new updates?"

Sheriff Thompson leaned back in his chair and folded his arms across his chest, "We are waiting for forensics to complete their reports. A complete sweep was done of the murder scene. They dusted for fingerprints and gathered trace evidence. Now it all has to be sorted through."

Mayor Jenkins asked, "Do we have a serial killer running loose?"

"I sure as hell hope not. If it is a serial killer, then there is a chance he will wait until things die down before striking again."

Chapter 17

After eating a sandwich for supper, Nicki continued cleaning. She worked late into the night, removing years of accumulated dust. After choking on more than her fair share of dust, she opened several of the windows and let some fresh air in. The impending storm sent a cool breeze through the house. In the distance, she could hear the sound of rumbling thunder. She didn't mind the storm, since it brought a reprieve from the heat. She watched as darkness swept across the yard, as if it had a life all its own, moving across the grounds like a shadowy mist.

As the clock struck midnight, she went upstairs and prepared for bed. Drifting off to sleep, she heard a coyote howl mournfully from somewhere deep in the swamp. A low moaning noise slowly roused Nicki from her deep slumber. The moaning was soft at first, but became louder at intervals.

Nicki looked around the dark room and shook her head. It had to be the wind outside. She became aware of the scent of lavender in her room. As the mournful cry became more intense, it quickly faded again. The only sound that could be heard now was the rhythmic ticking of the old grandfather clock.

Sleep eluded her. She tossed and turned, trying to get comfortable. Then, unexpectedly, she felt someone run a hand down her side. She bolted upright in bed. Her heart pounded ferociously in her chest. At the foot of the bed was a misty form. The translucent figure appeared to be wearing a nightgown from the Victorian era. There were little ruffles adorning the wrists.

The apparition let out a startling, unearthly wail that sent a chill down Nicki's spine. Unable to take the horrifying sound any longer, Nicki let out a shriek of terror. The noise must have been loud enough to startle the ghost because it immediately disappeared.

Throwing back the covers, Nicki reached over and turned on the lamp that sat on her nightstand and looked around the room. Knowing that she wouldn't be able to fall back asleep, she climbed out of bed and walked downstairs, turning on every light switch she passed.

After putting on a pot of coffee, she walked around the downstairs and contemplated where to start. She felt overwhelmed at everything that still needed to be done. Walking back into the kitchen, she grabbed the broom and began to sweep. Dust mites became infused with the light and danced through the air on yellow ribbons of light.

An intense feeling of being watched came over her. Had the ghost from earlier returned? As she looked around, she confirmed she was alone.

The sound of a woman sobbing broke the silence of the house. The sound seemed to surround her, coming at her from all directions. As she walked up the stairs, the sound grew louder. Once upstairs, the bedroom door that she kept closed due to its foul odor, blew open. A rush of cold, stale air whipped past her. The force of the wind had her gripping the handrail. As the breeze subsided so did the cries.

A glowing light from the room caught her attention. When she slowly entered the room, it seemed to grow colder. The musty air hung heavy and suffocating. Oscar, trailing behind her, let out a low growl, "Shh, boy, it's okay." However, Nicki couldn't even convince herself that everything was okay.

The smell of rotting flesh surrounded her, forcing her to swallow back the nausea rising in her throat.

Oscar unexpectedly lurched forward and barked fiercely, "Oscar, sit!" she commanded.

Oscar's barking ceased, but he stood guard and stared into the room. A far wall appeared to be glowing. The light pulsated in and out like a heartbeat. Nicki was baffled at the sight before her. "This isn't real. It can't be."

The wall only glowed for a short time, before returning to normal. Nicki stood there a few more minutes, waiting to see if the glowing would return. Walking over to the wall, she reached out and touched it with a shaky hand – needing to confirm that it was a solid wall. After several minutes passed by without another change, she walked back downstairs.

***

Several hours later, the sound of knocking woke Nicki. She eased herself up from the couch, where she had only fallen asleep a short while ago. At first, she didn't think she would be able to fall back asleep after what happened, but then at five o'clock this morning fatigue had won out.

She glanced at her watch and saw that it was almost eight o'clock in the morning. She opened the door to find Darren waiting to start his day. "I hope I didn't wake you, but you did say that you wanted to get started around eight o'clock."

Shaking her head, she stopped herself from telling him what had happened. She didn't want him to think that she was crazy, or worse – scare him off. "No, you are fine. I cleaned the house until early this morning. I must have dozed off and forgotten to set the alarm."

"Would you prefer that I come back later?"

Not wanting to be alone in the house after what had transpired earlier, she welcomed the company. "No, please come in. I will put a fresh pot of coffee on for us."

"I don't want to put you out."

"You aren't putting me out at all. Besides, I will need several cups of coffee to help me get through the day."

After letting Darren into the house, she walked into the kitchen and brewed a pot of coffee. Leaning against the counter, waiting for the coffee to brew, her thoughts replayed all that had taken place last night. The fear was still there, lurking in the depths of her consciousness. While she looked around the massive kitchen, she began to notice how many places there were for someone to hide, as well as enter this house.

Suddenly, Nicki realized that she wasn't alone. She sensed another presence in the kitchen. She looked around, expecting to find Darren, but instead saw no one. Yet she couldn't shake the feeling that she was being watched. The air around her turned thick and oppressive. Then just as quickly, the feeling dissipated and her surroundings returned to normal.

Shaking off the eerie sensation, she poured her and Darren a cup of coffee, and went in search of him. When she passed the grandfather clock in the foyer, she noticed that it had stopped keeping time. As if sensing her presence, it started keeping time again. She shrugged her shoulders and decided if it stopped again, she may have to find a clock repairman to look at it.

She had become quite used to the familiar tick tock from the pendulum.

Chapter 18

With a sinister smirk, he thought to himself, "The woman doesn't even know she is in danger."

Look at the way she walked with confidence. He would show her just how weak she really was. She would learn that he had the power.

She would die like the others. Begging to be spared; crying out in pain. She would be the helpless one now. He would show her what agony was. She would die at his hands.

There was no escape from him.

As she walked to her front door, she never glanced up from her phone. Probably texting. As usual, she was too busy to be afraid. That was her own fault and it would become her downfall as well.

Surveying his surroundings, he pondered why a woman her age would choose to live so remotely. There were no neighbors, no one to hear her scream.

She walked up to the door, punched in her password on the keyless entry and prepared to enter the house.

She was making this too easy. She never had the chance to scream. With one hit, she fell to the ground. Her head slamming into the door stoop.

He may not have given her the chance to scream, but there was plenty of time. Soon she would be screaming, crying, and begging for her life.

***

Erica Stevens awoke tied to her bed. Duct tape covering her mouth.

Her eyes flitted open. When she saw him smiling down at her, the tears quickly fell. Behind the tape, he could hear her moaning. Trying to talk, possibly beg. Perhaps she wanted to plead for mercy.

As realization entered her brain, her gaze turned to terror, then helplessness and back to tears.

He took the tip of the knife and glided it over her body. The blade never cut her. Not yet anyway. After all, he had plenty of time for that – all night as a matter of fact.

Besides, there was a method to his madness. And the method had to be followed.

While Erica had been unconscious, he had stripped her. As she pulled at the restraints, he let the knife blade tease her tender flesh. The pain instantly caused her to thrash, struggling to break free. The will to live was stronger than he had expected.

As the blood ran down her skin, the terror deepened in Erica's eyes. Oh yes, he would enjoy this kill.

Chapter 19

A steady rain fell from the night sky. It was a reprieve from the ill-tempered summer heat. The torrential downpour had only let up a few minutes ago. All that remained now was a low hanging mist over the streets. The last of the rain was almost invisible, only becoming perceptible in the streetlights.

Despite the recent rainfall, a heavy blanket of humidity hung over the city. As Detective Adam Veret breathed in the night air, he knew immediately he was home. Born and raised as a pure blooded cajun, Detective Veret loved his hometown. He even loved the constant humidity that hung over this state, the kind that made you sweat even on a winter day. It took moving away for him to discover how much he loved it here.

He even loved the run-down and dilapidated buildings that made up this tiny little town. He thought that the big city life was for him, but he had been wrong. He thoroughly enjoyed being back home. That was until now.

As he drove up to the crime scene, he observed the flashing red and blue lights of police cars parked around the entrance of the home. Next to the police cars was the crime scene van, the town's newest purchase.

While he made his way to the crime scene, his partner, Detective James Cook, walked up to him. The two detectives were polar opposites. Adam preferred to arrive at the crime scene dressed more professionally, from his tan dockers to his black polo shirt. Detective Cook favored a t-shirt, which had seen better days, and a pair of jeans that had more holes than he cared to count. Despite their differences, they made the perfect crime fighting duo. "Mon ami, this has to be the worst case I have ever seen."

Surveying the area, Adam stated, "I don't see the coroner."

Detective Cook shook his head, "No, he is on his way. He asked that the crime scene techs not touch any evidence near the body until he arrives."

"What do we know about the victim?"

Cook exhaled before speaking, "A caucasian female, age twenty-three, with severe lacerations to the body. From what I understand, gruesomely dismembered may be an understatement. Some of the officers have come out of the house looking a little green around the gills. We won't know for certain until the good doctor gets here, but it appears that she may have been alive when the dismemberment started."

Adam braced himself. As they were walking in, Officer Dan Guidry passed them on his way out, "I thought I had seen it all, especially when I was in Afghanistan, but this… this is nothing like seeing a body torn apart by an IED." His body gave way to a shudder. "That in there is a ghoulish nightmare. The crime scene techs are busy working and the coroner should be pulling up any minute."

One look at the crime scene and he knew he would never get this poor girl's image out of his head. The murder scene sickened him to the very core of his soul. From the pools of blood on the floor, to the strips of flesh clinging to the walls, the stench of bile was enough to turn even the most hardened cop's stomach. However, what seemed to affect him the most was the look on the victim's face, frozen in sheer agony.

It was as if he was experiencing every horror that she had been forced to endure before death took her away from the pain.

"How can anyone do this to another human being?"

"We are dealing with a first-rate psychopath." Adam moved in closer to the body, "The cuts are too clean. The killer knew what he was doing and had this well planned out."

"So you don't think this was a crime of passion?"

Shaking his head, "No, not at all."

Dr. Sam Metcalf walked in and looked at them with tired eyes "Detectives, sorry it took me so long. I wanted to make sure that I had everything I would need."

Nodding his head, Adam moved out of the way. A pair of EMT's rolled the gurney in behind him.

While Dr. Metcalf set out to do his work, he mumbled, "The amputations are clean and deliberate. There are no hesitation marks." As Dr. Metcalf continued preparing the body to be removed from the scene, his voice raised with emotion, "This poor girl was put through an unnecessary amount of torture. She was most definitely alive when he started dismembering her body."

Chapter 20

Nicki opened the medicine cabinet and looked over the bottles filled with pills, prescription and over the counter alike. It was now three o'clock in the morning and she desperately needed a few hours of uninterrupted sleep. She had over the counter sleep aids, but decided better of it and reached for the bottle of aspirin instead.

As she opened the bottle, she glanced at her reflection in the mirror. The recent lack of sleep had left her face more gaunt than normal. Her eyes seemed to be a little sunk in, and her pallor a bit pale. Her silvery gray eyes had lost their shine. Her brown hair lacked luster, especially pulled back in the tight ponytail she wore it in lately. Swallowing down two aspirin with a glass of water from the tap, she headed downstairs.

After pouring herself a cup of coffee, she walked onto the back porch. She breathed in the early morning air and caught a whiff of the pine cleaner that she had been using earlier, mingled with the sweet scent of magnolia trees that grew around the property. With the serenity of a new day, her thoughts inadvertently wandered to Tom. His death had taught her how short life can be and that no day should be wasted. When she saw this property on the internet, it was as if Tom had given her a sign that this was where she should be. So she took the life insurance money that he had left her and bought the plantation. What better way to honor Tom's memory, than to buy Rosewood and renovate it?

The storm that had been raging earlier was now a mere patter. Restless, she decided to venture into the attic.

Even after three months, she was still finding many hidden treasures. The attic housed remnants from the decades that the old home had stood. Rife with dust, it felt as if she had stepped into the past. It was a trove of forgotten riches. There were numerous trunks, civil war weapons and other items strewn about.

Dressmakers' mannequins were scattered about, dressed in clothing ranging from an antebellum ball gown from the civil war era to a Mardi Gras gown from the early 1950's. There was an antique sewing machine tucked in one corner, along with a wire crate containing toys from eons past. There was a trunk with wooden soldiers and dolls that would be a collector's dream, to croquet mallets, balls, and wickets.

As she explored the attic, she was surprised to find one area that had been arranged with a row of dormitory style rooms. Perhaps the rooms had been used for slave quarters for the household staff at one time.

Why Mrs. Fontaine hadn't left this place to a family member? After all, it had been in the family for generations. Perhaps she didn't realize what she had.

While going through the treasure trove of items, she thought she felt something tug at her hair. A gentle touch, something so light that it might have been imagined.

She looked around, but saw nothing. She was slowly going through the boxes when she stumbled across a box that sent chills down her spine. She recoiled from the object, as if merely looking at it was welcoming the evil that lived inside the box out.

Her heart pounded and her body tingled as her blood ran cold. She took a deep breathe and she tried to calm herself.

She closed the box back up; afraid to see anymore of the horrors it held. *What should she do with the items contained within the box?* The pictures didn't look that old and if they were real, then the authorities needed to know about them. Then again, if they were nothing more than someone's imagination, the cops would think a lunatic had moved into town.

Chapter 21

As the two detectives pulled up to the morgue a chill of apprehension ran through Detective Cook. Visiting the morgue was the least favorite part of his job. The place reeked of death and formaldehyde. No matter how hard the janitorial service cleaned, they could not remove the bloodstains from all the autopsies conducted long ago.

The place was in serious need of renovation, only there had never been enough money in the budget. The paint peeled and the only ventilation was a few sporadic windows up high.

They found Dr. Metcalf eating an oyster po'boy while he reviewed the pictures of the crime scene. Shaking his head, James asked, "How can you eat before an autopsy?"

Adding a dash of hot sauce to an oyster that had fallen out of his po'boy before popping it into his mouth, he smiled at the two detectives, "The bodies don't bother me, nor the blood. What does bother me is the lack of consideration our fellow man has for one another."

Slurping down the last of his iced tea, Dr. Metcalf directed the two detectives to the autopsy room. Upon entrance, they noticed two other bodies in the room with her, "Looks like you will be busy today, Doc."

Nodding his head, "Fight at the Faux Pas last night. These two decided to have an actual duel over a woman."

Dr. Metcalf surveyed the body, "It's a damn shame what this young woman went through." Dr. Metcalf started counting stab wounds. Next he carefully removed the paper bags from her hands. He scraped the victim's fingernails for evidence, putting each scraping in separate vials.

After he collected any evidence that had clung to the body, he washed off the body parts. The dried blood liquefied as it was drained away from the body. Then another set of photos was taken.

After the blood had been washed away, twenty-seven more stab wounds were documented between the lower and upper torso. Dr. Metcalf pointed out, "Most of the stab wounds are superficial. They are shallow, just puncturing the skin, going past the fatty tissue, but not going past the ribs."

After each of the wounds was measured and logged, Dr. Metcalf began the internal autopsy. When he made the "Y" incision, James stepped back. He could do without this part. He inwardly cringed as the snippers cut each rib. Examining each of the organs, Dr. Metcalf reported, "None of the stab wounds were fatal. She exsanguinated from blood loss yes, but it appears that it was from the dismemberment."

When the bone saw cut into the victim's skull, James regretted his decision to be present for the autopsy. Unfortunately, he could learn more from watching the process than he could ever get from reading a report. It helped to witness the wounds first hand. He could see the depth and force used to kill.

***

When James walked into the laundry room door of his house, he stripped down, and threw his clothes directly into the washing machine. It would take several washings before the smell of death was removed.

Walking naked through his small home, he headed to the restroom and showered until he used all the hot water. James glanced into the mirror above his sink while he brushed his teeth. He grimaced at the sight of dark circles under his eyes. There were also a few more newly acquired crow's feet and several more gray hairs at his temples.

He had been told that he looked like his mother's side of the family, but as he aged he was beginning to look more like his father.

That night he dreamed of a bayou full of blood and body parts. The vision of the victim's face haunted him. He bolted awake when he heard a noise on his front porch.

He grabbed the revolver from his nightstand, placed his hand on the butt of the gun, and stayed still. Who was outside his house? And why?

He eased himself out of bed, but remained low in a shooting crouch. He peered around as best he could in the semi darkness. There was enough light filtering through the mini-blinds for him to make out shapes. Shadows danced across the bedroom, but nothing else seemed to be moving. He carefully moved through the house, listening for any discernible noises. Everything remained silent.

When he arrived at the front door, he spotted a piece of paper on the floor. He waited a few seconds before he retrieved it. An old black and white photo stared up at him. Instant conclusions jumped to his mind. The photo appeared to be from the early 1900's, and definitely had to be self-developed. With the nature of this photo, it would NOT have been brought to someone to be developed. It depicted a dead woman who had been brutally tortured. Worse yet, the photo was eerily similar to the recent murders he was investigating. Which was impossible, wasn't it?

When he turned over the photo, instant chills snaked down his spine. *How old do you think i am detective?*

Chapter 22

While Darren was busy working downstairs, Nicki decided to work on the bookshelves in the library. The library could be one of the most impressive rooms in this place once it was cleaned. One wall was floor to ceiling mahogany bookshelves, stained to match the massive desk in the center of the room.

While Nicki cleaned the bookshelves with furniture polish, she noticed the back of a bookshelf felt loose. She was about to go get Darren, when he walked into the room, "I think that one of the bookshelves needs to be repaired. A back panel appears to be loose."

"Hmm, let me see. It may be an easy fix." After he inspected the bookshelf, he informed her, "I think that this is a fake panel.

Nicki looked at him quizzically, "What does that mean?"

"There may be a secret passage behind here."

Eager to find out, she watched as Darren looked for a hidden latch. After inspecting the shelves and not finding anything, he pressed his hand flat against the back panel and pushed. Nicki was disappointed when nothing happened. "Don't give up yet." Darren informed her, "It could be that this panel hasn't been opened in a long time." He took the weight of his body and pushed on the entire bookshelf. After the second try, it sprung open. Darren told her, "I wouldn't be surprised if this house holds all kinds of interesting wonders."

She suspected that his statement was completely true. He turned to Nicki and told her, "I'm going to run to my truck and get a flashlight."

When he returned several minutes later, he had a flashlight for her also. Once inside, Nicki wrinkled her nose at the cobwebs hanging from the ceiling, "I don't think anyone has been in here for a long time."

Nicki was surprised to find the small room crammed with various trunks, along with several vintage wooden garment rods with dresses covered with clear, plastic bags. Nicki untied one of the bags and freed the dresses from their confines, "Why would anyone leave these in here?" Taking in the intricate detail of the dresses, "This must have cost a fortune back then."

Curious to see what was in the trunks, she gasped in surprise, "This one is stuffed with clothes." Eager to see what was in another trunk, she quickly opened it. She was delighted to find some old photographs, letters dated at around the turn of the century, several old newspaper clippings, and what appeared to be an old leather satchel.

As Nicki started going through the treasures she found hidden in the trunk, Darren stated, "Unless you need me to help you with anything else in here, I want to get back to work."

"No, I think I am good for now."

For the next hour, Nicki searched through the trunks. She wondered why someone decided to store all of these treasures in this room instead of, perhaps, the attic.

Later that night, as Nicki drifted off to sleep, she heard a woman whimpering. The whimpering escalated into deep sobbing, and then to heart wrenching cries. Throwing off the covers, she eased herself out of bed and slipped on a robe. While leaving her room, she listened intently to determine which direction the sound might be coming from. When she walked into the hall, it sounded as if the noise was coming from the room she feared.

She cautiously opened the bedroom door and gasped at the sight in front of her. The wall was once again glowing. From the corner of the room appeared a round, luminous beacon of blue light. As the seconds passed, the light began to move through the room and towards the wall. Nicki watched as the light hovered near the wall before moving through the wall.

Nicki rushed to the other room, but was disappointed to find that the ball of light had disappeared. Curious as to whether or not the ball of light had returned to the previous room, she rushed back to it. When Nicki walked back into the room, she thought she had stepped back in time. A young woman in her early twenties sat on the edge of the bed, with tears flowing down her cheeks and onto her white, pleated nightgown. The woman stared at the ground, as if she was too afraid to look up.

The woman's eyes shifted, as if reacting to someone walking into the room. Nicki wondered if the woman had noticed her standing here. Nicki carefully approached the woman, "Can you see me?"

Instead of answering, the woman continued crying. "What's wrong? Please, don't cry."

The girl didn't flinch when Nicki moved closer to her. She kept her gaze transfixed on the door. She stared right through Nicki as if she weren't even there. When Nicki reached out to touch her, a high-pitched wailing sound filled the room. The woman abruptly stood up and started to back up to the wall. She held out her arms, as if pushing someone away. "Please, don't." she begged, "You don't have to do this."

Before Nicki could react, the woman started moving up the wall as she gripped at her neck. Her entire body trembled as if she were having some sort of seizure. She gasped out, "Please... stop." Then her entire body went limp. A man's laugh echoed throughout the room while the woman crumpled to the floor.

As the woman's eyes closed, the image in front of Nicki disappeared. When the vision returned to present time, Nicki knew for certain that someone had died in this house – possibly this room.

Chapter 23

A cacophony of sounds greeted Detect ve Cook as he walked into the precinct. It was as if everyone seemed to be having a conversation at the same time. There were also the noises of fingers clacking on keyboards, copies being made, doors opening and closing as well as shoes slapping against the old linoleum floor. The trill of the telephone let the receptionist know it needed to be answered.

Once at his desk, he absent-mindedly opened the case file, not really needing to. He had a photographic memory, could file away facts, conversations and crime scenes with complete ease. The information would be there whenever he needed - with perfect clarity. It was sometimes a gift, and sometimes a curse.

Walking over to his desk, Adam informed him, "Our first victim had a record. She was picked up for solicitation several times in New Orleans."

"So it appears that our killer found a victim whom he suspected was low risk."

Nodding his head, "Crime scene is still running the fingerprints in the home, but I wouldr't hold your breath on any leads. The place was full of prints, more than likely she continued her profession when moving here." Sighing, "My gut tells me, though, that this guy isn't done."

James couldn't help but agree, even though that didn't offer any solace.

"According to Dr. Metcalf's report, the dismemberment was done by a surgical bone saw, much like the one he uses during autopsies."

Running his hand through his hair, James stated, "So it could be that our killer has some medical training."

Nodding his head, "Dr. Metcalf believes the cuts had the precision of a trained surgeon, or someone who has had a lot of practice."

***

With determined steps, Nicki entered the police station. Voices shouted and phones rang. Basically, there was chaos everywhere.

Clenching the box, Nicki walked up to the front desk and said softly, "Excuse me, officer."

The cop never looked up.

Nicki cleared her throat and spoke louder, "Excuse me, sir."

Bushy eyebrows rose as the officer focused on her, "Can I help you with something, miss?"

"I may have something of interest for the officers handling the recent murder."

He looked at her suspiciously, "They are quite busy this morning. Is there something I can help you with instead?"

With trembling hands, she held out the box and stated, "I think there may be some information in here that they will want to see."

The officer glanced through the box, paled and picked up his telephone. "I'm sorry detectives, but there is a woman up at the front desk that you may be interested in speaking with. She found a box that may or may not be related to your recent killing."

***

This little bit of information piqued Adam's curiosity. At the front desk, he noticed a middle-aged woman pacing back and forth; every now and then she would glance warily at a box. Extending his hand, "My name is Detective Adam Veret. I understand you have something you would like to show us."

Shaking her head, "Not show, but give you. I don't want it back in my house. My name is Nicki Brady. I recently purchased the Rosewood Plantation."

Taking the box from the desk, he led Nicki to his small cubicle. "Please have a seat."

Running her hands up and down her arms, "I don't want the box back. At first I wasn't sure what to do with it, but I knew I didn't want to keep it in the house."

Adam peeked into the box and felt a small rush of adrenaline, "I'm sorry, but how did you find this?"

"I couldn't sleep the other night and decided to go through some of the boxes in the attic. This was up there. I'm honestly not sure what else could be up there. As soon I found this box I went back downstairs."

"Would you have any objections to my partner and I searching through the remainder of the boxes to see if there are any more like this one?"

Writing down her address, "Not at all detective. But promise me that anything you find, you won't tell me about, nor will you leave it in my house."

Shaking her hand, "I can promise you that."

"I will be home the rest of the day if you would like to come by. If you need to come another day, I wrote down my phone number as well."

After Ms. Brady left, he started going through the items in the box. There were photos, notebooks detailing the "research" and detailed diagrams. "I can't tell when the pictures were taken, but this sure looks like the work of our killer." He told James.

"Where do you suppose these bodies are at? We would have known if they were found."

"He probably has them buried somewhere. They could be on the property."

Shaking his head, "Well, I don't want to be the one to tell that woman she bought a house where a serial killer lived, and worse - possibly killed his victims."

"You and me both. We need to find out who owned the house before her and why they left the boxes there."

"I don't see our killer accidentally leaving these."

Nodding his head, "Me neither. Either it was intentional or he hadn't expected the move."

***

After Nicki left the police station, she let out a long sigh of relief. Neither of the detectives were what she was expecting, but especially Detective James Cook. The deep southern drawl added to his mystique. The detective was a handsome man. He had strong features that bordered on rough. He had a square jaw and high cheekbones.

The way he towered over her, she suspected that he was well over six feet tall. He had a faint scar along his left eye and wide, strong shoulders. Arms that were meant to wrap around a woman and take away their worries and fears.

***

Frank Ingalls watched as Nicki Brady crossed the street from the police precinct to Robicheaux's Pharmacy. From what he had learned, Jason Robicheaux's family opened the pharmacy in 1910 and had owned it ever since. Jason took over after his dad retired. This particular family came from old money and was one of the richest here in town. Frank had met Jason at a few of the town functions and he was a rather peculiar man.

He had heard that at one time Jason went to school to become a doctor, but when his father became ill, he dropped out of medical school and took over the family business.

Frank was curious as to why the new owner of Rosewood Plantation had visited the police precinct. He was also curious about the woman who had purchased the plantation from Mrs. Fontaine. He quickly walked across the street and into the pharmacy. He slunk over a few aisles behind her.

Once he saw an opportune moment, he approached her, "Aren't you the woman who purchased the Rosewood Plantation?"

Nicki looked at him, shocked by the question. Shaking his hand, she replied, "Nicki Brady."

Laughing, "Frank Ingalls, and don't worry, I am not stalking you. I happened to notice you walking across the street and wanted to introduce myself. I have always been fascinated with Rosewood Plantation. I am a reporter for The Harold here in town. I would love to write a story about the home, if you would permit me."

****

Nicki continued to look at Frank Ingalls. One look at Frank and there was no denying the man's mixed heritage. This handsome man stood well over six feet tall, had powder blue eyes and caramel colored skin. He was clean-shaven, fit, and trim. She had noticed that most of the men here preferred to wear jeans, but he looked completely comfortable in his dockers and tailored shirt.

She knew the whole town was interested in the person who had purchased the Rosewood Plantation, but she wasn't sure how to handle the sudden interest in her. She had wanted to find herself and thought moving here she could hide from the world. She laughed nervously and responded, "I'm not sure about a story, but you are more than welcome to stop by for a tour. But I must warn you, I am still in the middle of remodeling."

Frank looked at her and smiled, "Well, I guess for now I will have to take you up on your hospitality for just a tour."

Chapter 24

Evelyn Jefferson sat outside the restaurant and waited for her daughter, Nicki. She shifted uncomfortably on the iron bench as she checked her watch one more time. Nicki was never late, and here it was she had been waiting ten minutes past the agreed upon time.

She had missed her daughter terribly since she moved away. While she understood why Nicki moved, she wished it had been closer. As it was, it had been almost two months since she saw her daughter and even now they were meeting halfway for a few hours at dinnertime. She had hoped that Nicki would invite her to the plantation, but so far she had not extended an invitation.

Evelyn was worried about Nicki's decision to seclude herself in a place where she had no friends or family. A part of Evelyn felt that Nicki was running away from her feelings, and had hoped the move was merely temporary. She hoped that Nicki merely needed time to adjust to Tom's death. She desperately wanted her to return home, where she belonged.

Truthfully, though, Evelyn feared that Tom's death had left a permanent scar on Nicki's heart, one that would never completely go away. Tom's death showed Nicki that life could change at any moment. Her loving husband was gone, and she believed that she would have to face life alone. Nicki was not ready for Tom to die, but, then again, no one wants to lose a loved one.

Evelyn jumped up when she saw Nicki park. She rushed over to Nicki's car with tears in her eyes, "I'm so happy to see you, honey." Giving her a warm hug, "I've missed you so much."

Nicki hugged her mom back and took her hands in hers. "I've missed you too. Are you doing all right?"

Not letting her hand go, they walked inside the restaurant. "I'm doing all right."

****

On the drive home, as the heat of the day faded and merged with the dampness of the bayou, a rolling fog moved in. Her home rose against the mist and darkness while the moonlight danced across the road. While she had enjoyed the visit with her mother, she was glad to be back home. A part of her had wanted her mother to see what all she had accomplished, but another part of her didn't want to listen to her mother begging her to move back home.

While she unlocked the front door, Oscar let out an impatient bark. Chuckling, she opened the door, "What's wrong boy? Did you miss me?" Holding up the doggy bag, she asked, "Or are you more interested in finding out what treat I brought back for you?"

Oscar danced around her feet excitedly as she walked into the kitchen. "Okay, okay. You know that I couldn't forget about you." She opened the to go box and hand fed him pieces of the steak that she had left over from her meal. After Oscar finished his snack, she washed her hands at the kitchen sink. Afterwards, she poured herself a glass of wine and decided to watch some television in the back parlor overlooking the courtyard.

While she settled down on the couch, Oscar jumped up beside her and made himself comfortable. She stroked his fur absent-mindedly while she flipped through channels until she found an old sitcom playing. As she watched television, a shadow in her peripheral vision caught her attention. It appeared to be walking along the back wall. She stayed unnerved until Oscar's ears perked up and he let out a low growl. "It's okay, boy. It's just the moonlight." Even she had to admit that she didn't sound convincing. Getting up from the couch, she walked over to the french doors and looked outside. She was going to make herself crazy if she started jumping at every shadow that crossed her path.

Then, without warning, the channels on the television began changing. Shaking her head, she returned to the couch to get the remote. Only the remote wasn't there. A loud thunderclap shook the glass panels in the windows, while the volume on the television increased. A loud static noise blasted from the television speakers. Nicki got on her hands and knees, searching under the couch for the remote. Not finding it, she removed the couch cushions, hoping to find it quickly. *Where can that blasted thing be?*

A low snarling emitted from a dark corner of the parlor. "This is my house." stated a raspy sounding, male voice in the dark. Oscar immediately barked madly in the direction of the voice.

Suddenly, from the shadows the remote flew through the air and landed near her feet. Picking up the remote, Nicki turned off the television, and she said to Oscar, "Come on, boy, let's go to bed."

Oscar bounded up the stairs ahead of her. Nicki rushed up the stairs and into her room. She quickly propped a chair under the locked doorknob and let out a shaky breath.

Nicki hastily dressed for bed, and joined Oscar – who was hiding under the bed covers. She considered turning on the television to keep her company and help drown out the odd noises the house made at night, but reconsidered.

No sooner than she had fallen asleep, she started to dream. She was standing outside of the plantation, staring at the front door. It opened on its own, as if beckoning her inside. From the entryway, she could hear someone talking from upstairs, but she couldn't make out what they were saying. It was almost as if they were arguing. Then, suddenly, there were voices all around her. Indistinct conversations, the whispers were barely audible, then became clearer, "You have to help us."

A woman in white appeared before her, "You have to help them." Then a loud, horrified scream pierced the silent night. She tried to make herself wake up from the dream, but she seemed to be frozen in time. The lady's image faded away, taking the voices and screams with her. As they vanished, she was enveloped in a giant black abyss.

She woke with a start, covered in a cold sweat. She sat up in bed and gasped for air. The screams still rung in her ears. Oscar nudging her on the arm pulled her back to reality. She curled up to Oscar's warmth and tried to go back to sleep. She tossed and turned for several long minutes before she drifted off to sleep.

Chapter 25

The police precinct at midnight was mildly quieter than in the daytime. The main difference at night was the place smelled of pine cleaner.

Even at this hour there was still a handful of detectives working, hoping to close their open cases. Detective Cook was among those. Currently he was waiting to see if there were any hits in VICAP. This killer must have struck before, but where?

He had lost track of time as he scribbled several pages of notes in his notebook. So far there had been no hits. Hell, even the photograph left at his house had been a bust. The paper it had been printed on was nondescript. Since it had not been printed at a local store, there were no tags on the back. No numbers that would lead them to a specific printer. They were still analyzing the ink. The techs had dusted for fingerprints, but it had been wiped clean.

Unlike Adam, James had yet to get married. In his opinion, if you want to be a good detective then there was no way you could be a husband, or even a father. Adam was slowly trying to prove him wrong.

As James stared at the photos of the victim, he felt drawn to the woman's glassy eyes. It was as if they were pleading with him to find her killer. For a moment he felt as if they were connected. He would carry the weight of those pleading eyes around with him until her killer was found.

James couldn't understand how none of the neighbors heard or saw anything. The houses in that neighborhood had paper-thin walls. St ll, no one knew anything.

The victim's fellow co-workers didn't have much information either. She had left work alone and had no definite plans. No one had any idea if she had a current boyfriend. She had only lived here for a short time. She had moved here from New Orleans.

While it was true that most murders were committed by friends or relatives, this one was not. No, if his gut instincts were correct, they were searching for a serial killer. He prayed that they would find the killer before they had another body.

He leaned back in his chair and took a long drink of coffee. So far they had been able to keep the details of the murders out of the news, but it wouldn't be long before the media was all over the case. Some asshole reporter would find someone in either the police department or the coroner's office to talk. These women deserved better than to be a front page story.

When he took this job he never imagined that he would be investigating a murder as gruesome as this. Hell, he never considered a serial killer as being something that preyed on the citizens here. But this was also the kind of case he was good at solving. He had a talent for following the clues. Whether it meant studying people or evidence. He had a mind for it.

Before going home he stopped to grab something to eat. His refrigerator only held a few dismal contents and his freezer was empty of its usual microwaveable meals.

Once home, he dropped the pizza he purchased on the coffee table, grabbed a beer from the fridge and turned on the TV. While a sportscaster recapped the weekend's games, highlights flashed across the screen in rapid fire images.

While he ate his pizza, he opened his briefcase. There were a few more notes that he wanted to write. As he reviewed the material, he hoped to find something that he may have missed the first, second, third or even fourth time.

After several more hours of reviewing the material, James leaned back in his chair, frustrated that nothing jumped out at him. *Had his dad been right? Should he have chosen a different field?* His dad had been hurt when James had chosen police work instead of a promising football career.

Ever since James was little his dad had envisioned him as a star quarterback. Every chance he had, his dad would take James to the field to practice. Throughout school James's life focused around football, and football only. James had not been allowed to date, as his dad feared it would deter him.

All of that practice had paid off though. A scout had spotted James's talent one Friday night. He had earned a full scholarship to one of the top colleges in Louisiana. For once James had been appreciative that his dad had made him not only focus on football, but keep his grades up as well.

During college he had been a football star. While in college, he became interested in the law. He changed his major to criminal justice, much to his dad's disappointment. During one of the criminal justice classes, a Louisiana state trooper came to give a talk. After listening to the police officer, James knew what he wanted to do with his life.

To say that his dad had been angry when he decided not to pursue a career in football was putting it mildly. His dad still talked about how great it would have been to see his son play professional football. Even though his dad had been disappointed, James never regretted his decision. Working for the police department, he was making a difference in this world, something he doubted he would have done playing football.

Chapter 26

Nicki had mixed feelings about seeing Frank Ingalls again. She desperately tried to deny that she had found the man attractive. When he looked at her with that sexy smile on his face, she felt her knees grow weak.

She wasn't sure why, but something about him pushed her to delve deeper into his life. She could sense something lurking behind that easygoing veneer he showed the world. She was playing with fire. The man was trouble. Besides, she wasn't ready to start a romantic relationship with someone. She still missed Tom, and felt guilty about seeing another man. But the thought of seeing Frank again had her heart racing.

However, she was getting way ahead of herself. He probably was not even interested in her. And if he was, then what?

She tried to calm her nerves when the doorbell rang. Frank was at the door, "Thank you for agreeing to give me a tour of your home."

Smiling, she held open the door for him to come inside, "Just please remember that I am still in the middle of renovations."

Once inside, Frank let out a whistle, "I'm impressed that you even considered taking on such a monumental task. This house is huge."

"It is a monstrosity, but if you look past all the work that needs to be done, you can still see the grandeur of the place. The previous owner left behind some furniture and I've been slowly trying to restore that as well."

"You may have a new career in your horizon."

Nicki shook her head, "Not likely. However, it has been a learning experience. It also gives me something to do after my husband's death."

"I'm sorry; I didn't realize that you were a widow."

She was startled to see empathy in his eyes. When most people looked at her lately, they had more of a sorrowful look, instead of one that would offer comfort. It was also a look that could catch her off guard. Shaking her head, "My family keeps telling me to move on, but it is easier said than done."

"I lost someone important to me when I was young. He was the only person who seemed to understand me. He listened to what I had to say, and didn't ridicule me. I wasn't prepared when he died unexpectedly."

"I'm sorry. After watching Tom suffer from cancer, I would much rather die suddenly rather than live in that much pain."

"You may be right. But, still, I wish I had more time with him. He was such a great man. On the day of his funeral, I stood at the casket and waited for him to sit up and tell everyone that it had been a huge joke. He was a huge jokester, and never took anything seriously."

"Tom was the dreamer in our family. I was the serious one, always needing a plan and wanting everything planned out." She smiled as she reminisced about Tom, "He despised my lists, and he hated having to keep a schedule." Looking around the room, she confessed, "This was actually Tom's dream, one that I wanted to see come to fruition."

"You are an interesting woman, Nicki Brady, one that I would like to get to know better."

His statement caught her by surprise. Giving him a nervous laugh, she said, "Well, I guess I better give you a tour of the house."

"Yes, let's do something entertaining. Enough of this gloomy talk about death."

As she showed him everything that they had accomplished so far, an image of Frank holding her in his arms and devouring her with kisses flashed through her mind. She forced the image to go away and focused on what he was saying. "You have accomplished a lot so far. Have you discovered anything interesting while cleaning yet?"

His question threw her for a minute, but she was not ready to divulge to him what all she had discovered around the house so far, "Nothing special yet, some old photos and a few interesting pieces of furniture that needed to be refurbished."

"And no ghosts keeping you awake at night?"

Laughing nervously, "By the time my head hits the pillow at night, I am out. The one good thing about remodeling the house is I am exhausted when it is time for bed."

If he suspected that she wasn't being completely honest, he didn't push the matter, "I'm sorry about all the questions. I guess it is the reporter in me."

Nicki asked, "Did you always want to be a reporter?"

Frank shook his head, "Actually no. At first, I wanted to be a surgeon, but when I realized how much schooling it involved, I changed my curriculum."

"I've read some of your work; you do have a way with words."

Frank laughed, "I've always been a great bull shitter. That is one of the most important things in this business."

"I don't know why, but I envisioned a journalist to be a little more pushy."

He shrugged his shoulders, "I can be when I need to, but I have learned that it really isn't needed. My grandmother used to tell me that you could catch more flies with honey.

Nicki laughed, "Are you from here?"

"My family lived here when I was younger. We moved to Baton Rouge when I was a teenager. Before I decided to return to my childhood town, I worked in New Orleans."

"What made you move here?"

Frank responded, "I was working on a story about haunted plantations and began to reminisce about Rosewood Plantation. I learned that the local paper had a position open and decided to apply. I assumed it was fate telling me it was time to return home."

"Well, fate called me to this town as well. If I hadn't been able to sleep that night I might not have been perusing the internet or saw the real estate ad for this plantation."

As they finished the tour, Frank stated, "When you are done, this will be a beautiful place. The person who built this house took a lot of pride in what they did."

As he was leaving, he turned to her, "I have really enjoyed talking to you today. How would you like to go out to dinner tonight?"

Against her better judgment, "I would love to."

***

Frank was outside her door promptly at seven. She answered the door in a burgundy wrap dress that hit right below her knees and helped accentuate her body in all the right places. When Frank had left earlier, it had given her enough time to finish the chores she had planned for today, take a shower, and wash her hair. She had taken the time to style her hair where it fell in cascading waves down her back. Since Tom's passing, she hadn't cared about how she looked. Even though this wasn't a date, she had found herself wanting to actually look nice for a man. Besides, something in her gut told her that she should take everything about this man slowly – and carefully.

Smiling, she greeted him, "You are right on time."

"I enjoyed our talk so much, that I was eager to learn more about you."

Nicki slipped her hand into the crook of Frank's arm and allowed him to escort her outside. After opening the car door for her, he walked around to the driver's side. Nicki immediately fell in love with the black BMW 650i. "I had secretly wanted this car, but knew I could never afford it."

He laughed, "I decided to splurge when this car came out. I heard it calling my name from the showroom floor. This car was built for speed and handles the roads superbly."

"Before Tom passed away, he had bought me a Hyundai Genesis. While I love the car and would never dream of getting rid of it, I'm starting to wonder if an SUV or truck would be better when driving the plantation road all the time."

"You can get you an inexpensive truck for quick trips to town."

Nicki rested her head back against the headrest and took in the beautiful night. "That is true."

Frank found a parking space outside of Jacques, "I assumed since you haven't lived here long, you may not know about this place. Not only is the food delicious, but the ambiance is inviting."

Shaking her head, "No, I've never been here."

As they walked to the front door, Nicki noticed the growing line, "It appears to be full tonight.

Nodding his head, "I wish they accepted reservations. But we shouldn't have to wait too long."

Nicki was pleased to find that Frank had been true to his word. They only had to wait fifteen minutes before their table was ready. During that time, they got to know each other better. Nicki found herself opening up to this man a little more.

The restaurant was pleasant, and the background music was low enough where patrons could talk. After they were seated, Nicki smiled over at Frank, "This place is very nice. Thank you so much for asking me out tonight."

He picked up her hand and gently kissed it. She blushed at the romantic gesture, "No, thank you for agreeing to come out with me tonight. I really do want to get to know you better."

The waitress picked that moment to show up, "My name is Jessica. Would y'all like something from the bar and maybe an appetizer?"

Nicki ordered a chocolate martini and Frank ordered a manhattan, for the appetizer they both agreed on the spinach artichoke dip with french bread.

After the waitress walked away to place their orders, Frank focused his attention back on Nicki. He asked, "How do you like living in Lost Bayou?"

"I'm still getting used to things, but so far it seems to be a pleasant town."

Frank looked her in the eyes, "And the media coverage about the recent killings doesn't have you worried living out there all by yourself?"

Flabbergasted by his question, she shook her head and replied, "No, I guess I have been so busy with the renovations that I haven't thought about it."

"Well, from a professional standpoint, wish the police would release more information."

She laughed, "I can see where a reporter would find

that annoying."

Frank stunned her by changing the subject, "So have you considered opening the plantation as an inn when you are done renovating. You seem to be a natural at giving tours, and I bet you would make the guests feel welcome."

Now it was her turn to let out a laugh, "I honestly haven't decided what I want to do after the renovations are complete. For once in my life, I don't have a specific plan."

"So what did you do before moving here?"

"Before my Tom passed away, I worked as a chef at a popular restaurant."

"I'm impressed. So you could open a restaurant at the plantation? I know the locals would be interested in eating there, just in hopes of seeing a ghost."

For the next two hours, they enjoyed their food and conversation. On the drive back to the plantation, Nicki couldn't remember the last time she had such a pleasant night. She was glad she went against her better judgment and accepted Frank's offer. As she unlocked the front door, she felt his hand on the small of her back. Her heart fluttered nervously. "Thank you once again for allowing me the pleasure of your company. I hope we can do it again very soon."

She whispered, "Yes. I would like that very much."

Before they could say anything else, a gust of wind blew through the porch and knocked one of the potted plants over. Nicki jumped when the swing at the far end of the porch began to move on its own accord.

A shiver snaked down Nicki's back, "That's strange."

Frank looked around, knowing there must be some reasonable explanation, "It is more than likely the wind."

Nicki wasn't convinced that it was the wind. The air was unnaturally still around them.

In an attempt to break the embarrassing discomfort, she said, "Thank you for the lovely dinner."

"It was my pleasure."

After unlocking the front door, Frank took her hand in his and brought it up to his lips. "I really do want to see you again, Nicki."

Nodding her head, "Same here."

Smiling, he told her, "Well, then, I will call you tomorrow so that we can set up another date."

Once safely inside, Oscar let out a happy bark and danced around her legs. She absently bent down and petted him on the head.

After Nicki watched Frank drive off, she headed upstairs to get ready for bed. Sliding between the cool sheets of her bed, she picked up a book sitting on her nightstand to help her relax. As she opened the novel, the lights flickered on and off, "Great, this is not how I wanted my night to end."

Nicki placed the book back on the nightstand, kicked off the covers, and stepped out of bed. After slipping on a robe and a pair of slip-on shoes, she retrieved the flashlight she kept in the top drawer of her nightstand and moved towards the door.

When she opened the bedroom door, the lights flickered again. A chill wracked through her body as she shined the flashlight down the hallway. She took a cautious step into the hallway and searched both ways. Somewhere downstairs a door slammed shut, causing her to jump. Oscar began to bark wildly at the direction of the sound.

She crept towards the staircase, the flashlight shaking with her nerves. As she began to walk down the stairs, a strange raspy gurgling sound teased the night air. As fear consumed her very being, her breath came in short, quick spurts. "What the crap is that?"

An irrational sense of paranoia rushed through her. A hundred thoughts ran through her mind and became increasingly ridiculous as fear overrode her ability to think. She took slow, halting steps. Icy sweat built under her arms and across the back of her neck.

She walked cautiously, listening. The hairs on her arms prickled. A horrifying image flashed through her mind. She saw a hulking man bringing a knife down into a woman's body, repeatedly.

Nicki wrapped her arms about herself. Her mouth went dry. The floor groaned under her weight, and Nicki let out a small curse. Her eyes watered as she tried to focus on the poorly illuminated downstairs. She squinted in an effort to make out any threat that might be before her. Her body was alive with adrenaline. The gurgling continued as Nicki descended the stairs. Beside her, Oscar let out a menacing growl when the lights flickered once more. Nicki suddenly found herself surrounded by a gruesome sight, young women with pale, haunting faces. Most were making gurgling noises as they clawed at their necks, as if trying to remove some sort of restraint. A scream stayed lodged in Nicki's throat as she tried to back away from the apparitions surrounding her as their pasty skin glowed and their bulging eyes stared into the afterlife.

Out of the dozen or so lifeless figures surrounding her, two forms took more shape. Blood trickled down their bodies and multiple slash wounds were present. Her heart pounded in her ears. Discordant voices became clearer, "Nicki, we have something to tell you."

As she scrambled back up the stairs, her stomach began to churn and bile rose up in her throat. A whisper sounded in the distance. The voice came from somewhere downstairs, "Help me…"

Tripping on the first step, she stumbled as she turned to rush back to her room. She was hoping to hide from the apparitions and the voice that called out to her. This time the voice repeated louder, "Help me!" With lead weighted legs, she pushed forward as arms reached out in the darkness, "Please, help me."

When Nicki opened her bedroom door, hands reached out, trying to pull her back into the hallway, "You have to help me, please."

An icy chuckle sounded behind her and when she turned around, she had to suck in a deep breathe. Standing a few feet away from her was the shadow of a man. Not wanting to find out if he was an apparition or real, she bolted into her room, slammed the door shut and locked it. The doorknob rattled as she pushed the full weight of her body against the door. Without even thinking about what she was doing, she called

Detective James Cook. While she waited for him to answer his phone, she tried to calm her racing heart, "Detective Cook, it's Nicki Brady. I'm sorry to bother you, but could you please come over. Something strange is happening here and you may be the only person who can help me."

"I'll be there as soon as I can. Do you need me to send an officer over to your house?"

Gulping in a deep breathe, "I'm not sure if the man I saw was a ghost or real, but I think those women in the photos were killed here and I saw their ghosts tonight. They were begging me to help them."

***

While James didn't believe in ghosts, he was certain that something had scared Nicki Brady. He feared that if she did indeed see a man standing in the hallway that he has an intruder. Since James was still at the precinct, he rushed to the front desk, "Look, Nicki, I want you to stay on the line with me, okay? I'm going to send out an officer right away, and I will be there shortly."

"Oh... Okay."

Rushing to the front desk, he informed Officer Evan Jenkins, "Officer, I need you to get a patrol car to Rosewood Plantation, asap. There is a possible intruder, and she is locked in her room."

Nodding his head while he went to radio in the request, "Yes sir. I will have them there as quickly as possible."

Not waiting for confirmation, he spoke into his phone once more, "Nicki, they are on their way and I'm heading to my car. Do not open your bedroom door under any circumstances, unless you are absolutely certain that it is the police officers or me, do you understand?"

"Please hurry."

***

While Nicki waited for the police officers and Detective Cook, she could still hear the mournful pleas of the women. She backed herself into a corner of the room and watched as eerie shadows danced across the room. Nicki put a quivering hand to her mouth and sucked in a shallow breathe. Thankfully Oscar was next to her, snarling at the shadows.

The chair in the corner of the room began to rock back and forth, and then abruptly slid across the room to where she was sitting.

Nicki rushed to the bed and hid under the covers, hoping that Detective Cook got here quickly. The sound of approaching footsteps caught her attention. It sounded as if someone was walking inside the room. Her breath caught when she heard a man breathing loudly. She was too scared to peek from under the covers. Without warning the bed began to shake and she heard the sound of furniture moving inside her room.

A rasping sound came from the foot of the bed and Nicki felt the covers being lifted. A pounding at the front door caused the activity going on around her to cease. Thankful that someone was here, she rushed downstairs to answer the door.

There was no doubt in her mind anymore, she lived in

a house which divulged secrets when it saw fit. She was almost certain that there were a variety of entities that must live here, some from another era. In this house the lines of time were blurred as if this house was a portal to the past as well as the present.

Yet, since all of her money was tied up in the house, she must learn how to live with these spirits.

***

"Ma'am. I'm Officer Jenkins. Detective Cook asked that I come by and check things out for you."

Nicki opened the door wide, and greeted him, "Thank you for coming out."

As Nicki was welcoming him, a sound came from upstairs. It sounded like it came from her bedroom.

Officer Jenkins reached for the revolver he wore at his waist and instructed Nicki, "Stay down here, by the door."

While Nicki watched Officer Jenkins walk up the stairs, she could hear furniture being moved around in the bedrooms. The ghosts weren't afraid that she had a visitor at this hour of the night, and they weren't scared to let outsiders witness their activity.

It seemed like an eternity before Officer Jenkins came back downstairs, "I'm sorry ma'am, but I did not find anyone hiding upstairs."

As he was talking, a loud scraping sound came from the wall under the stairs. Officer Jenkins walked over and listened intently, "It sounds like you might have a rodent problem. If I were you, I would get some traps."

Before he could say anything further, the cabinet doors

in the kitchen began opening and slamming shut. With his gun drawn, Nicki followed Officer Jenkins into the kitchen.

They both watched in awe as the refrigerator door, cabinet doors and kitchen drawers opened and closed. The bar stools began sliding round the room and the lights started to flicker.

Officer Jenkins took in a ragged breath, and informed Nicki, "Unfortunately, there isn't anything here I can help you with. You may need the help of an exorcist, not a police officer."

***

James arrived at the Rosewood Plantation as Officer Jenkins was leaving the house, "I'm sorry, sir, but I didn't find any intruders – living that is."

James wondered what that remark was all about, but as Officer Jenkins was getting into his car, Nicki walked outside, "I feel like such a fool. I'm so sorry about all of this."

James could see that she was still trembling. He had to fight an overwhelming desire to pull her into his arms. Pushing it aside, he placed his hands on her shoulders. She was ice cold. She slowly began to warm under his touch, and when she looked up at him still with fear in her eyes, his resolve almost broke. "You don't need to be sorry. In fact, I would rather you call, no matter how ridiculous it may sound. After all, what we do know for certain is that a killer is preying on women."

He felt the involuntary shudder move through her body at the mention of the killer, and wanted to kick himself for mentioning it. "I feel like such a fool. I don't normally jump at things that go bump in the night."

"Why don't you tell me what happened."

Shrugging her shoulders, "I overreacted to a nightmare is all. And now I feel like a fool. I'm mortified that I even called you."

"Would you like me to stay the rest of the night with you?"

Shaking her head, "No, that isn't necessary. I'm humiliated about my reaction as it is. Besides, I'm fine. I swear."

"Feel free to call me anytime. Seriously, any time you need me – please, call."

* * *

As Detective Cook drove off, a part of her wanted to call him back. But if she wanted the ghosts to tell her what they needed, it may be better if she was by herself. She was certain that they were trying to tell her something – but what.

Knowing that she wouldn't be able to go back to bed, she went back into her bedroom and unscrewed all but one light bulb. This time, instead of the ghosts haunting her dreams, she hoped to summon them herself.

She sat in the center of her bed and watched as shadows danced around the room. She shrank back in fear, when the shadows seemed to develop bony fingers that reached out for her. While she waited for the ghosts to appear, the light in the ceiling fixture began to dim. She was beginning to suspect that ghosts somehow fed off the energy in the house.

When the light dimmed once more, she saw a man. He was dressed in a waistcoat and a stovepipe hat. He seemed to be looking around the room, as if searching for something. Then he moved toward her. She sat there unmoving, staring at him. At first she wasn't sure if he was a figment of her imagination or really there.

Suddenly, she was surrounded by women, some dressed in Victorian attire to more modern wear. Indistinct whispering came from the women.

For a moment, Nicki swore that she could feel a malevolent energy flowing from him. It was as if evil actually dwelled inside of him. When the man moved closer to her, a woman touched her cheek. "Nicki, you must listen to me. These are the victims of the evil that lives in this house. These women have all been killed here, or near here. While some had their bodies discovered, most have not. These women are trapped here, all hoping to help those who did not escape the heinous death forced upon them.

The light bulb unexpectedly burned with a brilliant explosion. The entire room was aglow, dust mites danced in the brilliant gold light. Then her surroundings went dark and the apparitions disappeared.

Chapter 27

Nicki woke up early feeling refreshed and ready to start her day. She walked into the kitchen and brewed a pot of coffee before letting Oscar out to perform his morning duties.

After pouring her a cup of coffee, she opened the kitchen door and called Oscar, "Come on boy. Let's go for a walk."

Oscar bounded over to her, and then took off ahead of her toward the bayou. As Nicki sipped her coffee, she stepped out into the yard. A few feet away, down the path, she turned back and looked at her home. The black windows watched with guarded eyes over the property.

Icy dew from the grass clung to her ankles and the hem of her pants as she continued her walk. Like the inside of the house, Nicki had been dividing her time to work on renovating the outside. The grounds were starting to look better with each passing day.

Continuing to the bayou, tiny insects fluttered away from her, shocked to be woken at this early hour. A solitary owl called out from deep in the woods. As she called out for Oscar another noise from the woods caught her attention. A shudder moved through her as the trees' branches moved in the breeze.

In the distance, she could hear Oscar barking, "Come on boy. Let's go inside and eat our breakfast."

Hearing the promise of food, Oscar came bounding from the woods. While they walked home, she listened for any noise behind her. Once back inside the house, she leaned heavily on the now closed front door. She took in several deep gulps of air in an attempt to settle her frazzled nerves. Before moving away from the door, she listened to the quiet house and breathed a sigh of relief when no ghosts made their presence known.

* * *

That night Nicki had a dream. She was back on the path, but instead of walking, she was floating high in the sky. She felt light and airy, weightless.

She watched in awe as the scene below played out in slow motion. She noticed a person laying on the ground. It appeared to be an unmoving woman.

The minutes passed slowly. The woman began to tremble, as if she were cold. Only it wasn't cold outside, it was sweltering. The woman's eyes flashed open and stared directly at Nicki. Her eyes had a dull, lifeless look to them.

Nicki stared at the image in disbelief. Without warning, the ground opened up and swallowed the woman whole. Nicki screamed and reached out to the woman, but it was useless –she was gone. Where the woman had once been was replaced by a blinding white light. So bright in fact, that Nicki had to cover her eyes.

Nicki bolted upright in bed and looked around. There was no ghost watching her, no blinding light to greet her – just darkness.

Chapter 28

Steam rose from the coffee cup in James's hand. He grimaced when the strong coffee hit his lips.

Rummaging through the papers on his desk, he let out a low groan. Everything was so disorganized, which was not how he liked to work. Normally he was organized and methodical to the point that it bordered on obsessive compulsive, but these last few days had been crazy. They had yet to get back to Ms. Brady's house to search the attic. They had not even ascertained how the box had found its way into that particular plantation. As far as they could tell, the house had been owned by an elderly woman who had sold the house to move into a nursing home. She had no children and her own husband had passed away years ago.

They were looking into anyone who could have had access to the house, but, unfortunately, the elderly lady had a stroke not long ago and could not tell them anything.

A clunk on his desk shook James out of his reverie. "Thought you might be hungry. It looks as if you slept here last night."

Opening the bag, he pulled out a bagel, "I went home about one o'clock this morning. I couldn't sleep though. I keep seeing our victim's eyes in my dreams. She was pleading with me to find the killer."

One look at his partner, and James could tell that he had trouble sleeping as well. There were bags under his eyes and he looked as haggard as him.

Smearing cream cheese on his bagel, James said, "Since we aren't getting any leads by sitting on our asses here, maybe it is time we paid Ms. Brady a visit."

Nodding his head in agreement, "I was thinking the same thing, mon ami. I'm not sure if the information we discovered in the box is from our killer, but you have to admit that some of the photos are eerily similar."

"As well as the notes that we found in there. So far the forensic techs have not been able to date the photos. They are fairly certain the photos are rather recent, but with them being stored up in the attic, it's hard to tell. The heat did a real number on them."

The drive to Rosewood Plantation was breathtaking. Cypress and oak trees dripping with moss lined the bayou. The water was so still the current was almost nonexistent. Only an occasional ripple of an animal or reptile disturbed the glass-like surface.

Up ahead, a large water moccasin slithered into the murky bayou waters as a large alligator watched the snake with intent.

It was peaceful, and secluded. If the killer was using the old plantation grounds to practice on his victims there would be no one to hear him. It was also the perfect place to dispose of the bodies. Hell, he didn't even have to bury them; the alligators would finish off any remains.

Adam was worried about his partner, "Mon ami you need a woman. You are working too hard. You need something to take your mind off your work."

James let out a laugh, "Trust me, the last thing I need is a woman."

Adam shook his head at his partner's comment. One of these days this man was going to meet a woman who would make him forget all about his reservations. She would turn his life upside down and he wouldn't know what hit him. "I'm just saying someone your age needs to get out. You live alone, never go out, and work your tail off. That is no life for a young man like yourself is all."

Shrugging his shoulders, "I have a life. I just don't want to get involved in a relationship is all."

***

As they pulled up to Rosewood Plantation, James looked over the impressive home now that it was daylight. Even by today's standards the house was massive. Homes back then were built to last. He wouldn't doubt that the nails were handmade and the joists which supported the house individually notched.

He let his mind wander, and imagined what it would be like to live in a house like this. Shaking his head, he told himself that those kinds of dreams were foolish. A house such as this was meant to be filled with children.

Knocking on the door, they patiently waited for Nicki to answer, "Detectives Cook and Veret, I am so glad that you came by. Detective Cook, again thank you for last night. I'm not normally spooked so easily."

James shook his head, "Anyone that had discovered those photos would be uneasy." While she held the door open for them to come inside, he continued, "We came by to search the attic if you don't mind. We would especially like to see exactly where you found the photos."

"Of course. But please, if you find anything – take it with you. You don't need to tell or show me what you found. I would rather not know."

Veret replied, "That is understandable."

Chapter 29

"Nicki."

Nicki had fallen fast asleep from the sheer exhaustion from today's work. She assumed the soft whisper of her name was something her mind had conjured up.

Without opening her eyes, she listened to see if her name was repeated. However, the only sound that she heard was the tick tock from the grandfather clock.

"Nicki."

Then she heard her name again, and heard it clearly this time. She opened her eyes, and a scream caught in her throat. A young woman stood at the foot of her bed. She was dressed in Victorian era clothes, stained with what – possibly mud? "Help us, please, Nicki." The apparition looked at Nicki with forlorn eyes. Nicki tried to let out a scream, but her voice remained frozen in fear.

Then sounds emitted from her. Pitiful moans – more of an infant whining.

"Please, Nicki, you have to help us."

Nicki didn't understand what this young girl was talking about. *Help who? And how?*

She closed her eyes and prayed that the vision disappeared. She tried to convince herself the apparition wasn't real.

"Nicki, please you have to help us. You are our only hope."

She opened her eyes. The apparition stood there, pleading with her to help.

"I don't understand. How can I help you?"

"Please, don't let him continue hurting the innocent."

"Who? What are you talking about?"

"This evil must be stopped. It can't continue."

"What evil? What are you talking about?"

When the apparition reached out to her, she recoiled inwardly. Sheets of icy fear surged through her. She swore the temperature dropped fifty degrees as the apparition moved closer to her. Hysteria started to rise in her when the ghost moved even closer to her, the bottom half of her body hidden by the bed.

Finally, she found her voice and screamed in pure terror. The ghost immediately dissipated into tiny dust mites that sailed on ribbons of moonlight filtering into the room.

Chapter 30

With the discovery of another box of pictures and detailed notes in the attic, Nicki quickly agreed to have the grounds inspected. While James and Adam surveyed the grounds of the plantation, Adam stated, "It would make sense for the killer to dispose of the bodies out here. It is remote."

Nodding in agreement, "But surely the old lady would have heard something?"

"I don't know, mon ami. There is a chance when she fell asleep, she was out cold. I talked to the nurse at the nursing home and she said that Mrs. Fontaine is hard of hearing and has been that way for quite some time."

Adam sighed, "Hopefully, sooner rather than later, she is lucid enough to answer some questions."

Near the back of the property they found what they were looking for. Adam pointed out, "It appears to be an old family graveyard." An old wrought iron fence encased the small patch of land and weathered tombstones. "This would be the best place to hide a body. That is, if they weren't fed to the alligators."

While they walked through the graveyard, Adam found what he was looking for, "Does it look like the ground has been disturbed here?"

Nodding his head, "It appears that a body had been buried directly into the ground."

"Whoever did this thought that they were being clever burying a body on top of a coffin."

Completing Adam's thought James stated, "They didn't take into consideration decomposition though."

Taking out his phone, "Nope. Most people wouldn't have noticed the grave was sunk in though." To the person on the other end of the line Adam stated, "This is Detective Adam Veret. I am at Rosewood Plantation. We need crime scene techs and the ground penetrating radar."

Afterwards he called Sheriff Thompson, "Sir, it appears that we found the killer's burial site."

***

An hour later Nicki watched as a forensics team began stringing crime scene tape around the old graveyard. Shaking her head, she sadly looked over the cemetery. The crumbling tombstones were in desperate need of tender loving care.

Elaborate ironwork swirls and patterns wove the length of the wrought iron fence that surrounded the area. Beyond the gravestones rose a mausoleum, reminiscent of a miniature cathedral. The tar darkened doors were fastened shut with a wooden plank. Tombstones were placed in no apparent order. They were all old and weathered. Some had chunks broken off while others nearly toppled over as the ground under bulged.

The old gate was rusty, but still opened. Unlike the rest of the property this area seemed to be impervious to weeds. The dry earth cracked in places.

She suspected the family had meant for it to be a pleasant oasis. Trees were planted as a barrier, sheltering it from the living or to keep the dead in, she wasn't sure. However, the crape myrtle trees did offer a barrier that defined the space attractively. Yet, she rarely traveled this way. Whenever she was near the graveyard an overwhelming sense of loneliness plagued her. She wasn't sure if it was because of Tom's death or the current neglect of the grounds.

This was the first time since the purchase of the plantation she doubted her decision. Had she been foolish moving down here and trying to start her life over? No, if she had stayed in North Carolina she would have seen Tom everywhere she looked. Nicki closed her eyes and breathed in deeply. *Hang in there girl. You can do this. Just put one foot in front of the other.*

No, she had made the right decision, but possibly the wrong decision in which property to purchase.

However, it was not as if the real estate agent knew that a killer had been using the grounds as his own personal dumping ground. Still Nicki couldn't help but wonder who would have ventured way out there to dispose of bodies. And then there were the boxes up in the attic. Why would they have hidden the boxes up there? Her imagination began to run wild. Could it be that they didn't expect Mrs. Fontaine to sell the property?

When she opened her eyes, she saw Detective Veret observing her, "Do you have any idea who the victim may be?"

Shaking his head, "No, but so far only one body has been found."

"But you expect to find more, don't you?"

Nodding his head, "If we can go by the photographs found in the attic, then yes, I would say there are a few more bodies buried out here."

"From what I understood, before I bought the property, it had been in the Fontaine family."

Nodding his head, "That is correct." Looking at the distraught woman, he asked, "Mrs. Fontaine hired Mr. Mayon to tend to the property several years back. Is that correct?"

Nicki confirmed this, "Yes. From what I understand he has worked for her for approximately six years now. After she moved into the nursing home, he would come check on the property regularly."

His jaw tightened as the intense Louisiana sun beat down on the back of his neck. James ran his hands through his hair, "Have you noticed anything strange lately. Perhaps someone on the property?"

"No, not really. A few visitors and the men I hired to start the renovation work."

***

James saw Chris Ford moving towards him and let out a silent sigh of relief. He was glad that Chris had caught the case. Even though the man may be as annoying as hell to talk to, he was a damn good forensic tech. If only the man knew how to take a joke, but he was too book smart for his own good. He had to analyze everything you told him. He was the only person James knew that could actually ruin a good joke.

"I hear you found a body that doesn't belong here."

Nodding his head, "That is what it appears to be."

"How was the body detected?"

James nodded his head towards the machinery, "Ground radar. I instructed the men to wait until you arrived before digging up the site."

James knew that if anyone had indeed touched the area there would be hell to pay. Although normally laid back, Chris Ford could show his temper if anyone laid a hand on his crime scene.

"Has more than one body been found?"

James informed him, "They just finished marking the grave. They are getting ready to inspect the rest of the grounds."

Nodding his head, Chris told him, "Well, this is going to be a slow, tedious process. I only allow hand shovels and small brushes when excavating a body."

Chris immediately began taking shot after shot of the scene from multiple angles before he would even allow the body to be removed.

* * *

True to his word, five hours later the sun was beginning to set. Crime scene technicians were busy arranging portable floodlights powered by generators. Soon this area would be covered in darkness, making it difficult to work even with the lights. Right now James was wishing they had thought to bring enough bug spray for an army. Being this close to the water the mosquitos were going to be a bitch.

James watched as Chris stood up and stretched his back. They had been working over the burial sites for hours now, meticulously removing and sifting through the dirt.

All the remains found were nothing more than skeletons. The flesh had decomposed. So far only two complete skeletons had been found and there were three partial.

A noise behind him caught James's attention. Nicki smiled over at him, holding up a cooler, "I thought perhaps y'all would be hungry right about now. I made sandwiches and packed some cold drinks."

As if on cue his stomach let out a loud rumble, "You didn't have to do that, but I am sure that everyone here will be extremely grateful."

Nodding to her car, "There are also a couple of thermoses of hot coffee in case anyone needs a pick me up."

Adam moaned in anticipation, "A cup of hot coffee sure would hit the spot."

Over by the forensics van, Adam began setting up a makeshift eating area for those working the scene.

Nicki looked at all the activity buzzing around her, "I'm almost afraid to ask if you found anything."

While James unwrapped one of the turkey sandwiches Nicki had made, he stated, "This will be a long procedure. I am not sure how much longer it will take."

Biting into the sandwich, he swore it was the best sandwich he had ever had. He didn't realize how hungry he had been. After he took a sip of the hot coffee, he began to feel almost human again.

***

Chris winked over at Nicki, "Thanks for the food, ma'am. It sure did hit the spot."

Nicki looked at the man, grimacing at the dirt clinging to his clothes. A shudder of fear ran through her at the reason why he was on her property. She couldn't help but think about the victims they had found. Had they been killed on this very property or were the bodies merely disposed of here. Would the police be able to identify who they were? Did they have family or friends worrying about them? As hard as it was to lose someone, the not knowing what happened to them had to be far worse.

After Tom's death, she had been lost. Sleep had been impossible and she had no appetite. Even now his death hurt her, but at least she knew what had happened to him. The families of these poor victims never had a chance to mourn for the deaths properly. She would make sure that they received a proper burial. She hoped the detectives could find out their identities so the families and friends could finally know what happened to their loved ones.

James looked at the woman curiously, "What made you buy a house way out here?"

Shrugging her shoulders, "I needed to get away from where I lived. Every time I turned around there was something to remind me of Tom. Then one night I saw the real estate ad for Rosewood Plantation. The price is what lured me in."

"Have you decided what you are going to do once you are finished with the restoration?"

Shaking her head, "I haven't thought that far ahead." Staring back in the direction of the house, "When I first moved in I could envision myself running a bed and breakfast," waving her hands towards the cemetery, "but now with the bodies having been found I'm not sure." Sighing, "Although it will be difficult to sell a house when prospective buyers find out bodies were buried here. Then, if it turns out the killer killed those very victims here, I doubt the house will ever sell."

***

James nodded his head in agreement, thinking to himself it would be hard to get people to spend the night out here as well if a killer had indeed used the property for his killing grounds. "It doesn't bother you living out here all by yourself?"

"No, actually I find it peaceful." Shaking her head, "Well, that is up until now."

The sadness that filled her eyes had James wanting to reach out and comfort her. Hell, having her this close to him affected James more than he would care to admit. "Hopefully we can get out of your hair quickly."

With a touch of sadness in her voice, "No, having you here doesn't bother me in the least. Actually, it is quite comforting. What bothers me is not knowing when the killer was on the property last."

Adam took the woman's hands in his, trying to bring her some comfort. He had never seen his partner look as out of place as he did right now, "So far all we know is that the bodies had been buried a while back. No fresh bodies have been found."

A shudder passed through Nicki at the thought of bodies having been unearthed here, "I guess that is a good thing. I hope the killer doesn't come back, though."

Adam nodded his head in agreement, "We will have someone keep a close check on things out here."

James spoke up, "I will personally come look in on you every night until this killer is caught."

Holding up her hands, "No, no, no that really isn't necessary detective. You have your hands full trying to find this killer and not having to come babysit me."

"We know that this killer used this property at one time and it is my duty to make sure that you are safe."

Adam looked at his partner dumbfounded. He had never seen James behave like this. A slow smile began to form on his face. Could it be that his partner had become infatuated with Ms. Nicki Brady?

Adam looked at the woman with sympathy, "I hope that these murders don't change your feelings about Rosewood Plantation or Lost Bayou. This is a great little town to live in and the house needs laughter in it. It needs someone to wash away all the bad that happened here."

"Even if I wanted to, I doubt I could get back the money I paid for the house." Straightening her back, "Perhaps you are right Detective Veret. Maybe I can make Rosewood Plantation a happy place once more. It would be nice to dispel this shroud of gloom that seems to hover over the house like a cloud."

James shook his head, "Still, I don't like the fact that you are living out here all by yourself with a killer running loose."

Chapter 31

Running her tongue provocatively over her lips, she asked, "You want something special cher?"

"Strip!"

While she stripped, she started to wonder if there was something really wrong with her latest customer. Fear snaked down her spine as she shed her clothes. If she didn't need the cash so bad she would tell the man to get lost. Maybe he wasn't that bad.

It could be he was shy around women and not sure how to find a woman on his own. Then again, he could be a man of the cloth from New Orleans seeking out "services" of women from neighboring towns. One thing this business had taught her was that even some of the most religious of men had strange sexual fantasies.

Her fingers lingered momentarily on the bra straps. "Keep going," he ordered.

As the bra fell to the floor, she pondered why the attractive men who sought out her services were so quirky in their ways. The man sitting in front of her was very handsome, with a slightly over-weight body. If it wasn't for the way he acted around her, she would never suspect something even a little off about him. It was only after she had been in the room for a few minutes that she began to realize something was odd about him. It was a shame that someone as handsome as him was also spooky as hell.

She finished undressing and waited for his next set of instructions. In this business, she never knew what to expect. Some men liked for her to perform a little strip tease for them. Some men watched as she touched herself, but this man, he wasn't like any of the others. It was almost as if he was devoid of any emotions. It was eerie the way he watched her with those cold eyes of his. Trying to speed things up, she reached for his crotch, "Did you want to have a little fun?"

Brushing her hand away, he stood up, "Get on the bed."

Doing as she was told she watched as he took out some restraints, "Bondage will cost you extra."

Without hesitation he took out an extra one hundred dollar bill from his wallet, throwing it on the nightstand.

Fear congealed her blood when she saw him take the scalpel out of his bag. *Oh dear God, what did he plan on doing with that?*

Writhing on the bed, she tried to loosen the restraints. Terror moved through her body when he made the first cut. White hot pain took her breath away. She screamed against the gag, praying someone would save her.

When she looked into his eyes, she knew that he was going to kill her. There would be no knight in shining armor to rescue her.

If only she could free herself from these restraints. The pain coursed through her body like molten lava. The intense pain was almost too much for her to handle.

Gloved fingers forced her eyes open while an intense light was flashed into her eyes. The brilliance of the light seared into her eyes as halos of yellow began to dance in her brain. Even when she closed her eyes, she could see those halos of light.

Her heart nearly stopped when the sharp blade cut into her again. She tried to pull her arm away as this man cut into her flesh. Yet all she could do was feel the searing pain while he amputated her arm.

She screamed unmerciously against the gag. How could no one hear what was happening to her in this room? Yet, no one was coming to her rescue. It was as if they were ignoring what was happening in here.

Blood flowed freely from her body now.

Chapter 32

Peter Sampson couldn't wait to drop his line in the water. He had been dreaming of this fishing trip all week. He told his wife, Amber, nothing was stopping him from going fishing today. Come rain or shine he was getting his boat in the water.

As he went to set his boat in the bayou, an object floating in the water caught his attention. He pulled out his flashlight and shined it over at the object to make sure that he wasn't getting ready to walk up on an alligator. He felt himself grow weak from the sight in front of him. While he made the sign of the cross over the body, he called 911 to let the dispatcher know a dead body was in the bayou, or to be more exact, part of a body.

***

James ruefully drove to the crime scene. He glanced over at his partner and noticed that his face showed no emotion whatsoever. James tried his best to keep himself detached from an emotional situation, at least long enough to do his job, but it was difficult for him to hide his emotions.

James gripped the steering wheel a little tighter. His gut clenched in dread as he once again prepared to face a lifeless soul violently taken from this earth. It took a soulless bastard to maliciously kill another human being.

With the discovery of the latest victim's body, he was convinced this killer had no intentions of stopping. He would even bet his next paycheck that this guy was poised and ready to strike again.

By the time Adam and James made it to the crime scene, the sun was rising. Police cars lined the street as uniformed officers combed the area for clues.

James walked stoically over to the bayou, passing crime scene technicians along the way. "Have you found anything yet?" The cop shook his head and carried on. Thankfully, the media hadn't caught wind of the latest murder. Hopefully, when they found out, the scene would be processed and the body removed.

Even before looking at the body, they knew what they would see. The killer's calling card had become all too familiar. Once he saw the body parts, he started barking orders. "I want this entire area combed for clues. For once, I hope this guy left us something to go on."

James carefully surveyed the crime scene and started the meticulous, precise task of assessing the scene. One of the crime scene techs hollered, "We have tire treads not far from where the body was found. They are further down the road than our boater was, so they may belong to the killer."

James and Adam followed the young tech to see what they found. When they arrived, another tech was busy preparing to cast the tire tracks, "We also found some footprints leading away from where the car was parked. We can't guarantee that these belong to the killer, but if you follow the path, it leads to the bayou."

James looked in the direction of the footprints. Could it be that they were finally catching a break? "The body has been here a couple of days though. Surely, the tire tracks and footprints from the killer would have washed away by now?"

The tech shook his head, "It hasn't rained in a few days. It looks like nature helped preserve the rest for us."

Adam exclaimed, "I'll be damned. Let's cast everything in case this was our killer. If nothing else, maybe we can find out what kind of tires are on the vehicle."

Dr. Metcalf arrived while they were making it back to where the body was located. He looked over the body and let out a sigh, "It's a damn shame. She looks so young." After Dr. Metcalf finished examining the body, he stated, "I don't see any scars, marks or tattoos that will make it easier to identify the body right off, but maybe after a more thorough exam, I will find something."

It took several hours for the forensics team to finish combing the area; unfortunately, they didn't find much to go on. Their only clue could be the tire tracks found and James wasn't putting too much hope into that either.

By the time James and Adam walked into the police station, they looked as if they hadn't slept in twenty-four hours. Neither man took the time to shower this morning so they desperately needed to freshen up; unfortunately, that luxury would have to wait. There was still a lot to do before either man could head home.

Chapter 33

Adam caught his partner as he entered the precinct, "Don't get too comfortable. Dr. Metcalf called. He has the preliminary reports done on the victims from the graveyard."

"Did he identify the bodies found on Rosewood Plantation yet?"

Shaking his head, "No, they are still listed as Jane Does."

They moved down the hallway of the medical examiner's office at a brisk pace. James tried to think about anything other than the antiseptic smell that permeated throughout the place. They found Dr. Metcalf busy working in his office.

Shelves were jam packed with various books, and papers lined the desk and floor. Dr. Metcalf looked up from his computer, "Detectives, thank you for making it before the end of the day."

James asked, "What did you find out?"

"I inspected the bones carefully, hoping to find something to help identify these victims. I had hoped we could find out if maybe there was a birth defect that could be found from the bones or even job related anomalies."

Adam asked, "Did you find out anything?

"The victims were buried in the cemetery anywhere from one hundred years ago to as recent as five years ago. Because of the age of some of the skeletal remains, there is no way they were murdered by your killer. This man would have to be ancient."

James asked, "You mentioned birth defects or job related anomalies. Anything there help you?"

Shaking his head, he grimly stated, "No, not really. Two of the girls did a lot of walking in high heels. Could have been a waitress or a..."

Adam cleared his throat, "Or a lady of the evening."

Nodding his head in agreement, "There is that too. Unfortunately, we don't know for sure which she was."

James stated, "So it appears that this is another dead end for us."

Dr. Metcalf replied, "I haven't given up on identifying these victims. I want to see them identified just as bad as you do."

Chapter 34

Nicki walked into her bedroom and let out a long sigh. Her rigorous cleaning was paying off. When she looked around, she could see a remarkable difference. It felt good to witness her hard work, but her muscles were protesting today.

She walked into the bathroom and started running the hot water for a bubble bath. While the tub filled with water, she walked back into the bedroom for a change of clothes. Oscar, who had made himself comfortable in his favorite corner of the room, jumped up to follow her.

A glance at the clock on the nightstand showed that it was almost eleven o'clock. She had worked later than she intended, but the end result had been worth it. From the bathroom, she heard the plumbing creak and then the water stopped running. Groaning to herself, she hoped the plumbing wasn't going to become an issue.

When she walked into the bathroom, a shiver ran through her. It felt as if the temperature had dropped in the tiny room. *Not something else...* She had to bite back a scream when Oscar took a stance at the door and started growling, "What's wrong boy? There is nothing there."

The room quickly warmed so she began to wonder if it was her imagination. Yet Oscar still stood by her side, standing on guard. Fear snaked down Nicki's back. She stared at the faucet like it was a terrifying creature. *Now how in the world did that happen?*

She spun around the room, surveying her surroundings. Nothing seemed disturbed. She walked into her bedroom. The closet door was cracked open, but nothing seemed out of the ordinary.

Then the curtains fluttered. *Almost like someone was hiding behind them.*

Her first instinct was to call Detective Cook, but then common sense kicked in. She had been here all day. She would have heard if someone had entered the house. Besides, Darren would have told her if he saw someone inside the house. *It's an old house with drafty windows, is all.* Perhaps she would invest in upgrading the windows and doors sooner rather than later.

But how did the water turn off in the bathroom? As she walked back into the bathroom, she stared at the tub faucet. Goosebumps broke out on her arms. *What if someone WAS in the house?*

She stood there frozen, unsure what to do next. Her feet felt heavy. The logical side of her reminded her that there was a reasonable explanation, but her paranoid side feared that a murderer was in the house.

She listened intently for any noises coming from the house, but all that greeted her was silence. The smell of rot pervaded the room. It seemed to be coming from her bedroom.

Nicki felt like she was a child again, afraid of monsters hiding under her bed. Or worse – an insane killer with a rusty knife.

She shook her head, attempting to dispel the image. She turned on all the lights in her room to vanquish any shadows. She was standing by her nightstand when the curtains moved again. And again. Reminiscent of someone poking them from the other side.

Nicki flinched, stepping backwards. Clenching her jaw, she told herself that it was from the drafty window.

But, what if…? She thought about the unsolved murders – and worse the pictures that she found. She stared at the windows, the curtains remained still.

"Do it." she ordered herself.

Nicki didn't move, "Go on, do it."

Nicki set her jaw and in one motion, opened the curtains. Nothing there.

She felt a cold wind lift her hair. She laughed; it had to be a draft coming in from a small gap in the window.

As she walked back to the bathroom, a movement from the corner of her eye caught her attention. The dust ruffle on the bed was fluttering. Almost as if something had disturbed it. *Perhaps Oscar had crawled underneath the bed.* Except Oscar was still standing beside her with his guard remaining up. The low growling he had been emitting had stopped, but the hairs on his back were still raised.

Nicki stood still, paralyzed with sheer terror. Her heart jumped into her throat as she attempted to swallow down the fear.

There is NOT a crazed killer under the bed. Yet, there was room for someone to fit under there. The bed was high off the floor. *Had the killer returned for his pictures?*

No, if someone was in the house, Oscar wouldn't be standing here merely growling. He would have warned her instantly when she had an intruder.

But why had the dust ruffle moved?

Nicki got on her hands and knees at the foot of the bed.

What are you going to do if you find someone under there?

Stop it! There won't be.

But what if there is? What if he makes his move when you lift the dust ruffle?

No, it was just the air conditioner kicking on that caused the movement.

But, what if it wasn't?

Nicki reached for the fabric and jerked up the dust ruffle. No one grabbed her. The space under the bed was empty except for a small plume of dust that she waved away.

Nicki let the ruffle drop and sighed in relief. Standing up, "Come on Oscar, let's get ready for bed. We have had enough adventure for one day."

She walked back into the bathroom and started her bath water once again.

***

Sleep came fitfully. The minutes seemed to tick by in silence. A frigid air stirred around her while she drifted off to sleep. She reached down and pulled the covers up to her chin. It didn't help, she remained cold. She bolted awake when she felt a cold breath on her cheek.

She sat up. A faint light, in the shape of a misty white figure faded in and out near her side of the bed. It was soft at first, offering a pale illumination to the room.

Steam from her breath floated into the air and slowly dissipated in front of her.

The shape undulated inside the light, reminiscent of a small chick struggling to break free from the hardened confines of its shell.

Terror gripped Nicki's body when the light moved closer. It lingered at the edge of the bed, swaying back and forth before stopping. Long, skeletal fingers slowly punctured a hole in the light. Bony fingers pushed through the opening.

Nicki's screams echoed through the house when a silhouette of a woman stepped through the light. The woman stared at Nicki, never blinking. The look on her face was one of heartbreak and longing. She never spoke. She simply stood there, as if waiting for something. But what?

Something inside of her compelled her to interact with the ghost. This woman meant her no harm, Nicki was certain of it. "What's your name?"

The woman turned her gaze to Nicki, but didn't utter a word.

"Why are you here?"

Again, no response.

"Did something happen to you in this house? Is that why you are here?"

The woman's mouth opened partially, and uttered three faint words, "Please, help me."

Goosebumps crawled up Nicki's arms. *This can't be happening.* "How? How do I help you?"

A single tear trailed down her ashen cheek.

"Please, can you tell me anything else?" Nicki asked. "I don't know how to help you."

"You must help us," the young woman pleaded, a second time.

Before Nicki could ask her any more questions, the apparition vanished. Determination moved through Nicki. She would find a way to help this woman. She would figure out how she died, and more importantly, who was responsible for her death.

Chapter 35

The silk blouse clung to her full breasts, and the black skirt rode up her legs. Her chestnut hair pooled at the side of her face. Underneath her eyes was smudged black by her mascara. The telltale sign of a bruise was beginning to show on her cheek.

He waited for her to wake up. As she began to stir, he stood over her, "I was beginning to wonder if you were ever going to wake up."

As he continued to smile down at her, he could see the fear showing in her eyes. "Please let me go."

Shaking his head, "Not yet, cher."

"Please let me go. I won't tell anyone, I swear."

Fresh tears rolled down her cheeks. Her lips quivered, as if sensing that her life was about to come to an end.

He watched while she futilely tried to free herself from her restraints. Her breasts bounced with each movement, "Please, why are you doing this to me?"

Taking the knife from its sheath he glided it down her body. He watched as any fight left in her drained from her eyes. Her pleas were now merely a hoarse whisper, "Please. Please. Please."

As he gagged her, he knew that she had no more spirit, no more fight left in her. He had wanted to wait longer before his next kill, but the indefinable hunger had tracked him down once more. Lately his appetites clawed at his insides, demanding to be satisfied.

He traced her lips, then her eyes before moving down her body. When he made the first cut, she screamed against the gag. Blood splattered on his face. With each dismemberment his heart pounded harder in his chest.

He fed off of her pain, off of her terror. The smell of her spilled blood was better than any drug he could buy.

***

Searing pain consumed her body. Her lungs were on fire and the only sounds that could escape from her throat were pathetic yipping noises. They were a waste of precious energy. Tears blurred her vision. She futilely attempted to blink them back and swallow the knot caught in her throat. The light trickling in through the threadbare curtains gave the room a surreal, garish look. When he slashed at her with the knife once more, she felt the blade move through her body again. He cut at her face, arms, and stomach in a frenzied madness.

Death was near. The scent of her blood charged the air as the coppery taste coated her mouth. Death loomed nearer as the killer stabbed her once again. He was relentless, ruthless, and pure evil.

Chapter 36

"Cook."

The dispatcher informed him, "Detective Cook, a maintenance man found the remains of a woman at the park."

The sleep cleared his mind when he heard the news. *Damn!* There went his morning. He jumped in the shower, brushed his teeth, combed his hair, and dressed in a blur. He was out the door in less than fifteen minutes.

James guided his Dodge Charger along the meandering roadway that led to the park. This was one of his favorite parts of town. There were massive ancient oak trees with gnarled branches dripping with Spanish moss. The bayou curved around the outskirts of the park like a snake.

He parked his car alongside the crime scene tape that cordoned off the scene. Patrol cars with flashing blue lights lined the area.

While he watched the growing crowd, he knew that it would be one hell of a day. As with most small towns, word spread like wildfire. They all knew about the discovery of the body and must be wondering who it was. James scanned the crowd. *Which one of these fine, upstanding citizens was the killer?*

He winced at the expression of dread on the face of the young cop guarding the area. James informed him, "If you need help with crowd control call someone in. We need to try and send these folks home."

"Yes, sir. Sheriff Thompson has some officers heading this way."

He heard Frank Ingalls from The Harold call his name, "Detective Cook, do you have any idea whose body has been found?"

Of all the stupid questions, "I just got here Frank. You probably know more than me right now."

The scent of death hung heavy in the air. The smell assaulted his senses. He approached Dr. Metcalf, who was currently hunched over what remained of the victim. A crime scene tech was busy photographing the body and surrounding area.

"What do we have doc?" asked James.

"The killer was vicious. Once again, he cut the body into pieces."

The remains of the woman lay sprawled near one of the large oak trees in the park. The sight of the corpse disgusted James. What remained of her upper torso was propped against the tree like a rag doll. This crime was particularly heinous, its perpetrator barbaric. What drove someone to commit such an atrocity?

This time, the killer took his time to stage the body. It worried James that the killer no longer cared if he hid his work. Would he continue to display his kills?

While Adam observed the scene, he stated, "The killer has changed the game plan again."

James observed the growing crowd, "The press is going to eat this up."

Adam agreed, "They are dying to get a close look at the body."

"That's why the prick dumped her here. He wanted a place with shock value."

Adam clenched his teeth as he said, "My nephew plays here. Any kid could have found her! That burns me up."

"Our perp wanted to make sure the body was found. I do believe he has grown tired of hiding his work."

"Yeah, he's ready for attention. This was an in-your-face-coppers dump."

James had to agree. They were lucky a jogger, or worse a kid, had not stumbled upon the body. Looking down at the body, he couldn't help but think of what a waste this murder had been. She had been beautiful.

Adam shook his head in disgust, "Sometimes I really hate this job."

"Same here, bro."

James studied the scene with clinical eyes. The killer more than likely subdued the woman and bound her before she had a chance to fight back. Her small demeanor made her the perfect prey.

After one final look at the victim, James asked Adam, "Is the maintenance man still here?"

"He is sitting in his truck. I asked him to wait until the scene was processed before leaving in case we have any more questions for him."

James walked over to the truck with Adam, "You found the body?"

"Yes, sir, I was coming to empty the trash cans and saw something propped up against the tree. I wasn't sure what it was and went to check it out. I have never seen anything like that before. Who would do that to someone?"

"Did you touch the body?"

"No, sir. I did not even get close to it. I called 911 and sat at the table nearby so I could keep anyone else away from the area. No one else needed to see that."

Adam asked, "When you got here, did you see anyone else around?"

The maintenance worker ruefully shook his head, "The park was empty. People usually wait until mid-morning to head this way. You mainly get your lunch crowd during the week. They stop to eat their lunches and stuff. Some moms bring their kids to play on the swings and slides, but it is usually after school when it really gets busy. That's why I empty the trash in the mornings. There are less people, and I can clean up quickly."

"Have you seen anyone new hanging out around here, maybe checking out the area?"

"Not that I can recall. This is a small town and most of the locals hang out here sometime during the day. The kids come to unwind after school before heading home to do their homework during the week. On the weekends, they come to play and get out of the house. A bunch of people come at lunchtime to eat and talk. Parents meet and talk here while their kids play in the afternoons. Well, that is until now, I do not look for too many people to come here after they hear about the body. I have a feeling it will be empty for a while."

James looked at the poor man, "Go home. If you think of anything else, call or stop by the station."

"I'm going to go on back to the maintenance shed. Have to let my supervisor know what is going on. I didn't think to call him. He'll probably flip his lid."

Adam watched as the crowd seemed to grow by the minute, "I think half the town is out here now."

James looked over at the crowd, "Hopefully they will head to work or back home soon. They must have something better to do than wait to hear who is dead."

Adam shook his head, "Maybe they'll get tired of waiting and leave." Even as he said the words, he didn't believe them. Everyone would be too shaken up with the discovery of another body.

Sheriff Thompson walked over to the two detectives, "If the crowd starts to bother you, I can have Officer James run them off."

James shook his head, "Let's hold off Sheriff. I have Officer Evans taking pictures of the crowd along with the crime scene. Besides, if we run them off now they will think we are trying to hide something."

***

Brenda Jackson watched from the passenger seat of the van as reporters swarmed the area. Inspecting her reflection in the rearview mirror, she stepped out and prepared her attack.

Looking into the camera, she reported, "Today authorities discovered another body, this time in our beloved park. Undoubtedly, this killer holds no area in the picturesque town sacred." Looking over the park and the detectives working the case, Brenda went on, "And to make matters worse, so far none of the detectives working the case want to make any comments. Women, we need to take a stand. After all, this maniac is hunting us!"

***

By the time, they had made it back to the precinct they had an hour before the autopsy was to begin. James could not believe they had spent half of the day at the crime scene.

Chapter 37

Nicki tossed and turned as she drifted off to sleep. It wasn't long before she started to dream. She was walking through a dense fog, as gray and opaque as a shroud. In the distance she could hear a mournful cry.

The ghostly apparitions started to rise from the ground. She was surrounded by them, but they walked past her, as if they were being beckoned by an unknown source. She cringed inwardly at the sight. Their skin was as gray as the mist enveloping her. Their eyes were nothing but black, hollow sockets.

Nicki found herself being pulled along with them. The fog was reminiscent of a thick soup. She imagined this was what it was like to wade through the murky swamp water.

In the distance a bright light started to radiate in the fog and took the form of a woman. She called the hordes of the dead to her and they slowly moved towards her. As they neared her, she spread her arms and they parted. The woman was trying to speak to Nicki, but she couldn't understand what she was saying.

Then the apparitions were strewn apart in front of her, reminiscent of a doll torn apart by an ill-tempered child. Heads were tossed in one direction, arms in another, and legs in yet another direction. The detached heads now had eyes that cried tears of blood. Their lips moved in silent prayer.

The lady continued to plead with her, but Nicki was too afraid to move. She feared the dismembered arms would reach for her, try to trip her.

Nicki woke up with a start to a cold bedroom; she shuddered at the idea of removing the covers from her body. Taking a deep breathe, she threw off the covers, walked over to her closet and rummaged for a thick sweater.

Walking into her bathroom, she turned on the light and grimaced at her reflection. Not only did she look haggard, but as she quickly undressed for a hot shower she immediately noticed several bruises scattered over her arms and legs. She didn't even recall bumping into anything, but obviously she must have.

To make matters worse, her normally docile dog had chosen to hide under the couch rather than in the room with her. Whenever she tried to carry him into her room, he protested vehemently. It was almost as if he was frightened of the room. He only reluctantly came out of his hiding spot when he was hungry, thirsty or needed to go outside to do his business. However, once outside it normally took some coaxing on her part to get him back inside.

On the nights she could coax Oscar to sleep in the bedroom with her, he would cautiously slink into the room, look around, jump into bed and dive straight under the covers. Lately he rarely sought out affection from her and would growl and moan in his sleep. Even when sleeping, he moved about restlessly. Come morning, he would cautiously leave the bed and bolt from the room without looking back. He immediately bounded down the stairs and went straight to the front door to be let out.

There had even been a few times that Nicki had witnessed Oscar enter a room, bare his fangs, and emit a low growl while he stared wide-eyed into thin air. A couple of times he even went into an attack stance, ears straight up and the fur on his fully extended body stood up the best that it could. The threatening, ominous sounds that emitted from his body were like none that she had ever heard before. He would attack thin air before quickly retreating to a hiding spot.

Now that the boxes were removed from the house and Nicki was certain she wouldn't stumble upon any more grisly photos, she was ready to explore the attic. She was delighted to find an old rocking horse, still in good shape. There was also an old writing desk crammed with moldy papers.

One box contained several old candles and holders. Unfortunately the candles had melted into large blobs, ruining any chances of salvaging the holders.

In one trunk she found several turn of the century Victorian patterns as well as some material. While rummaging through the trunk, she found an old tin box, more than likely used for needles. However the box was heavier than she would expect for holding a few needles. Curious, Nicki tucked it into her jean pocket for further inspection later.

While moving around boxes, she came across an old sewing machine and a dressmaker's mannequin. Nicki made a mental note to move the sewing finds to one of the smaller rooms. There were enough antiques in here to showcase one of the smaller rooms as a Victorian sewing room, one that would have been used when the house was first built.

Excitement bubbled up inside of her as she envisioned what the room would look like with her recent finds. Even the writing desk needed to be brought into one of the rooms. Between the antique store she had stumbled upon the other day and the treasures she had found here, she could set up quite a few rooms for display. *Oh how fun it would be to offer tours in this house.* She would be preserving a part of history that time was starting to forget.

As she stepped out of the attic, she didn't notice the apparition standing in the doorway, watching her. The apparition was more of an indistinguishable mass rather than an actual form. When Nicki collided into it, its intense odor and frigidity knocked her backwards.

She immediately breathed in the frosty, foul odor emitting from the entity causing her body to be wracked with violent coughs. Shaking her head, she assumed she'd stirred up more dust than she realized.

Once back downstairs, Nicki carefully opened the tin box she had found. Inside was an old pocket watch. Before she could inspect the watch further there was a knock at the door.

The sight of Detective James Cook brought an immediate smile to her face. For some reason Nicki had found herself drawn to this man and it scared her. She wasn't ready for these feelings. "Detective, what a surprise."

"I hope I am not bothering you this evening, but I did tell you I would check in on you."

Opening the door wider, "Won't you come in Detective? Would you like a cup of coffee?"

As James entered the house, he shook his head, "I don't want to put you out. I wanted to make sure you were okay after all that happened here the other day."

A noise from upstairs caught their attention, James asked, "Do you have any idea what that was?"

"No… No, I don't."

Upstairs, Nicki gasped at what she saw. The clothes that she had recently washed and put away were scattered around her room, "What the…"

Without warning, Oscar let out a low, menacing growl towards the bedroom door that Nicki kept closed until she could repaint it. James asked, "What is that room?"

Nicki replied, "Another bedroom, but it smells rather musty so I keep the door closed until I can repaint it."

Pulling out his gun, he instructed Nicki "Stay here. I want to go check it out and make sure that no one is hiding in there."

Nicki's heart pounded furiously inside of her chest. She thought things were starting to settle down, now this. She had no idea why her clothes were scattered all over the room, or even what could have caused that noise. She had been home all day today and hadn't heard anything until now. Could it possibly be the ghosts letting her know something? But what? Why wait until Detective Cook arrived to make a statement?

***

When James opened the door, the smell of decay assaulted his senses. His gut instinct told him that someone or something had died in this room. He couldn't help but wonder what this room would look like when sprayed with luminol. If there had ever been blood present in this room the luminol would show it. Now the trick would be to convince Ms. Nicki Brady to allow the crime scene techs to do this very procedure.

***

While James searched the room, Nicki began to pick up her scattered clothes. The mere thought of something or someone going through her things had her nerves strung tight. She had to get to the bottom of this mystery. Everything she owned was tied up in this house. If she merely walked away, she would lose everything. She owed it to Tom to make his dream come true. But if it turned out there were gruesome murders here, could she truly see herself living here? Could she bring peace to this house after the nightmares that took place here?

Nicki had been so deep in thought she didn't hear James walk up behind her, "I didn't see anything in the room."

Placing a hand over her racing heart, "Goodness you scared me." Shaking her head, "I don't understand who or what could have done this."

Her vulnerability must have had him feeling protective towards her. James pulled Nicki close to his body.

Nicki found herself falling for this man, but soon guilt took over her body. How could she ever love another man after Tom? He had been her whole life. He was

the knight in shining armor she had dreamed of. But
now he was gone, taken from her too soon. She
quickly pushed away from the warmth of James's
body.

James shook his head, "I'm no expert, but I don't see
this being done by a ghost. Are you certain that you
didn't hear anyone in the house today?"

Shaking her head, "No, I have been home all day and
the house was quiet."

"Well, after seeing this there is no way I am allowing
you to spend the night here by yourself."

"No, Detective Cook that's really not necessary. I don't
want to put you out. Surely you have someone at
home waiting for you."

James shrugged his shoulder, "There is no one at home
waiting for me, and even if there were, I wouldn't feel
right leaving you alone in this house at night. At least
until we know what caused this."

***

While he helped Nicki pick up the clothes, he caught a
whiff of her perfume. The scent was intoxicating.
Perhaps he should have insisted she check into a hotel
room until this mystery was solved. Being around this
woman could bring him nothing but trouble.

Needing to distract himself from being so close to this woman, he began searching her room, "You know some of these old houses have secret passageways." James began tapping on the walls, waiting to see if he heard a hollow sound. He called out, "I think I found something."

Nicki was astonished to hear that, "What? Like a secret door or something?"

Shrugging his shoulders, "I'm not sure, but I don't think whoever put this here wanted it found. It is sealed tight."

"Then how are we supposed to open it?"

"Well, if the passageway had been built at the same time as the house there would be a lever of some kind."

Nicki searched for some kind of lever with James. After a few minutes James stated, "You know this room is actually much smaller than the other bedrooms. It is as if someone had purposefully sealed off the room."

Nicki shouted out in exhilaration, "There is a smaller room that I thought was the nursery right next door. However, unlike the other rooms there is no door connecting these two rooms."

James rubbed his chin as he thought, "Hmmm, that is odd. I do believe that someone sealed up this area."

A curious Nicki excitedly asked, "So what do you think we should do?"

"Let's search the other rooms and see if we can find any other hidden doors." In the next bedroom, inside the closet James found what he was looking for, "I found another hidden door, but this one doesn't appear to be sealed shut."

James pushed the door with his shoulder, forcing the heavy door open. The rusted hinges groaned in protest. Finally, the door yielded to James's weight with a loud snap, almost throwing him off balance. Stagnant and musty air escaped from the dark passageway. They both stared at the h dden passageway in shocked silence. James stated, "We may be able to find out if someone is getting in and out of your house."

A shiver of fear ran down Nicki's spine at the thought of a stranger coming and going as they pleased in her house, especially if that person was a gruesome killer. James asked, "Do you have a flashlight by any chance?"

"Hold on and I will go grab it." Nicki rushed into the kitchen for the flashlight, making it back to the bedroom in no time. "Here you go, sir."

While James inspected the passage, he noticed it was laden with dust more than a century old, "It doesn't look as if anyone has been in this area in ages."

They entered the dark passage and crept along the corridor carefully. The walls and floor were made of solid wood. Several cobwebs hung like shrouds from the ceilings and crevices. The deeper they moved inside, the fouler the air smelled.

Nicki was intrigued with the passageway running inside the house, "Why do you think a passageway is here?"

"If I remember correctly, during the 1800's several homeowners had the passageways built in their houses as an escape route. The passageways would lead out to the barn or another building so that the family could escape if needed. It was a way of adding extra security in case soldiers decided to raid the house in the middle of the night."

As they made their way further down the passageway, James stopped her, "Look! Someone or something has been down here. See the marks in the dust."

Swallowing down her fear, "Perhaps it was a mouse or something?"

James shook his head, "No, these look like footsteps and they appear to be fresh."

Apprehension began to fill Nicki, "I don't suppose a ghost would leave footsteps behind would they?"

"No, I don't think so."

Nicki wasn't sure what to think of the fresh footsteps in the passageway, "Maybe the caretaker, Jake Mayon, knew about the passageways and he is the one who left the footprints."

James thought about that for a minute, "That could be. It wouldn't hurt to ask him."

After a few more steps they made it to the end of the passage. "If this is the end of the passageway there would be a trap door."

They immediately began looking for signs of a door. Up above them James found a large iron ring with the remnants of a rope tied to it. The door was barely visible in the murky darkness. It took several hard pulls before the trap door let out a loud squeal. The smell of dank, damp earth greeted them.

James shone the flashlight in the area, "It appears that this comes out in an old workshop of some kind."

As they made their way out of the passage and into the old workshop, Nicki looked around. "So if someone did know about these old passageways, it would be easy for them to gain entry into the house?"

Grimly, James nodded his head, "I'm afraid so."

"Should we figure out some way to board this passageway shut?"

Rather harshly, James replied, "No! If he is coming in and out of the house this may be the perfect way to trap him."

Nicki let out a long sigh, "Do you have a plan on how to do that?"

"No, but it won't take me long to put one together."

Already, James's head was turning. He planned on finding out if the computer techs had some surveillance he could set up in the tunnels. His pulse was racing at the possibility of catching this killer in his own game.

Once they were back in the house James went straight up to the room with the sealed door, "It appears that someone sealed this door from the passageway. If you have no objections I would like to try and tear down this wall."

"I want to solve this mystery as much as you. I say we see what is in here."

Once James found a sledgehammer in the old tool shed, he began to punch a hole in the wall. A musty, stale odor imbued the room, as the hidden room was made visible. Nicki peered over James's shoulder into the opening he had created, letting out a loud shriek, "Oh no...!"

James looked up to see that Nicki's face had turned ashen white, "What's wrong?"

Nicki pointed inside the tiny room. Propped up against the wall was a pair of mummified remains. Goosebumps prickled up and down Nicki's body.

James moved in closer to inspect the skeletal remains, "These weren't left here by the killer. The clothing is from more than likely the Victorian era."

Cobwebs and dust covered the remains. Nicki pointed to a box on the man's body, "It looks as if someone threw the box in here as well. James carefully removed the box, handing it to Nicki. She slowly opened the box and gasped when she found a ring inside, "It is gorgeous and very old."

James took the ring out for closer inspection, "It doesn't appear to have ever been worn either. The gold is in too good of shape."

"Can you imagine what this ring must be worth now?"

"I imagine it cost this gentleman a good bit back then too. Fine jewelry like this was too expensive for the common man to buy."

While Nicki looked at the two skeletons, she exclaimed, "I wonder if this is Aurora and her lover."

Nicki continued to tell James the story of the two lovers.

James ran his hands through his hair as he listened to her story, "It could be that the husband caught the two lovers during a tryst and killed them in a fit of rage."

"That would explain why they were never seen. He sealed them inside the house."

Taking his phone out of his pocket, he explained, "I am going to call the crime scene techs to come in and remove the bodies. There is a chance the coroner can date the bodies."

Nicki nodded her head in agreement, "At least we can give these two a proper burial."

Chapter 38

As Nicki opened the bedroom door, she stated, "There are fresh sheets on the bed and fresh towels in the bathroom. Are you sure that you are okay with sleeping here?"

"I don't like that you are living out here all by yourself with a killer on the loose."

James was glad that she had chosen to give him the room next to hers, that way he could hear if she made the slightest noise during the middle of the night. He loathed the idea of her sleeping out here all by herself.

She gave him a smile, "I will be fine."

"Well, in case you do see anything, at least I am right next door."

Walking to her room, she replied, "Good night Detective Cook."

"Just remember that I am right next door if you need me."

"Thank you. Knowing that you are here will help me sleep a lot easier tonight."

He watched as she walked into her room and closed the door. James went into his room and looked around. He unholstered his Glock 22 and placed it on the nightstand next to the bed.

***

While James took his shower, Nicki slipped outside to enjoy the bayou and moonlight. The glow from the moon shimmered across the water. A light breeze flirted with the leaves in the trees. Nicki listened to the gentle sloshing of the water. It was such a perfect romantic night and she found herself missing Tom. Sitting here beneath the canopy of trees, she watched the fireflies dance and reflected on how isolated the plantation was. This was the first time she found this fact disarming.

As she studied the murky water of the bayou, she found herself wondering what secrets it held. She watched as a low clinging fog moved over the dark water. She found herself mesmerized as it moved over the land. For a moment Nicki thought a figure was beginning to take shape in the fog.

When she entered the house the water from the shower was no longer running. She tiptoed to his bedroom door and heard nothing but silence. He must be asleep. She looked at her watch and gasped, she had been outside longer than planned.

She decided to take a quick shower to wash off the dust and grime of the day.

Once the water was hot, she stepped into the tub and let the warm water run down her back. The soothing water turned ice cold as the temperature in the bathroom dropped twenty degrees. The sound of the television playing in her bedroom started to become louder as she turned off the water. She hoped the loud tv didn't wake her guest. She could have sworn she had the volume low when she stepped into the bathroom. Then she heard the channels switching and laughed to herself. Oscar must be sitting on the remote.

A loud raking sound pierced through the night air. It was reminiscent of metal nails scraping against a chalkboard. As the sound moved closer to the bathroom, a shiver of fear ran down her back. She took a deep breathe and wrapped her fingers around the shower curtain. As if in slow motion, she pulled open the shower curtain a crack and peeked out. She saw her clothes crumpled on the floor and Oscar standing at the now open bathroom door. She shook her head; she swore that she had closed it.

"Oscar, you scared the crap out of me!"

Oscar cocked his ears and stood there. Suddenly, Oscar pulled his lips back and snarled, bolted out of the bathroom and straight into the bedroom. Wrapping a towel around her still wet body, Nicki went after Oscar in hopes of calming her skittish pet. As she entered her bedroom a cold draft passed over her body, sending goosebumps up and down her arms. Nicki's muscles tensed in fear as she looked around the room. She swallowed down a lump of fear and called out, "Oscar, come on boy. Where are you?"

A strong smell of cigar smoke annihilated her senses and was quickly replaced by the comforting scent of her husband's favorite cologne. The scent surrounded her. "Tom, is that really you?"

She waited for his response as tears built up in her eyes. As if sensing his owner's discomfort, Oscar came out from his hiding spot and rubbed his body against her legs. Realizing that Tom was never there, that it was only her imagination, Nicki pet Oscar's head and dressed for bed.

As she lay curled up in bed, her mind drifted back to all the work that needed to be done to the plantation. She wished she had seen it in its original grandeur. What a sight it must have been!

When sleep came, she found herself in the midst of a dream. The women were there once again, staring at her mournfully. Out of nowhere, a man came into view. He didn't appear to be from this decade. He had muttonchops on his cheeks and a clean-shaven chin. He appeared to be approximately early forties and stood a little taller than the women. There appeared to be traces of gray showing right above his ears. He seemed to be attractive until he turned towards her.

She shuddered in fear at the black, soulless eyes staring back at her.

As he moved closer to the bed, he pulled a knife out of mid-air. The blade gleamed against the darkness of the room. The women began wailing in fear, "You must stop the evil that lives here. It is the only way we can find peace!"

The man let out a menacing laugh, "You foolish women. No one can stop us. No one will ever be able to stop us." As he laughed, the dream dissipated into thin air.

The next morning, Nicki woke up later than she had wanted. She let out a groan when she saw that it was almost eight o'clock in the morning. She had wanted to awake early, in case Detective Cook was an early bird. She felt responsible for him spending the night here.

As she walked downstairs, she heard Darren outside, busy pounding away with his hammer. While she finished setting out everything for the coffee on the counter, she heard someone whistling, followed by footsteps. By the sound of it, either Darren or James was nearby. She called out, "Coffee is ready."

Not hearing a response, she peered into the foyer to see that it was empty. She could have sworn she heard someone. Shrugging her shoulders, she went in search of the men. In the foyer, she felt a cold breath on her shoulder. Swallowing hard, she looked back and a shiver went through her. No one was there.

Before she could search further for the men, she heard a car coming up the driveway. She wondered who that could be at this hour. She stepped out onto the porch and watched as a red Mercedes stopped in front of the house. Once the dust settled around the vehicle, a rather large man stepped out. The way he carried himself had Nicki believing the man more than likely never worked a day in his life.

***

Charles Guilliot looked at Rosewood Plantation with pure envy. The house should be his. If only his damn aunt had left it to him like he had planned. This place would be perfect for a bed and breakfast. He had everything planned out, this place would have made him a fortune, and then his aunt had to go and sell it.

He would make the current owner believe the house was haunted. Perhaps then, he could buy it cheap.

He had to convince this woman to leave. People would clamor to stay in a place that was rumored to be haunted. On top of that he had made sure that the Rougarou legend had been the talk of the town lately. He would have even more people wanting to stay out here in hopes of catching sight of the mysterious creature. He may even be able to charge triple what rooms normally go for in this area.

He moved with determination and purpose to the front porch. The glare he gave her packed a powerful punch of discontent. Nicki met the man's hateful stare head on. A scowl was plastered on his face as he looked at her accusingly.

In a harsh tone, he stated, "My name is Charles Guilliot. This should have been my house and I am having my attorney file the necessary paperwork for me to take over my aunt's financial matters. When she sold this house to you she wasn't of sound mind or body and we shall prove that."

Nicki bristled at his harsh comments, "You can try, but when I bought this plantation Mrs. Fontaine was very much aware of what she was doing."

"Hmm, we shall see about that. I aim to prove that you coerced my aunt into selling this house to you."

"I did no such thing. Your aunt went through a real estate agent to sell this house. If the agent felt that she was not of sound mind or body I am certain that they would have said something."

Scoffing at her, "You would be better off leaving this place and forgetting that you ever saw it. I aim to make this house mine."

Shaking her head, "I won't do that. I plan to return this place to its original grandeur."

Pointing his finger at her, "Listen here, lady; you better take heed to my warnings. Strange things have been known to happen in this house."

***

As the man stomped back to his car, a chill washed over Nicki. She could swear someone was watching her. She cautiously looked around praying she didn't see anyone. Her breath caught with a gasp. There in the trees, near the bayou, was a man staring back at her. With him hiding in the shadows, it was too hard to make out his appearance. He stood motionless with his arms at his side. There was a disheveled look to him.

James walked out of the house, "What was all that commotion?"

Shrugging her shoulders, "It was nothing."

The man disappeared before Nicki had a chance to tell James about him. Perhaps it was only her mind playing tricks on her.

***

Moving deeper into the swamp, briars grabbed at his jeans as he plunged deeper into the underbrush and he made his way to his hiding spot. He made his way carefully to avoid slipping and falling in the foul smelling muck. He let out a curse as a clump of sodden moss slapped him straight in the face.

As of yet this woman had not left. He would have to amp up his efforts quickly. He wanted her gone!

Chapter 39

Nicki found herself thinking about all that had transpired recently. After pouring herself a cup of coffee Nicki stepped out onto the back porch. The rising sun neared the distant horizon as soft pinks and orange hues began to streak the dark sky. She took a deep breathe, inhaling the fresh air.

The scenery of the bayou helped lift her spirits. She HAD made the right decision purchasing this plantation. This was simply a speed bump in her path.

She heard the back door open and watched as James stepped outside, "I hope you slept well last night."

James cracked his neck as he looked over Nicki, "You should have woken me. I don't like you being out here by yourself."

Nicki merely shook her head, "I am not letting what happened stop me from renovating this house. I will not be scared off of this property. Besides, if the killer had really wanted to kill me, he would have done so by now."

"I don't know. We still have no idea how long he stalks his victims."

Not wanting to talk about the subject anymore, Nicki asked, "Would you like me to cook you breakfast?"

"You don't have to do that. I am good with a cup of coffee."

Laughing, "Well, that I can handle.

As they headed back inside a feeling of being watched overcame Nicki. The hairs on the back of her neck stood on end and her skin had goosebumps running up and down her body. Her gaze moved to the swamp. There was no movement there that caught her attention. Shaking off the feeling, she hurried back inside.

The sound of a hammer greeted her. "I didn't even hear Darren come inside this morning."

James shrugged his shoulders, "He arrived around seven. I'm not sure I like how he has the run of the house while you are asleep. But he went straight to work when he got here."

Wanting to greet Darren, she walked into the living room to find him hard at work, "Good morning. I'm sorry that I didn't hear you arrive this morning."

Glancing over at James's direction, he stated, "I figured you may have had a late night and decided to get right to work."

After finding the hidden passageways Nicki found it a little unsettling the way Darren moved around the house so quietly. Had he perhaps known about the passageways? Could he have been the one to scatter her clothes all over the place?

Shaking off the unsettling feeling, she asked, "Well, can I at least get you a cup of coffee or cook you breakfast?"

Darren shook his head, "I'm good. I want to get a little more done this morning." With that he walked off.

Turning around, she collided into James. Losing her balance, he caught her by the waist and pulled her to him. The look he gave her could melt a glacier. Silence thickened as his unrelenting stare missed nothing in her eyes. Her heart pounded in her ears. Powerless to fight the need rising inside of her, she wrapped her arms around his neck and pulled him to her. His chest was rock hard and welcoming. Looking deeply into his eyes, "I shouldn't be doing this."

Shaking his head, "No, you are right. This would complicate matters."

Nicki tried to sound convincing, "I don't want this."

James smiled at her, "Neither do I."

They were both lying to each other. She saw the desire in his eyes. Her eyes glowed with the same passion. There was a smoldering fire burning inside of her. The flames rapidly spread through her body. For the first time in a long time, she wanted another man.

His arms curved around her back, clutching her as if he never wanted her to leave his arms. She found herself not wanting him to let her go, not until he doused the flame inside of her.

He whispered in her ear, "If you truly don't want this, then you must stop me." He touched her lips with his. With a desperate moan, she greedily accepted his kiss. She shuddered in response. He tasted as if he was made for sin.

His touch sent her pulse racing. Not wanting the kiss to end, she ran her hands through his hair as the kiss deepened. She felt her body melting against his. They lost themselves in the long, slow kiss.

As they ended the kiss, Nicki looked deep into James's eyes. She could see the passion he felt for her. It turned her blood to hot lava. Every nerve in her body responded to his touch.

Was she ready for a romantic relationship? Swallowing hard, she pushed away from James. "I guess I should get in the kitchen and cook us breakfast before we starve to death."

He let his hands drop from her waist, and she instantly missed their warmth, "You don't have to do that. I need to get to work anyway." Looking into her eyes, "I didn't mean for the kiss to go that far."

Sighing, "I am a big girl. I knew what I was doing. You didn't make me do anything I didn't want to do."

Nicki watched as James drove off to work. It had been so tempting in his arms. Maybe cleaning would take her mind off her out of control libido.

A sudden desire to explore the attic came over Nicki and she rushed upstairs. Several hours later she was shocked to find James standing in the attic doorway, "Oh my goodness. What time is it? I got so busy in here I wasn't paying any attention to the time."

He looked around at all the piles, "I take it you found some interesting items?"

Nodding her head, "Now that I don't have to worry about finding any more gory surprises I have found some real treasures. I even found some old photos that would be perfect to display around the house. It looks as if items have been stored up here for years and no one even bothered to check and see what was up here. Instead, they piled more stuff in the space."

"Do you need any help?"

Nicki pointed to a back corner, "I did find an old trunk that seems to be almost buried in the corner back there."

As they drug the trunk out of its hiding place they stirred up some dust, "Whew, it's been a while since anyone has been in this particular area."

Nicki fanned the dust from her face, "As long as we don't find any bodies, I will be fine."

She gasped in delight at the treasures the trunk held. There were old clothes and letters in the trunk as well as some old photographs. "This appears to have been Aurora Fontaine's trunk. Her husband must have had it stored up here after her death."

As they headed back downstairs Nicki caught a heady scent of James's rich maleness. Once they were downstairs, James closed the distance between them. He pressed his mouth to hers. At first, the kiss was gentle, soft as a butterfly's fluttering wings. The chaste kiss was merely an appetizer.

He pulled her closer to him, devouring her with his mouth. Heat skimmed along her nerves as his hands slid up and down her body. Any objection she may have had floated away with his touch. Later, she may be sorry, but for now, she couldn't resist his kisses.

She let out a low, throaty moan as he kissed her neck. Warmth filled her deep inside, flaming up higher and higher. His lips took hers once more and long forgotten passion ignited in her body. Her body became a vessel for passions as his hands moved up and down her spine. Her body melted into his and her blood boiled over with desire.

As his hands caressed her breasts, her legs turned to liquid. Her breath caught as his hands slipped underneath her shirt. He cupped her breasts and squeezed softly. As his fingers teased her nipples, she shivered with delight. His touch felt so good. She wanted nothing more than for this feeling to go on forever. Her body craved his touch, but then images of Tom flashed through her mind.

As if sensing a change in her emotions, he pulled away, but still kept her in his embrace, "Nicki?"

Holding back the tears, she said remorsefully, "I'm not sure I'm ready for where this is leading."

He nibbled on her neck, before smiling down at her, "I understand, and the last thing I want to do is rush you." Tilting her chin up, he gently kissed her on the lips, "But when the time is right, you will know it. And I promise you it will be spectacular."

Nicki laughed, "I hope that I can live up to those expectations."

Chapter 40

The perilous night gave him a thrill. Like a hungry animal stalking its prey, he waited for the perfect moment to strike.

He hid in the shadows. The darkness of his car cloaking him. He had been following her for over a week now – waiting and watching.

His heart pounded violently in his chest. He became overwhelmed with a feeling of euphoria that few would ever understand.

He looked at the clock and noticed she would soon be going to bed. It would soon be time to act. He quietly left his vehicle and stood in the shadows of the trees outside of her house. Nightfall brought no relief from the heat wave that plagued the state. His shirt clung to his back, already damp with sweat.

He watched as the lights in her house were turned off. He caught a hint of movement in her room. Moving cautiously along the shadows to her back door, he quickly opened it and entered the house. He had been in her house while she was at work and knew the way. He headed straight to her bedroom.

Moving efficiently, he pulled out the ketamine soaked rag and held it over her mouth and nose before she had a chance to react. The drug quickly weakened her.

Keeping to the shadows, he easily carried her back to his car.

He drove to his favorite spot, not paying attention to the speed limit. He reprimanded himself; it would be hard to explain an unconscious woman in the back of his car.

He pulled down the long narrow road that led to the plantation. This had been the perfect place to practice his skills and it was time he returned. Trees dripping with Spanish moss shrouded the old plantation home, cloaking his every movement. The old woman had no idea what he had done here. Even when she had put up the house for sale, no one seemed to want to take on the monstrosity and expense of renovating it.

This would be his biggest challenge yet, though. Working under the nose of not only the current owner, but the detective searching for him also. The rush added to the thrill of the hunt, more than he anticipated.

A heavy fog hovered over the bayou. A smoky mist made its way to the house. The damp air was a perfect marriage of the murky bayou water and the fragrances of confederate jasmine and gardenia. He turned off his lights and pulled up to his hiding spot in the dark. He didn't need light to show him the way. He had the area memorized.

He hastily brought the unconscious woman to his workroom. He placed her bound and gagged body onto the table, moving quickly to secure her.

He carefully arranged his tools on the cart. He ran his hands down her body before bending down to inhale the scent exuding from her body. Even unconscious, her body seemed to emit the insidious aroma of fear.

He tingled with anticipation at the thought of dismembering her body. He made sure the gag sealed her mouth closed and zip strips restrained her arms and legs to the table. The smell of her fear had a powerful effect on him. Her scent enveloped the room.

He wheeled the cart over to her. He picked up the filet knife and made a long incision down her torso.

He watched as the blood flowed from her body. She bolted awake from the pain. Her eyes widened in pure, unadulterated terror. Tears streamed down her cheeks. He watched her breasts rise and fall with each breath she took.

After he finished dismembering her body, he took her body parts to the bayou. A noise echoed through the trees. An early morning fisherman must be on his way to try to beat the impending heat and humidity of another scorching summer day. The sun's first rays were still hours away.

With a devious smile, knowing what he had accomplished under the detective's nose – he disposed of the body in the bayou. It felt good to be back home doing what he enjoyed best – killing.

Chapter 41

Death was a normal part of life, especially here in the bayou. Death lived in the shadows, and moved silently as a snake. But this killer brought a new meaning to death. He moved through the town silently, killing efficiently and leaving no evidence behind. Just like the bayou that ran through the town, the killer was vast with secrets.

As James stared at the crime scene, he said a silent prayer that they could keep this latest murder under tight wraps for as long as possible. Once it became known that another murder had taken place, all hell would break loose.

James parked behind a police cruiser, settled his hat on his head, and headed towards the boat landing where the remains of a woman had been discovered. James carried his height with a forceful stride that made his stature seem even more intimidating.

There was no denying that Lost Bayou had a killer on the loose. He feared that his suspicions were correct and that Rosewood Plantation was the killer's playground. And worse, even with James staying there at night, the killer was still using it.

He winced at the expression of dread on the young, rookie cop's face. "I take it you were first on the scene?" James asked.

"Yes, sir, a boater called it in. He was going to launch his boat and found the torso drifting in the current."

Looking at the young officer, James informed him, "Make sure that you keep out any nosy reporters who may want a better picture."

"Yes, sir."

"Do we know who the victim is?"

"Jenny Robinson, sir. She is a local waitress."

James noticed the forensic techs were already busy taking photographs of the remains as well as the crime scene. His partner, Detective Veret, was walking the scene looking for any evidence that could have been left behind by the killer.

He approached the coroner, Dr. Metcalf, hunched over what was left of the victim. "What do we have doc?"

"It's the same as the previous victims. The mutilation of the body occurred while she was alive."

As James looked down at the victim, he felt his stomach clench. There was faint bruising on her face, which possibly came from a blow from the killer. "How long has she been dead?"

"I'm estimating that time of death occurred around two o'clock this morning."

***

As Veret finished his appraisal of the crime scene, he walked over to the body to join Dr. Metcalf and his partner, Detective Cook. Looking down at the body caused Veret's stomach to churn. He could actually feel a chill reach to his soul. "Mais, we need to keep this quiet for as long as possible."

James asked Dr. Metcalf, "Did you happen to see any trace evidence on the body?"

"The water washed most of the evidence away. Fortunately, a few fibers were found caked with the blood of the wounds. But there is nothing really remarkable or distinctive. I will have those rushed to forensics for you. There were no hairs, bite marks nor any defensive wounds noted on the body either."

***

James and Adam made it to the morgue a few minutes before the autopsy was to begin. Upon entering the morgue, they both noticed the drop in temperature. The bone penetrating cold seemed to hang onto every breath one took just as death hung onto the victim.

Adam confided to his partner, "This place gives me the creeps."

James merely nodded as he adjusted to the smells around him. Before entering the autopsy room, they peered through the viewing window to make sure that Dr. Metcalf was ready for them. Inside the room, what remained of the latest victim was laid out with a white sheet pulled up to her chin.

Dr. Metcalf greeted the two detectives, "Detectives you are just in time. I was about to begin." When Dr. Metcalf moved the sheet down to begin the autopsy, it was all Adam could do to keep from losing his lunch all over the autopsy room floor. He thought that looking at the crime scene had been bad, but the harsh lights of the autopsy room made the mutilation appear even more grotesque.

Adam shook his head as he asked, "What kind of monster could do this to another human being?"

James looked over at him grimly, "Unfortunately, another human being."

So far, they had been able to keep all the gruesome details out of the paper, but James knew that it wouldn't be long before something was leaked to the press. When that happened, the shit would really hit the fan.

James looked over at Adam, "How many more women must die before he makes a mistake and leaves us a clue?"

***

James thought he knew what hell was, but that was before he had to tell Jenny Robinson's parents about their daughter's death. It had been heart wrenching to watch the light die in their eyes. It broke his heart when Mrs. Robinson crumpled to the ground in tears with her face ravaged with grief. It had taken all of his strength to accept Mr. Robinson's outstretched hand as he left.

Although, this wasn't his first time to notify someone that their loved one had died, it never got any easier. Every time, it felt like a punch in the stomach. It was almost as if somebody was ripping out his own heart.

He let out a shaky breathe and blinked his tired eyes as he tried to concentrate on the computer screen in front of him. He wanted to do one more search through VICAP. There was no way this killer was starting out. He was too precise in what he did not to have killed before.

James let out a deep sigh when he saw the results of his recent computer search. He had struck out. There were no murders being reported anywhere in the country that resembled the way his victim was mutilated and murdered.

He nodded his head as Adam made his way to his desk, "I can't believe that this killer isn't showing up on any of the sites. There is no way that this guy just started killing like this."

Adam shrugged his shoulders, "Who knows? It could be that he has been hiding the bodies before now."

James rubbed his temples. He felt a monster of a migraine coming on. Sighing, he looked at his watch and realized that it was almost midnight. Stepping up from his desk, he decided to head home and try to get some sleep. "Well, mon ami, I don't know about you, but I say we call it a night."

Adam turned off his computer, and agreed, "I don't know if I will be able to sleep but I plan to try."

Chapter 42

Sheriff Thompson looked up from his desk and tried to hide a scowl. Mayor Jenkins was walking towards his office. Why couldn't the man simply pick up the phone to check in? Mais non, he had to drop by with no warning. It was not as if they didn't have a lot going on right now.

Mayor Jenkins walked right into his office, "Sheriff, do you have any more information regarding these murders?" he asked without preamble.

Before Sheriff Thompson could even stand up from his desk Mayor Jenkins sank into one of the visitor's chairs and grabbed one of the files from Thompson's desk. *Mon dieu, of all the nerve!*

Thompson stacked the remaining files neatly in front of him, "Nothing that you don't already know, sir. I wish you would have called before heading over here, I could have saved you the trip."

He watched as Mayor Jenkins shrugged his shoulders, "I had planned on coming over this way anyhow. I wanted to check on the progress of this case personally. Lately, my phone is ringing off the hook with worried constituents wanting answers. I want this man stopped before he can kill again."

Sheriff Thompson stiffened at the tone, "Sir, with all due respect, we are working this case the best way we can."

"Do you think we need to consider bringing in the big guns?"

Sheriff Thompson shook his head, "No, sir. This isn't something they would be interested in right now. Besides, no outsider is going to know the people here in this town better than our own. We will put the pieces together and find this killer. Unfortunately, we are looking at someone local who is committing these murders. My main concern, right now, is I don't want the word serial killer leaked to the press. We don't need to put this town into a panic."

"People are already getting scared. I can hear it in their voices every time they call."

Sheriff Thompson informed him, "They may be scared, but no one is beginning to panic. We don't need all hell breaking loose."

"And what do you propose I tell these concerned citizens?"

Sheriff Thompson tried to keep the irritation out of his voice, "You can tell them Lost Bayou's finest are diligently working on catching this killer. Ask them to please keep their doors locked at night, be careful, and pay attention to their surroundings." He left out the part that they should all mind their own business. There was no need to ruffle feathers any more than they already were.

Sheriff Thompson ran a hand through his hair, "Look, sir, I know this is frustrating, but we are doing our job. These people are busting their asses to get this case solved. They stay late and come in early. The budget for overtime pay has gone out the window. Every man is working on this investigation. Everyone in this department wants to catch this killer. We are doing the very best we can."

"Yet you still don't have a suspect for even one of the murders?"

Thompson let out an exasperated sigh, "No, sir, not yet."

"You don't need me telling you how to do your job, but I want this killer stopped and it's not just me. The citizens of Lost Bayou also want to see some action. We can't afford any mistakes. I don't want this guy walking so make sure you get solid evidence when you bring someone in. I have no desire to see a guilty person walk away on a technicality."

"You don't have to worry, sir, I know my job."

Mayor Jenkins stood up from his chair, "Keep me advised would you? The town council is on my case. I don't want it to appear to anyone that y'all are sitting on your asses."

Relief washed over Sheriff Thompson as he watched Mayor Jenkins walk out of the office. He had no doubt the man would be back here soon, though.

Chapter 43

Bruce Breaux enjoyed being a librarian for the past forty years. What other job allowed him the opportunity to share his favorite pastime with others – reading. He didn't even mind that working here had transformed his once thin physique into a rotund waistline. He traded his belt for suspenders, which he could choose from various colors and patterns. The children particularly enjoyed when he wore a pair decorated with their favorite cartoon character. Now if he could only get some of these adolescents who prefer to wear the saggy pants to wear suspenders, or even a belt, instead of showing everyone around them their underwear.

***

Nicki walked into the library determined to find some information on the house, or at least newspaper articles on women missing, or worse murdered, in the area. What she was really looking for, though, was photos. She hoped to recognize some of the ghosts at the house, and put names to the faces. Perhaps if she could address them by their names, they would talk to her.

At the front desk, she asked the man standing behind the desk, "Excuse me, but I am looking for any old newspapers that you might have, or any information regarding Rosewood Plantation."

Bruce asked her, "Hmm, any year in particular?"

Shaking her head, she replied, "No, I'd like to go back as far as I can with regards to the history of the plantation. As far as the newspaper articles, I'm not sure."

Bruce inserted his thumbs beneath his suspenders, running them up and down. "Well then, follow me. I will show you where we store the newspaper archives. Perhaps you can start there."

Bruce led her to the back of the library, "Are you one of those history buffs?"

Laughing, she replied, "No. I recently purchased Rosewood Plantation and am interested in learning more about this town and the plantation." The way the librarian looked at her when he asked the questions had her on guard. Deciding to change the subject, she asked, "Have you worked here long?"

"Over forty years. I suppose I should retire, but I enjoy sharing the job of reading with the younger generation."

"That is very admirable of you. I love reading whenever I have the opportunity."

Bruce opened a door to the left and extended his hand, ushering Nicki inside the tiny room. "The boxes in this room contain a copy of every published newspaper." He waved his hand toward a computer, "The more recent copies have been saved on the computer. Unfortunately, we haven't had the time or the budget for the earlier years."

The sheer number of boxes overwhelmed her, but at least everything appeared to be in chronological order. Bruce informed her, "While you are reviewing the newspapers, I will see what information I can find on Rosewood Plantation for you."

"I appreciate it."

At the door, he turned around, "I hope you find what you are looking for. The papers have all been preserved inside plastic sleeves, they are the originals so please be gentle."

Since some of the pictures appeared to be rather old, Nicki decided to start looking in the 1950's era. It wasn't until September of 1954 that she found something - a headline regarding a young local woman who had gone missing.

Dominating the center of the front page, in black and white, was the picture of a woman – smiling and full of life – but unfortunately it did not resemble the ghosts of the frail, panic-stricken women she had seen so far.

This young woman was twenty-four with raven black hair.

As Nicki perused more newspapers, she felt disheartened to see that three more women had gone missing that year – with no clues as to their disappearance. It was as if the women had disappeared into thin air. None of the women had been heard from, but no bodies found either.

Chapter 44

As James sat in Sheriff Thompson's office with Adam, he couldn't shake the feeling of being back in high school and waiting for a lecture from the principal. Judging from Sheriff Thompson's stance, the man had grown impatient, "You mean to tell me that we have no leads."

James huffed, "For now, we still have no leads. The computer search turned up zilch. There wasn't even a hint that this MO has shown up somewhere else. It doesn't help that this killer has left nothing behind at the crime scenes. All we have are the photos found at Ms. Brady's house and the photo someone dropped off at my house. But unfortunately we can't even pin those on the killer. We haven't even been able to ascertain where they were taken as of yet."

Sheriff Thompson looked at the two detectives, "That isn't the answer I want to hear. I need results that I can bring to the higher ups. They are riding my ass hard right now."

Adam shrugged his shoulders, "We are doing the best we can, sheriff. This guy isn't giving us anything to go on."

James informed the sheriff, "We have been comparing photos of all the bystanders at the crime scenes in hopes that one particular person has been visiting each and every scene. If the killer has been at each scene, there is a chance the photographer caught a picture of him."

Sheriff Thompson stated, "There is also a chance that an innocent bystander has been at each and every crime scene."

"But the killer will be more involved in watching us rather than the body. He has already seen what he did with the body; he will want to know how we are taking in the surroundings."

"So you are looking for people who are observing you and not the body?"

"Yes, sir."

For the next several days, James read the papers and watched the news to ensure none of the details of the case had been leaked. While he did find a few articles regarding the murder and later the investigation, none contained any pertinent details. Most of the articles focused around how the police were not being forthcoming with the details.

James wished that these reporters would take into consideration that a murder investigation happened in stages. The first twenty-four hours were spent examining the crime scene and interviewing witnesses, if there were any. The next day, they had to review any evidence in hopes of identifying a potential suspect. Unfortunately, if there were no witnesses or evidence, it was almost impossible to identify a suspect. The sad truth was that the kil er was more than likely already on the hunt for his next victim.

So far, their files on the murders were slim. While they did have the autopsy reports, crime scene photos, interviews and a vague timeline, there wasn't much else to help fill in the blanks.

***

Brenda Jackson slammed down the phone as she reached yet another dead end. She knew there was something unique about these killings, but so far she hadn't found anyone willing to talk to her. There had to be one person anxious to talk. There was always someone that liked to gossip a little more than the others. Someone who wanted the limelight.

She looked at her watch and noticed that it was almost five o'clock. If she could get to the funeral home as people were leaving work, she might find someone that would share their information.

Once at the funeral home, she checked her makeup and hair before stepping out of her car. Satisfied that she looked more like a model than an investigative reporter, she headed into the funeral home.

Inside the funeral home, the heady scent of flowers could not hide the odor of death. Soft music played from unseen speakers giving the place more of an eerie feeling rather than a calming one. It also didn't help that it was freezing in here.

Brenda noticed the funeral director, Mr. Peter Haskins, busy polishing the caskets he kept on display. His smile seemed to freeze on his face when he saw her walk in. From the corner of her eye, she also noticed a heavyset woman walking out the front door. She must have been curious as to who Brenda was because she stopped to stare at her openly for a few minutes. She made a mental note to bring the woman something to eat, and see if she would open up more. If Mr. Haskins didn't give her any information, maybe, she would. She had already tried to get the receptionist to talk to her, but the old biddy was a pit bull when it came to guarding secrets. So far, Brenda hadn't been able to get any information from her.

"Mr. Haskins, I was wondering if you could give me any information on the bodies that have been released to your care. How were they killed?"

Mr. Haskins shook his head grimly, "This is such sad business cher. The police have asked us explicitly not to release any information concerning the bodies. We must comply with their wishes."

His statement caught her attention, "Why don't they want you to release information about the bodies?"

Shaking his head, "I'm sorry cher, but we are under strict orders not to talk to anyone about these cases. This is a small town after all, and I don't want to upset the police."

Brenda could tell that she wouldn't get any information out of this man. "Well, thank you for your time Mr. Haskins. I am sorry to have bothered you."

"I am truly sorry that I couldn't help you."

Outside, she breathed in the fresh air. She would have to try the other woman and hope that she had better luck talking to her.

Chapter 45

Nicki looked around the completed rooms and was proud of her recent accomplishments. The kitchen was gleaming, as were the old hardwood floors. The house was starting to feel more like a home. It had taken a lot of work, but when she walked in the house now she was welcomed with the smell of furniture polish and fresh paint.

Nicki was busy putting way the cleaners when her phone rang. She smiled to herself when she noticed that it was Detective Cook, "Are you calling to say that you will be late tonight?"

He sighed, "I may be late tonight."

"Rough day, I take it?"

"The worst."

Nicki felt sorry for the man, "You really don't need to babysit me. I will be fine. Besides, if the killer wanted me or this house, I'm sure he would have made a move before now."

Rather abruptly, James stated, "No, this is a psychotic killer. Just because he hasn't made a move yet, doesn't mean he won't."

Nicki tried to make the man see reason, "If he is using this property to kill his victims, then he has had more than enough opportune moments to kill me as well."

There was a period of silence while he contemplated what she said. The faint lines around his lips deepened and his brows furrowed, "Still, I don't like that you are living out there by yourself."

Nicki gently reminded him, "Some of his victims lived in town, and no one heard him while he was murdering them."

She inwardly grimaced after realizing what she had said. She should know better than to speak before thinking. She hoped she hadn't hit a raw nerve with that last remark. "I don't mean that you aren't doing anything to stop him. It's just that I am just as safe here as I would be in town."

"I know you didn't mean it the wrong way."

"No, I didn't. You have a tough job and I don't want to come between you and stopping this maniac."

"It is also my job to make sure the citizens of this town are safe. Perhaps my best chance of stopping him may be staying there."

Nicki reiterated, "I love having the company, but I don't want you to feel obligated to stay here. Your first priority should be stopping this maniac, and not me.”

“I am a man of many talents and can do both. I promise you that.”

Trying to break the mood, Nicki joked, “A man of many talents, hm?”

He chuckled, “I promise you my talents wouldn’t disappoint.”

Nicki blushed at the comment, “No, I don’t think you could disappoint anyone. However, I am a bit rusty, and may not live up to any expectations a man may have.”

It was James’s turn to laugh, “Lady, I don’t think any man would ever be disappointed in having you.”

A somber look flashed across Nicki’s face, “Perhaps not, but sometimes I fear I had my one chance at happily ever after and it was robbed from me.”

“I may not have known your husband, but I am certain that he would want you to continue to live even though he is gone.”

Shaking her head ruefully, “I am trying. The best I can do right now is take it one day at a time.”

"Don't rush yourself into anything you aren't comfortable with. When the time is right, you will know it."

Smiling, "Thank you James."

Nicki heard some noise in the background and James replied, "Nicki, I need to go, but please make sure all of the doors are locked. I will also have an officer patrol the area."

"Goodnight, James. Be careful out there."

Chapter 46

James had warned Nicki that morning he would be working late again. While she knew he didn't expect her to wait up for him, she decided to spend her time cleaning the butler's pantry. She wanted to remove the layers of paint on the shelves and restore the wood to its previous beauty.

Darren had already said he would sand the wood down when she had finished stripping the shelves so that she could stain the wood.

After she finished removing the last coat of paint, Oscar let out a low growl. Nicki listened intently to hear what Oscar might be growling at and she heard footsteps at the front door.

"Come on boy. I do believe Detective Cook has made it home."

Nicki tried to calm her racing heart. She was getting comfortable having Detective Cook staying the night, but she knew that once the killer was found he would no longer need to stay here. Before he could knock, she greeted him at the door. Smiling warmly up at him, she informed him, "Oscar let me know that you were here."

As he walked inside, Nicki's hand moved across his body. His muscled arms were straining the material of his shirt. She could see the holster and his weapon, reminding her that he had a dangerous job. *A dangerous job for a dangerous man.*

She would never admit it to him, but having him here had made her feel safe. And reminded her that she was a woman. But she wasn't ready to feel those emotions again. No, she should take a few steps back. Put some distance between them.

Oscar gave the detective one more low growl before moving behind Nicki. James smirked, "You know, I don't think he likes me staying here."

"It must be a male thing, he growls at Darren also."

"He doesn't like sharing you with anyone else."

"That could be." Sadness filled her eyes, "He may be afraid someone is trying to take Tom's place also."

James shuffled his feet at the mention of her husband's name. Wanting to ease the tension that had moved between them, Nicki asked, "Would you like a snack before you go to bed?"

Sighing, he said, "It's been a long day. I better call it a night."

As they headed upstairs, the house became filled with sinister shadows. Nicki found herself wondering which shadows were real and which ones she conjured up from her imagination. She was beginning to suspect that this house did indeed have souls trapped between worlds. Unexpectedly, a loud boom of thunder rattled the house. Her hair stood on end as the air around her became charged with electricity.

James noticed her discomfort, "Sounds like a bad storm is moving in."

Oscar must have feared the same thing, as he was making sure he was right under Nicki's feet. She tried to comfort him, "It's okay boy. The storm will pass before you know it."

When they made it to the second floor, the lights flickered and then went out, bathing the house in darkness. A flash of light from the window caught her eye. Walking over to the window, she peered out into the night and saw another quick flash of light near the bayou. She strained to see who, or what, was causing the flashes of light. "Do you see that?"

"It's probably a fisherman trying to beat the storm."

An unexpected gust of cold air blew across her. The breeze reminded her of one that stung your lungs when you breathed it in. A strong sense of foreboding washed over her. It was as if she was being watched. Before she could move away from the window, a frightening scream echoed through the night. She jumped as another scream sliced through the night.

She heard James chuckle, "Relax, that was a panther. They run rampant in this area. I'm surprised you haven't heard one before now."

A loud cackle sounded next to Nicki's ear. "Okay, Mr. Smarty Pants, what was that?"

They turned toward the sound to find that no one was there. James informed her, "It was probably the wind."

"If you say so."

Taking another step forward, she saw a shadow move in front of her. Her heart was now pounding so fast, that she could hear the sound reverberate in her ears.

Whispering to James, "Are you going to tell me that is the wind?"

Nicki froze in fear as the shadow moved closer towards her. As the shadow grew even closer, the smell of cigar smoke began to permeate her senses. Instinctively she took a step backwards as she tried to calm her racing heart.

As the shadow continued to advance, another form began to take shape. As the shape took form she gasped and rubbed her eyes. Oscar sniffed the air as his fur raised and he released a low growl.

Before Nicki could react, James stepped in front of her as he shined his phone down the dark hallway, "I think the storm outside is casting shadows."

"You are probably right."

He asked, "Will you be okay tonight?"

Patting Oscar on the head, she replied, "I have my fearless protector with me."

Chortling, "If you say so."

Once in her room, Nicki could smell the heady scent of cigar smoke in the air, but there was another familiar scent mixing with the smell of smoke. It was a scent she remembered well, the scent of Tom's favorite cologne. She kept telling herself that this was her imagination playing tricks on her, "Tom?" Even as she asked the question, she knew what the answer was. She witnessed his death, buried him with a heavy heart. But then part of her began to wish that Tom's apparition had come to be with her.

Fighting back tears, she listened as outside the storm began to pick up. With every streak of lightning casting eerie shadows and the thunder shaking the house, Nicki rushed back downstairs. She walked into the kitchen as the lights came back on. Maybe a cup of hot tea would help her relax. She placed a cup in the microwave, leaned against the counter, and watched the seconds slowly count down.

She glanced around the kitchen through down swept lashes as she waited for her tea. This kitchen would be beautiful once it was completed. A movement by the butler's pantry caught her attention. Her pulse quickened as a dark shadow took shape.

Nicki quickly ran to her room, locked the door, and ducked under the covers. The heck with her tea. It may be merely a childish reaction, but for now, all she wanted to do was hide under the covers and pray the ghosts left her alone.

Chapter 47

While waiting for his coffee at the local café, James read an article in the paper. He immediately saw red. He wanted to throttle that damn reporter. He carefully read it one more time:

> *Women, you need to lock your doors and please take the necessary precautions. Men, you need to watch out for your wives, girlfriends, daughters, sisters, and mothers. A serial killer is stalking the women of this small town. One who disposes of the bodies in the murky bayous and leaves their forgotten corpses for the wildlife. Three bodies have been found so far and until the police catch this madman, there is no telling who his next victim may be.*

He let out a string of curse words before storming out the door. Where the hell did this man come off saying that there was a serial killer running loose? Three murders did not mean that they had a serial killer; even though he was certain of it.

This damn reporter had jumped the gun on this one and this article was going to cause mass panic. The phones would be ringing nonstop today. Everyone would want to know exactly what the police department was doing to protect the citizens of Lost Bayou.

While he agreed that people need to be wary and the public had the right to be informed of the murders, there was no reason for this reporter to put fear into citizens.

Sure enough, when he walked into the station, the phones were already ringing off the hook. The poor receptionist looked frazzled and it was only seven o'clock in the morning. James heard the sheriff call for him and Adam, "Get in my office now."

Once they were in his office, he closed the door, "It is not even eight o'clock, and the place is a madhouse. Can you imagine what it will be like by lunchtime?"

They answered in unison, "Yes, sir."

James was as pissed as the sheriff was. He despised the fact that Adam and he were the unfortunate recipients of his anger.

"I want y'all to find this murdering son of a bitch before this turns any more chaotic."

Again, they replied in unison, "Yes, sir."

The sheriff asked, "Do we have any more information yet?"

James replied, "No, sir. It looks as if all the murders were committed by the same person. However, none of the bodies had trace evidence to help pinpoint a killer. The women were killed somewhere else and disposed of at the site they were discovered."

Chapter 48

James scanned the area before heading to the body. He took in each face he saw. There was a chance one of them could be their killer. He learned long ago that perps liked to watch cops work the crime scene. If he was here, it should be easy enough to spot him since there were very few people out this way.

The officers working the scene all had their backs turned away from the body. None seemed to be able to watch as the coroner prepared to move what remained of the poor woman's body. From behind him, he heard another vehicle pulling up and let out a list of swear words. It appeared the press had caught wind of the murder. It wouldn't be long before they moved in like vultures, pushing their boundaries to get a picture.

He informed the young officer patrolling the scene, "Keep them as far away as possible. Move the crime scene tape if you need to. I don't want them anywhere near this scene." James knew that word of the murder would spread like wildfire and soon they would have even more bystanders. He did not like how this killer was escalating, and fast.

As he moved closer to the scene, the officers moved aside. Dr. Metcalf merely looked up at him as he resumed his work, "The killer probably had hoped the alligators would drag her off. If it wouldn't have been for the runner finding her body so soon, I doubt we would have even known there was another victim."

James looked across the bayou, "I wonder how many he has dropped here before now. It appears to be a perfect spot for him – alligator infested and remote."

"It would be the smart way to dispose of a body in this shape. The alligators would look at the bodies as merely a tenderized meal for them. All they need to do is drag the remains to their hidey hole and let nature do the rest of the work."

James looked at the body in dismay. Unfortunately, they still didn't have enough to come up with a profile on the killer. All he could do was work the crime scene as best as he could in hopes of getting into the mind of this killer.

He looked up at the morning sky. They would be here at least until lunchtime. James took out his tablet and started taking notes. Adam was already talking to the young boy that found the body. He was still pale and shaken up, but he was at least coherent enough to answer questions.

All around him, the crime scene techs were busy collecting evidence and taking pictures. There were so many areas that clues could be hiding or already possibly blown away. Every piece of trash would have to be collected as it could be the one clue that lead them to the killer. They could at least be thankful that it hadn't rained yet so some of the scene had been preserved.

Every person working the scene had a varying shade of grim on their face. Even now, few looked in the direction of the body. He understood how they felt, though. It was hard for him to look at the body as well.

James was glad to see Chris Ford heading up the crime scene investigations unit again today. With his sharp eye, he would ensure that no evidence went unnoticed. He had become an invaluable asset to the department.

James heard Chris instruct the technicians, "I want this entire area taken in a grid formation. Everyone works in twos, and we check each quadrant twice by a different set of eyes."

Adam walked over James, "The witness didn't see anyone in the area this morning. Our killer probably dropped off the body up there a ways and the current carried her down until she was caught in the cypress trees."

"The killer was probably hoping that an alligator would be in the mood for an early breakfast. Dr. Metcalf is about to move the body."

Adam let out a long sigh, "Damn, but this is getting frustrating."

Dr. Metcalf walked over to the two detectives as his assistants removed the body, "I won't know the exact time of death until I get her on my table. You should know that his surgical work is getting better."

As they drove back to the station, Adam told James, "I don't like waiting for this guy to make a mistake."

"I keep having these nightmares that this guy kills several women here before disappearing and leaving this case unsolved."

***

Brenda Jackson watched the crime scene with extreme interest. This case could be exactly what she needed to get her noticed. CAJN may be a small station in Lost Bayou, but there was a chance the story would be picked up by a larger network. She rearranged her hair and looked over at her camera man, "I'm telling you Jude, something isn't right about these murders. The cops aren't even talking about it. There is no way they would be stonewalling us if this was a simple murder."

Jude Anderson adjusted his video camera in case he could get a good shot of the body as it was being moved. "My gut tells me there is something the cops don't want revealed."

Brenda chewed on her bottom lip as she watched the scene in front of her, "Several of the cops actually look green."

Jude shrugged his shoulders, "Why don't you try calling the morgue or even the funeral home to see what they have to say about the bodies? I'm sure you could persuade someone over there to talk to you."

Brenda made a mental note to call both the morgue and the funeral home as soon as the name of the victim was released. She had already tried going in person. "That was a wasted trip," she thought sourly. Maybe if she made a call instead, she could pretend that she was a friend of the family who doesn't want to bother the grieving family members and would like to send flowers. If she talked to them long enough, maybe they would give her a little more information than they should.

Chapter 49

James looked at his watch and sighed. As much as he hated Nicki Brady sleeping out there with no protection, with the discovery of the recent body, he felt a deeper responsibility to work the case. Besides, his gut was telling him that the killer wouldn't strike again tonight.

He called Nicki, "It's James. Don't wait up for me tonight." Sighing, he stated, "We had another murder."

Nicki gasped, "I'm so sorry. But please do not feel obligated to spend the night here just to babysit me. I'm fine, really."

"Make sure that all of your doors are locked. If you need me, do not hesitate to call."

***

After hanging up with James, Nicki let out a long sigh. She had become rather comfortable with James spending the night, but she also understood the importance of his job. Besides, she would much rather see James work this case and catch the killer. Then everyone would feel safer at night.

"Come on, Oscar. Let's go outside."

As soon as Nicki opened the front door, Oscar bounded outside. She sat down on the swing and slowly rocked as Oscar meandered around the front yard. He would stop here and there, but mostly pranced around the yard, sniffing every blade of grass.

A cool breeze tickled her face, "You must help them."

Nicki's blood ran cold. "How can I help them?" she asked as her heart pounded furiously in her chest.

"You must stop the evil that lives here!" the exasperated voice exclaimed.

Before Nicki could ask anymore questions, Oscar came bounding up the stairs to the front porch growling.

Patting him on the head, Nicki looked around for any apparitions. While the ghosts were definitely communicating with her, she was still unclear as to exactly how she was to do what they wanted. She feared that something terrible had happened at Rosewood Plantation and the only way these events would stop replaying was for the mystery to be solved.

Opening the front door, she called Oscar inside, "Let's go to bed boy."

Nicki woke in the middle of the night to find it freezing in her room. Even with the air conditioner running full blast, it normally wasn't this cold in the house. She yawned and watched as her breath turned into a white misty vapor in front of her.

She pulled the blankets over her and buried her head in the pillows. Suddenly, the temperature in the room dropped another ten degrees. She peered out from under a small gap in the covers and saw no movement in the room. She got out of bed to check the thermostat.

As she left the bed, she felt something from underneath reach for her ankle. Her heart stopped. She slowly looked down and saw the dust ruffle gently swaying back and forth. Swallowing hard, she worked up the courage to look under the bed.

Slowly peeking under the bed, she was relieved to find the area empty. Still cold though, she walked to the bedroom door. She was startled to find the door handle freezing. It was even colder in the hall. Her skin prickled with chilly goose bumps. Her breath evaporated before her. She bit back a scream as a cold hand brushed across her face. She flinched away from the ghostly hand and jumped as a door downstairs slammed shut. Something whispered in the dark near her left side, but the words were incomprehensible. She heard strange noises coming from downstairs and they were moving up the stairs towards her. She wasn't sure what was making the sounds.

As she headed for the stairs, she noticed that the first floor was cloaked in darkness. No moonlight was even filtering inside. She shook her head, trying to figure out what she was doing. She should wait until the light of day. This was not something she should be trying to do alone in the dark of night.

At the stairs, she noticed that the temperature had dropped even more. Her feet became numb as she walked barefoot on the hardwood floors. Her fingers were actually becoming stiff from the extreme cold. She could literally breathe icicles.

Ping... Ping... Ping. A piano began to play from downstairs. The music was surprisingly cheerful. She felt drawn to follow the cheery notes. As she made her way downstairs once again, giggling noises sounded from upstairs and something bounded down the stairs, blowing right past her. The front door mysteriously opened and closed.

The downstairs was once again submersed in silence. The air around her dropped several more degrees. This time she feared her blood may actually freeze from the cold and here she was in only an oversized t-shirt.

Suddenly, she felt a pair of cold hands on her body, caressing her all over. She went to brush them away, only to realize that no one was there. She rushed over and turned on the light switch. The room was instantly blanketed in light. The room began to grow warmer and the house was once again still.

Ping. Ping. Ping. As she climbed back into bed, the piano music began to play once again, but this time it was single, hollow notes.

As she drifted off to sleep, a voice whispered in her ear, "You aren't welcome here." A cold hand wrapped its fingers around her neck and began to squeeze. In horror, Nicki struggled against the cold grasp of the person on top of her. A piercing shriek filled the room and the apparition disappeared.

Knowing she wouldn't be able to go back to sleep, Nicki threw off the covers and got out of bed. She hastily put on some clothes and walked downstairs to brew a pot of coffee. She may as well start cleaning the house. A part of her wanted to call James and ask him to come over, but she knew he needed his rest if he was going to catch this demented killer.

Chapter 50

James lay wide awake in bed, his thoughts drifting off to Nicki. He wondered if she was wide awake as well. He rolled over and punched his pillow down as he tried to force himself to go to sleep. Thinking of Nicki resting in bed right across the hall didn't help him.

Unable to sleep, he gave up and went to brew himself a cup of coffee. Between the case and Nicki, his mind wouldn't rest. At his bedroom door, he froze. Heavy footsteps were coming down the hall. As he listened to the footsteps, he realized they were too heavy to be from Nicki. He went back to his nightstand and grabbed his gun. He peered out the door and saw the long hall was dark and empty. James walked into the hall, watching and listening.

James felt someone behind him; it was a cold breath on his neck. He whirled around only to see that the hallway was still empty, but yet, it had a menacing look somehow. The footsteps continued back down the hall leading towards the stairs.

James crept into the hall, wondering if the killer had decided to break into the house. After thoroughly searching the house, James wondered if he'd met a ghost.

As James walked into the kitchen, he saw Nicki sitting at the bar pouring herself a cup of coffee, "Couldn't sleep either?" She asked.

Could it have been her he heard walking downstairs? But the footsteps sounded too heavy to belong to her. Nicki poured James a cup of coffee and handed it to him. As they went to sit down at the bar, the kitchen door blew open. Nicki held out her hand and told him, "I got it. I could have sworn the door was locked."

As she went to close the door, she became paralyzed with fear. Standing in the yard was the silhouette of a woman, or at least, what appeared to be a woman. The face was blurry, but a figure stood there watching her. As Nicki continued to stare at the figure, it stayed perfectly still.

There was an eerie glow coming from behind the figure, silhouetting it even more. James walked up behind Nicki to see what was going on. The figure started to walk down the pathway that led to the bayou. Nicki whispered, "Please tell me you see her?"

James instructed her, "You stay here. I'm going to follow her and see where she is going."

"No way I'm staying here."

James grabbed a flashlight from the kitchen drawer and instructed her, "Stay behind me at all times."

They watched in awe as the figure floated over the ground, "Where do you think she is going?" she asked.

Shrugging his shoulders, "I don't know, but I'm hoping she will lead us to where the killer's hideout is."

The mysterious figure hovered in midair before moving further down the pathway. "I think she really does want us to follow her."

"Let's see where she takes us," James agreed.

The further they moved down the pathway, Nicki felt a change in the air around them. The figure stopped moving and hovered over a small hill in the woods. "Why do you think she stopped?"

"I suspect there is something she wants us to find."

A shudder moved through Nicki, "Should we check it out tonight?"

Shaking his head, "It's too dark out here. I'm going to go in the morning." James thought to himself, where I can observe the surroundings and make sure that no one is going to attack.

Chapter 51

He crouched in the closet and waited for her to come home. Sweat pooled beneath his gloves. He had studied her patterns long enough to know that she came home every night at midnight and climbed in bed by one.

Anticipation coursed through his body as he eagerly awaited her arrival. As he waited, he reminisced. His professors and, worse, his family, never believed that he would ever become a skillful surgeon. No one thought that he had the ambition or intelligence for that profession. Well, he would show all of them how good his surgical skills were.

He heard the door open and knew that his time was near. When the light came on in the bedroom, he moved deeper into the closet; he wasn't ready to be discovered. He must wait until she was asleep before he made his move. Her screams would only alert the neighbors.

The muscles in his stomach tightened as he listened to her every move. It was almost too much to have to wait, but making his presence known now was too risky.

When he heard the water running, he fantasized about her getting undressed and stepping into the shower.

He waited for an hour after she had climbed into bed before making his move. He had to struggle to contain her, the will to live must have given her a boost of adrenaline. "Stop fighting me and I won't kill you. If you scream or say a word, you are dead. Do you understand?"

Unadulterated terror stared back up at him. It was so intense that he could actually smell the fear in the air. As the words penetrated her mind, tears filled her eyes.

He took a deep breathe in and began the meticulous work on the body. As much as he wanted to resume working on the body at the plantation, it was too risky to move her there. Instead, he would be forced to perform the act here. As he left her house, he wondered how long it would be before someone discovered the body.

Chapter 52

Warren Caulfield looked at his watch and wondered once again where the hell Brittany Segura was. It wasn't like her to be late, especially this late. He let out an exasperated sigh and called her cell phone one more time. He let out another curse when it went straight to voice mail. *Where the hell was that girl?* He should have known not to hire a twenty-one year old to be a bartender. He already had problems with his young waitresses showing up to work on time.

He really didn't want to serve drinks all night either. "Jessica, since you talked me into hiring your friend, Brittany, I want you to head over to her house and bring her ass into work."

Jessica reached behind the bar and grabbed her purse, "Yes sir."

Why was she late? All Brittany could talk about was working as a bartender. For some insane reason, she thought it was a fascinating job. She enjoyed trying out various cocktail recipes.

When Jessica pulled up to Brittany's house, she noticed that her car was still in the driveway. She walked up to the door and knocked loudly. When she didn't answer, Jessica assumed she was either in the shower or still sound asleep. She knew that Brittany kept a spare key under the front door rug. Opening the door, she called out, "Brit, it's Jessica. You awake?"

Not hearing an answer, she moved deeper into the house. Her bedroom door was closed and she knocked loudly on it before entering, "Brit, it's Jessica." When she entered the room, she felt the earth open up beneath her. Her screams echoed through the neighborhood.

It didn't take long before a multitude of police cars and flashing lights were in front of Brittany's house.

****

As James walked up to the house, Chris Ford walked up to him, "We have determined that the killer entered the house from the back door. He broke out the window and reached in to unlock the door."

James walked around to the backyard as the crime scene techs combed every inch of the property for clues. They were leaving no stone unturned as they searched for clues. Every piece of furniture was being dusted, and the floors were being inspected for shoe prints. The photographer was making sure to take photos from every angle before the body was removed.

Officer Morales walked up to James, "We have talked to all the neighbors; unfortunately, no one saw or heard anything out of the ordinary last night."

Back in the house, Officer Taylor called out, "We found where he was hiding." As James and Adam walked into the room, they noticed him pointing to the closet. You could see the impression of where the man must have sat for hours waiting, "We will be sure to dust and photograph this area well." Officer Taylor stated, "It looks as if he was here for a while from the indentation left. Surely, we have to get something from this."

After all their hard work, they only walked away with a few clues. From the size of the shoe prints, they were dealing with a tall, burly man and, that their killer was a very patient person.

Chapter 53

The next morning as Darren was busy working on the upstairs, Nicki started cleaning some more furniture that she had found tucked away in one of the smaller rooms upstairs.

While Nicki was hanging the mirror she had recently cleaned, a reflection caught her eye and drew her in closer. Dizziness overcame her and everything started to spin out of control as her perception blurred.

It was as if she was looking through a murky mist. An unexpected and overpowering urge to turn around and run overcame her. A dark figure appeared and moved towards her in slow motion. Light and shadows began to weave throughout the room. The closer he came to her, she began to feel incredibly weak and disoriented. Nicki instinctively turned around, but no one was behind her.

She could barely breathe as the dark figure in the mirror continued to move towards her. Without warning, strong arms reached out from the mirror and grabbed her neck. The grasp was so strong that Nicki could barely let out a moan. Then as quickly as the shadow appeared, it disappeared.

That night sleep eluded her. She laid in bed and listened to the various sounds the house made. Instead of calming her, it ate at her nerves.

The bedroom was only illuminated by the soft moonlight that filtered in from the window. Ominous shadows danced across the walls. A chill swept across her body. She thought she heard a man whisper her name, but she shook it off.

She found her thoughts drifting back to James. He had such a strong, commanding presence. There was something so intriguing about him. She felt a connection to him that she hadn't experienced since Tom.

Unexpectedly, her bed began to shake, jolting her out of her reverie. Her fear grew to mammoth proportions as the bed began to levitate. Her heart was pounding inside of her chest. Without warning, the doors in the room started to open and slam shut. A loud piercing voice resonated in the room, "Leave this house now! You are not welcome here."

Goose bumps began to climb up her body. Before Nicki could react the intrusion ceased and her surroundings returned to normal.

Chapter 54

The morning sky was overcast with a dark shade of gray as James drove to the funeral home. The funeral of Brittany Segura was today. Her parents had planned a memorial even though they couldn't have a proper funeral for their beloved daughter. In place of a casket, a life sized picture of Brittany had been placed in the viewing room.

James was shocked to see that so many people had turned out for the young woman's memorial. The room was filled with an assortment of carnations, roses, and lilies. A soft rendition of Amazing Grace was playing in the background as James walked over to the police photographer. "Take pictures of every man or woman attending the funeral. Afterwards, we can compare them to the pictures of the crime scenes."

Officer Morales asked, "Do you really think the killer will be here?"

"I don't see how he can resist."

As they finished their conversation, more people arrived. Grief set heavy in his heart as he watched Brittany's parents receive condolences from family and friends. As Brenda Jackson walked into the funeral home, James saw red. He hoped like hell this woman wasn't planning to write an article about the grieving family. Walking over to her, he took her by the elbow and firmly escorted her out of earshot from everyone else.

Brenda tried to remove herself from his powerful grip, "I see the police are busy on the job."

In a harsh whisper, "Why are you here?"

Looking up at him, "I came to pay my respects like everyone else. I suspect that you are hoping the killer will stop by to pay his respects as well."

James glared down at the woman, "I think it would be best for everyone if you went home."

Shaking her head, "I came here to pay my respects and I plan to do just that. I knew Brittany, and I think it is a shame what has happened to her. There are rumors going around that she had been mutilated."

"I hope you will keep those rumors to yourself Ms. Jackson."

Brenda smiled at the detective slyly, "Now, Detective, I am a reporter after all. It is my job to report the news."

"It would benefit you to not report any rumors that you may hear until they are substantiated."

Brenda placed her hands on her hips, and huffed, "And if I call to ask you to substantiate the rumors, will you?"

"Not at this time I won't."

Nodding her head, "That is what I figured. The people have a right to know what is going on in this town."

Not giving him a chance to have the last word, she turned on her heel and walked into the packed viewing room.

Sadness washed over James as the family continued to receive condolences. Adam replied, "I hope she can rest in peace."

"She may be resting in peace, but I won't be able to rest until we have this son of a bitch behind bars."

***

He watched as family and friends stopped by the parents to express condolences. It was exhilarating to have the police in the same room with him and they were unaware that he was the one responsible. They probably didn't even suspect him; no one did. They all considered him to be an insignificant person – if they only knew the truth.

As the women walked around him, he wondered if one of them could be his next test subject.

Chapter 55

After returning home from grocery shopping, Nicki put away the groceries. Next she began putting away the freshly cleaned laundry. Now and then she paused to see if she could get a sense of the ghosts again. Perhaps it was her quest in life to help them find peace and move on.

Nicki closed her eyes and imagined the ghosts like she had seen them before. It was horrible to think about how those women might have died.

She couldn't imagine the type of person it would take to commit such horrendous murders. And where were they killed? Where someone wouldn't have heard their screams? Surely someone tortured like those women would have screamed unrelentlessly. She swore the room in the photos looked like a basement, but as far as she knew this house didn't have one. Very few homes here did.

She shuddered at the thought of the fear that had seized the women. None of those women in the photos had died quickly and the pain must have been horrendous.

When she opened her eyes, darkness had settled over the room. A breeze wafted in and lifted the curtains. A woman stepped from the shadows and watched her sorrowfully.

Nicki stood there, frozen in place. Perhaps this was a figment of her imagination. After all, she had desperately wanted to see the ghosts of the women again. Anticipation and fear rushed through her body as she waited for the ghost to speak. But before the ghost could make her move a howling wind blew through the room and swept the apparition away.

Chapter 56

James sighed as he surveyed the murder board. They had centered their investigation on the victims and their lives, trying to find some sort of connection and so far they had had no luck. They had talked to friends and family members of each victim to see if anyone had noticed anything out of the ordinary before their deaths, but no one had noticed anything.

He despised the fact that they were at a complete loss for these murders. They had found no significant clues as of yet. None of them liked the fact that they had to wait for another person to be murdered in hopes of finding any pertinent evidence.

As far as the duct tape used in the crime, it could be purchased at any store around the country so that wasn't any help either. A small amount of DNA had been found on the duct tape when the killer had used his teeth to cut the tape; unfortunately, that wasn't enough to go on.

So far, they had no suspects. The trail grew cold with each passing day. The killer had obviously done his homework and had covered all bases. Regardless of the lack of clues, James continued forward as best as he could with this investigation.

They had started looking into each person who had recently moved to Lost Bayou hoping to find someone with a history that needed to be looked into further, but they had found no one who fell into that category. There were only a few new residents, and there were also a few people who had moved back to town after living away for several years. The only person catching James's interest was Mrs. Fontaine's nephew, Charles Guilliot. He had access to the plantation prior to Nicki purchasing it. But then again so did Jack Mayon.

Chapter 57

"Oscar, come on, let's go to bed, boy."

Oscar bounded up the stairs, and went straight for the bedroom door. At the doorway, he stopped abruptly. The hair on his back began to rise as he got a crazy look in his eyes before letting out a menacing growl."

Nicki bent down and patted him on his head, "Oscar, what's wrong?"

Oscar abruptly bolted into the room and hid under the bed. Nicki couldn't believe what had happened. She kneeled down at the bed and tried to coax Oscar out, but he refused to leave his hiding spot.

After Nicki finished her nightly routines in the bathroom, she walked into the bedroom and was relieved to see Oscar on the bed.

"I'm glad you are feeling better."

Before settling in for the night, Nicki walked out onto the balcony. She stood by the railing and watched as the moonlight danced across the yard.

She took in a deep breathe and enjoyed the scenery. As she watched the tranquility of the night, she thought of Tom. She hoped he was watching her from up above and not still roaming this earth.

"I wish you were here my love. You would have loved this adventure, ghosts and all." She still couldn't believe that Tom was gone. Life could take you down paths never expected, but she wanted to make sure that this one dream of Tom's was fulfilled.

The aroma of cigar smoke teased her nostrils and she looked around. There was no one there, and the smell had dissipated as quickly as it came.

Although physically exhausted, Nicki was still too restless to fall fast asleep. She picked up the book she had on her nightstand and decided to read for a little while.

She found it hard to believe how dirty things could get from neglect. Even though Mrs. Fontaine had lived here, she had been unable to keep up with the daily upkeep. It shouldn't be too much longer before she had the home cleaned, but it would be several more months before the renovations were complete.

***

Nicki's eyes snapped open as the dark interior of her bedroom came into focus. She wasn't sure exactly what had woken her, but something had. She looked at the closet door to make sure that it was still closed. The only sound she heard was the distant rumble of thunder. The storm that had been predicted for later in the morning seemed to be moving faster than anticipated.

Her heart caught briefly in her throat. She swore she felt a cold breath on her shoulder and turned to see if anyone was there, but she was alone.

She reached over, turned on the lamp that was on her nightstand with a shaky hand, and looked around the room. The book she had been reading was still right where she left it.   Unaware that she had been holding her breath, she gently released it. She suddenly felt silly and laughed at herself for being scared over nothing.

Perhaps it had not been a wise decision to read a murder mystery before bed. The house seemed to come alive with shadows. Although the dark had never bothered her before, she didn't want to start seeing things that weren't really there.

As she settled back down in bed, another noise caught her attention. It was a low, ominous creaking sound. The closet door was slowly opening. She lay there, frozen in fear as the door continued to open. An eerie crunching sound emitted from the closet as grotesque fingers slowly appeared one by one around the door's edge. When the footsteps began and started to move towards the bed, Nicki somehow found her voice and began to scream.

A voice called out to her, "Nicki…" Her heart started pounding in her ears. The apparition continued to taunt her, "Nicki…"

It sounded as if someone was right outside her door. She slowly got out of bed and opened the door. The hallway was dark and empty.

"Nicki…" She swallowed hard before looking back. This time, the voice had sounded as if it was right behind her, but no one was there.

"Nicki…" This time the voice sounded as if it was coming from her room. Once again, she stepped into her bedroom, and found it empty. Panic welled up deep in her, her heart skipped a beat and her breath caught as she turned to dart downstairs. Nothing stopped her dash out the front door and down the porch steps. Once she was in the driveway, she turned to look at the house expecting to see someone chasing her out the door.

Instead, there was nothing there; there were no figures looming at her from the windows and no eerie glow coming from the house. As she calmed her racing heart, she continued to stare at the house. She dared something to show itself. When nothing happened, she decided it was safe to go back inside. As she walked back inside, she tried to convince herself that she had imagined hearing her name being called out.

Knowing she wouldn't be able to go back to sleep, Nicki decided to paint one of the bedrooms on the second floor. By the time she was done, she was covered in flecks of paint.

Miraculously, she managed to get it on her and the wall, but none on the floor. She walked to her bathroom to take a good shower. It didn't take long for the bathroom to fill up with steam.

She lathered soap all over her body and began to scrub at the specks of paint on her skin. As she rinsed off the soap, she inspected her arms to see if she had managed to remove most of the paint. What remained should wear off rather quickly. But what shocked her was the long scratches on her arm. *How did she get these?*

She lathered shampoo in her hair and stepped under the pulsing water to rinse away the soap. She winced as a stream of soapy water ran into her eye. She put her face into the stream of water to rinse the soap out of her face. Instead, she managed to cause it to burn even more. Thankfully, she had a towel hanging from the shower rod and reached for it. As she was rubbing her eyes, a chill swept over her and goose bumps crawled up her skin.

She cautiously peered through the shower curtain to see a young woman staring at her. Her lips opened to scream, but no sound came out. The woman's body parts began to drop to the ground. Next her face began to decay as Nicki watched in horror. As the face rotted, the eyes disappeared and only black, empty sockets stared back at her. Then the vision dissipated into thin air.

Cold water pulsating on her body shook her out of her reverie. She turned off the water and stepped out of the tub. She wrapped the towel robe around her wet body and looked around the bathroom in a haze of confusion. She searched for the ghosts as she walked out of the bathroom and into the bedroom.

Still unsettled from the vision in the bathroom, she plopped herself onto the bed and stared at the ceiling. It was still hard for her to fathom that there were spirits in this house.

That night her sleep was disrupted by scattered dreams and nightmares. She found herself in a dark room, but it wasn't one that looked familiar to her.

A voice pleaded from somewhere in the dark abyss, "Help me."

A shiver ran down her spine as the cry turned to a shrill pitch that hurt Nicki's ears. She covered her ears as the air in front of her began to sway. The darkness pulsated with life around her, and the air became icy cold against her skin.

In the darkness of the room, a hazy vapor took form. The shape changed from a swirling outline of smoke and light to that of a young, but haggard, woman. Her dark brown hair appeared stringy, and her face contorted into a mask of pain. As the woman dragged her torn body closer to where Nicki stood, her complexion transformed into black, decomposing flesh. Her hair fell in clumps; the dank smell of death permeated the air.

As she stepped backwards, she became paralyzed with fear. A man appeared behind the woman, or at least she assumed it to be a man. The face was blurry, but a figure stood there watching her. As Nicki continued to stare at the man, it stayed perfectly still.

She had an overpowering urge to turn around, but instead watched as the scene in front of her changed. A dark figure appeared to be working on something in slow motion. Light and shadows wove throughout the room.

Her whole body shook as the brutal vision became clearer. She cried out, "No. Please stop. Don't do this."

She could barely breathe as the dark figure continued his work. She felt helpless as he hacked at the body in front of him.

A woman materialized on the side of her, "I tried to warn the lady what he was doing here, but she wouldn't listen. I knew what he had done to the others. I saw what all of them did. They were all bad men!"

The man turned towards her. There was a saw in his hand, with blood dripping on the floor from the blade. He let out a menacing laugh as he taunted her, "Come closer, and see what I've done." Then he turned to the woman standing next to Nicki and gave her a sinister smile, "Evil can never die. It will always live here."

The woman turned to Nicki, "Please, you have to stop the evil that lives here. You have to help us, help all of us."

Nicki bolted awake, forcing the dream to fade away. She breathed in deep, ragged gasps. She opened her eyes wide and forced herself to take in her surroundings. She had to find that room. It may be the only way to learn who was killing these poor women. Nicki was certain the women were killed on this property, but where? The room didn't look like any that she had been in.

Tossing the covers and sheet aside, she swung her legs over the edge of the bed, walked to the french doors, and opened them. The night air was comfortably warm, fragrant with the aroma of the nearby magnolia tree, and hinting at the humidity that would cover the area in a few short hours. She glanced over at the magnolia tree and breathed in the scent one more time. The tree was loaded with large, creamy, waxy white blossoms that were as large as dinner plates. The white blossoms glistened in the moonlight against the broad, leathery dark green leaves.

Chapter 58

As Debra Hanson walked home, a noise behind her caught her attention. It was a slight noise, but loud enough for her to hear. She looked behind her and saw a movement from deep in the shadows of the night.

Out of the shadows stepped a man. She looked at the person one more time, "Don't I know you?"

She never had a chance to scream. Her body slumped to the ground as he knocked her out. He duct taped her mouth closed and drug her deeper into the dark alleyway.

***

As Tony Matthews backed into the alleyway to pick up the dumpster, he caught a glimpse of something in his rearview mirror. It looked as if someone had scattered their trash around the dumpster, leaving it for someone else to dispose of. As much as he despised picking up the wrongfully placed trash, if he didn't – it could cost him his job.

As he neared the dumpster, he immediately stopped. It took a minute for the sight to register in his mind. He stumbled back to the cab of the truck and dialed 911.

The dispatcher asked, "What is your emergency?"

He stammered, "There is a dead body between 1st and Main St."

"I'm sorry, sir, but did you say a dead body?"

He replied, "I'm not sure if it is a whole body or not, but there are bloody body parts near the dumpster."

"Okay, sir, I am going to dispatch a unit your way. Can you please stay on the line? I will need to ask you a few more questions."

"Yes, of course. I will go to the street to direct them to the body."

"Thank you, sir."

In a daze, Tony walked to the street to wait for the police. It didn't take long before he heard the sirens of the police car. When he saw the red and blue flashing lights, he waved over to the car and watched as the officers stepped out of the car.

He told the policemen, "The body is next to the dumpster. If you don't mind, I would like to stay here."

***

Officer Robert Wilson and his partner Graham McKey walked toward the dumpster. Officer Wilson immediately took a step backwards when he saw the body. The gruesome sight would be forever imprinted in his mind.

He got on his radio and informed the dispatcher to let Detectives Cook and Veret know that they were needed at the crime scene as soon as possible, "It looks as if their killer has struck again. You may want to tell them that she was killed at the same location she was found."

The dispatcher responded, "I will let them know. I will dispatch the forensic techs as well."

Officer Wilson started cordoning off the crime scene. After the scene was secured, they walked back to the driver to take his statement.

* * *

Detective Adam Veret was stepping out of the shower when his cell phone rang. He shuddered involuntarily when he saw the dispatcher's number, "Veret."

"Detective, I am sorry to bother you, but there has been another murder. Officer Wilson said your killer has struck again."

Adam listened to the details as he dressed. He stepped into the kitchen to find Melanie pouring him a cup of coffee.

He hung up his cell phone and informed her, "We have another murder."

The drive to the murder scene took mere minutes. Lost Bayou wasn't that large of a town, and he only lived minutes from the crime scene. The sun had recently risen and the wet dew still glistened on the grass. The early morning streets were slick from last night's rain. Dark, ominous clouds hung heavy in the sky with the promise of rain. They needed to act fast if they hoped to preserve any evidence before the clouds opened up and washed away their crime scene.

Adam pulled up behind the black and white police cruiser. Looking around, it appeared that half the force was here.

Officers Wilson and McKey were the responding officers. Adam asked Officer McKey, "Can you fill me in on what you know?

"Yes, sir. The body was discovered by the gentleman over there, Mr. Tony Matthews. As he was backing up to the dumpster, he saw something in his rearview mirror. He got out of his truck to pick up what he thought was trash, but when he got closer, he saw the body parts and immediately called 911. He swears he didn't go close to the body. Forensic techs are busy working the scene to collect as much evidence as they can before it rains."

Adam noticed Officer Marston taking photos of the crime scene, "Officer Marston, can you take pictures of the crowd as well? I want to see if we have anyone overly curious or even disinterested?"

"Yes, sir."

Their killer was getting more brazen. He was quick and efficient in his killing, and now, he didn't care if he did it out in the open. He was becoming bold and they may get lucky because of that.

Looking down at the body made Adam reconsider his decision to switch from robbery to homicide. He was quickly learning that working homicide was not for the faint of heart.

As the ME's office prepared to remove the victim, James arrived. He walked over to his partner, "Sorry I am late. I thought I had a profile of the killer, but this murder changes everything. He's getting more comfortable with his killing and, by the looks of it, more efficient."

"I agree. We may need to increase patrols. If he is starting to kill these women right here on the streets, we might catch him in the act."

He watched as the forensic techs made sure the hands of the victim were bagged so the nails could be clipped. He hoped that she had a chance to fight back. Maybe they would get lucky and find some residue of foreign fibers or hair. As the ME'S office moved the body, the forensics team was casting footprints and scouring the area for any evidence that may have been left behind.

The roar of approaching vehicles caught their attention. James let out a groan and looked over at Adam, "Looks like the press is here." He nodded his head towards the street. The feeding frenzy was about to begin. Van after van pulled up.

Adam understood how he felt about the press. They may have a job to do, but lately all they did was get in the way of the investigation. James informed him, "Let the sheriff and mayor talk to the press. Those two know how to work the press. There is a chance this latest murder will ignite the whole town into a manhunt for the killer."

Adam nodded his head in agreement. This latest murder would create chaos and panic with the residents of this little town.

James watched as the forensic techs completed their work and loaded up the samples they had taken. He wondered how much of what they found here would actually be linked to this crime, but they had done a thorough job of gathering everything they could. It was a long shot that anything collected today would even lead them to the killer, but they could hope for a hair or a fiber in the collection that would break this case.

As they made their way back to their cars, the reporters called out to them, "Detectives, is it true that there has been another murder?"

"Detectives, what can you tell us about the murder?"

"Detectives, can you at least let us know who the murder victim is or how she was killed?"

"Detectives, can you answer any of our questions?"

Click. Click. Click. The sound of cameras in action filled the air. James stopped to look at the reporters. They stopped bombarding him with questions and waited to hear what he had to say. A television camera instantly focused in on him, "Sheriff Thompson will make a statement shortly; unfortunately, at this time, I don't have any information to give you."

"Come on detective, you can't give us any information?"

James shook his head, "Not at this time."

As the body was loaded into the coroner's van, camera flashes nearly blinded him. The coroner had already informed him that as soon as he arrived back at his office, he would perform the autopsy. James already informed Dr. Metcalf that they would be attending.

As soon as James and Adam stepped into the precinct, Sheriff Thompson was waiting for them, "Well, is it the same killer?"

Adam replied, "It is. Dr. Metcalf will be performing the autopsy in a few minutes and we want to be there for that. When he is done, we will come back here to finish our reports."

He nodded his head, "Good, good. Let me know as soon as you hear something. I need to make a press conference as soon as possible, but I would like to have some answers first."

Chapter 59

After this morning's rigorous run, James was eager to jump in a cool shower when his phone rang. He groaned when he saw that it was the dispatcher calling, "Cook."

"Detective, we got another body."

So much for a long shower, "Where is it?"

"It is at the Welcome Center."

He informed the dispatcher, "I'm on my way. Have you called Detective Veret yet?"

"Yes, sir. He said that he would meet you there."

As he was heading to the crime scene his phone rang once again. It was Adam, "Damn, man, I'm on my way."

"The killer is escalating. There was a lot of mutilation done to this woman's body."

By the time he reached the crime scene, it looked like a full-blown circus. Not only had a crowd of bystanders shown up, but the media were crawling all over the place. They were all trying to catch a glimpse of the dead body. *Great, more media coverage.* It wouldn't be long before this case went national and when it did, everyone would constantly be looking over their shoulder.

He saw Adam standing near the body. He remained quiet while staring down at the deceased. As he stood next to Adam, he winced when he saw the remains. The carnage was brutal.

Adam informed him, "I believe our guy has snapped. This is another dumpsite. I do believe he is starting to enjoy displaying the victims. All we can do right now is pray that he messed up and left some evidence we can use."

James watched as the medical examiner's office zipped up the body bag. The victim's lifeless eyes revealed the horror she went through only hours before. If only the dead could speak and tell them who did this.

Adam pursed his lips, "I don't like that the killer has decided that he wants these bodies found. He is taking great pride in the display. He wants the shock value."

James agreed, "This is a local. He is definitely stalking these victims beforehand. A stranger in town would stick out if he was caught skulking around at night for any reason. No, this is someone that knows this area who no one would question as to why he was out and about."

Adam surveyed the crime scene. The crowd of onlookers had increased. *Who in the crowd was the killer.*

James speculated if Rosewood Plantation had something to do with these murders. But what? With Nicki living there now, he didn't see how someone could be using the plantation to murder these women. Nicki would surely hear someone screaming. Unless the killer is using a part of the property further away from the house. Perhaps they should inspect the other parts of the property more thoroughly.

***

The next morning as James read Frank Ingall's article in The Harold, he questioned how he obtained some of his information. Was he merely going off the rumors that were spreading around town? Something still didn't sit right with James when it came to Frank Ingalls. Perhaps he should do a little more digging into the man's background. So far, the man had been a closed book. Maybe it was the fact that he was a journalist and they generally tended to keep many secrets, only revealing them when it was necessary. Still, someone should know something about his past.

Chapter 60

As Nicki was outside sweeping the porch, the rain began to fall. The large drops pelted the ground in front of her. A large gust of wind blew off of the bayou, sending leaves across the yard. The gnarled branches shrouded with moss stretched towards the sullen sky. The swaying trees looked more like skeletons than sturdy sentinels guarding the plantation. As the fog began to form over the bayou, it reminded her of a swarm of angry ghosts gliding along through the murky water.

Lightning streaked across the sky as the approaching storm bathed the old house in flashes of surreal blue light. The atmosphere around her suddenly seemed charged, threatening, and ominous.

As Nicki walked back inside, she noticed how chilled the house felt tonight. Even the lightning flashing through the room had her feeling uneasy. It created ominous, gloomy shadows that danced around the room. Outside the porch swing creaked softly as it gently swayed.

Nicki jumped involuntarily as a loud boom of thunder shook the house. Suddenly, a loud moaning echoed through the house; Nicki wasn't sure if it was from the wind outside or the ghosts inside voicing their complaints once again.

Another deep moan moved through the house, which sent chills down her back. The doors began to slam shut with a loud bang. A cold draft blew across the room, carrying with it a malevolent feeling. Another flash of lightning illuminated the house as the storm rolled in from the bayou. Shadows began to dance wildly in obscene contortions.

Nicki could feel the overpowering presence of evil all around her. A large black shadow seemed to be making its way around the parlor as a foul stench began to permeate the air. Nicki gasped as a hazy apparition materialized in the center of the room. Bones came from the darkness of the shadows and took form. Tendons began to connect to the bone. They started to move on their own accord as muscle and skin took on a human shape. The apparition's skin glowed with a sickly green, demonic color. Nicki shuddered in fear at the image in front of her.

Nicki instinctively stepped backwards as the apparition moved towards her with outstretched arms. Nicki became paralyzed in fear as it moved even closer to her. The apparition let out a deep moan and the room was instantly saturated with a putrid stench as black shadows reached out for her from its open mouth. The house continued to shake as the storm outside picked up.

The eyes that stared at her were filled with palpable hatred. The glaring eyes tore at her soul with gut wrenching guilt and self-loathing. Her body became overcome with a tempest of emotions manifesting themselves in a vile cesspool of bitter hate. Nicki grasped her heart as her soul was being pulled into an all-consuming abyss of hell. She cried out, unsure of how much longer she could take this emotional abuse. Her heart was beating so fast that she feared it would explode out of her chest.

She wasn't sure why the apparition felt so much hatred for her, but it seemed to consume the surrounding air. The apparition reached out and began to lash out at her with skeletal fingers. She cried out as the sharp nails tore into her tender flesh.

Without warning, the apparition let out a loud howl that sounded guttural and unearthly. The lightning outside began to streak violently as thunder rumbled deep in the sky. As the storm picked up, the apparition shrieked with an uncontrollable maelstrom of violent choking rage. The air became putrid as lightning exploded though the windows with pulsating light. The rain outside came down in torrents of water.

"Be gone from here woman. If you do not leave, you will meet the same fate as the others. I will KILL you."

Nicki watched in amazement as two more figures took shape in the shadows. A young woman took form and stepped forward as she warned, "I knew my time on this earth was short lived. I had to die, because I suspected what he was doing. I had feared that he was having an affair, but I never imagined what he was actually capable of. I followed him that night, watched him discard her. I was too scared to stop him, though. But his evil still continues. Can you hear me? Do you understand me? I was too scared to stop him then, but now I must warn someone that it is still happening. Oh please, can you hear me? Someone has to stop the evil that dwells here. The last woman tried to stop the evil that lived here, but she was unsuccessful. You have to do it."

The sound of screams filled the air. The eerie noise surrounded her. Before Nicki could fathom what was happening, the scene faded. As the apparitions dissipated, Nicki began to fear that what happened may have some importance to what was currently going on in Lost Bayou. Could it be that this woman just confirmed her fears, that those murders had taken place here, in her house? But where would the murders have taken place on the property? The room where the pictures were taken didn't look familiar. Was there another hidden room somewhere in this house? And what did she mean by the last woman had tried? Had Mrs. Fontaine suspected what was happening here? Is that why she decided to sell and move away? Perhaps it was time to have another talk with the former owner.

Curious, Nicki walked into the front parlor and started banging on the walls. Perhaps they had missed a secret passage. Then, as she was searching for any sign of a hidden room, it hit her. A bone chilling fear settled deep in her stomach as reality set in. She actually suspected that something horrifying had taken place here.

She spun around, as if convinced that an evil entity was with her at this very moment, watching her every move. As if it was hiding in the dark, crouched and waiting to make its move.

When a knock at the door sounded, she jumped in fright. She cautiously walked to the door and looked out the window. She let out a sigh of relief when she saw Detective Cook, "Am I relieved to see you."

Concerned, he asked, "Why, did something happen?"

Shaking her head, "No, not really. I just realized that there is more than likely a killer using this property, murdering innocent women."

"But did the room in the photos look familiar?"

"No, that's just it. It didn't look familiar, but it could have been remodeled years ago."

"But some of those photos were taken over two decades ago, maybe longer. Our killer would be an old man by now. I honestly think the person murdering the women currently is middle aged.”

Shrugging her shoulders, “Maybe so.” Nicki didn’t want to tell him about her visit from the ghosts, knowing he wouldn’t believe her.

“I had stopped by to see how you were doing and wanted to see if you would like to go grab a bite to eat.”

Smiling, she stated, “You know you could have called.”

Shrugging his shoulders, “Maybe I wanted to see your pretty face.”

Laughing, she informed him, “Maybe some actual human company is what I need for a little while.”

Nicki grabbed her purse from the entryway table before stepping outside. After locking the door, she walked side by side with Detective Cook to his car. As he opened her door, he asked, “Do you have a preference on what you want to eat?”

“Since you are the local, I will let you choose. I am easy.”

Smirking, he asked, “Oh really? Perhaps we should eat here then.”

Slapping at his shoulder, she replied, “You know that is not what I meant.” She braced herself before asking this next question, "But after supper do you mind stopping by the nursing home. I wanted to ask Mrs. Fontaine a few questions."

That piqued James's interest, "I suppose we can, but you know she may not be lucid enough to answer any questions."

Sighing, "I know." But Nicki hoped she could shed some light on the mystery unfolding before her eyes.

On the ride to the restaurant, they talked about how the remodeling was going. In the back of her mind, though, Nicki found herself wondering if the previous owners had problems with hauntings as well. Could that be why Jake didn't want to work on the renovations? Was he afraid it would upset the ghosts? But, then again, it was hard to tell anything with Jake. He showed no emotion when he talked to her. While he was an interesting and arresting man, it bothered her somewhat about his lack of emotion.

When they arrived at the restaurant, Nicki was relieved to see that there wasn't a long line. As they were ushered to their table, she noticed that most of the tables were occupied with happy couples. Looking at the smiling couples caused her heart to ache. She shook off the feeling of sadness and forced herself back to the present.

After the waitress took their orders, Nicki and James fell back into the pleasant banter they had enjoyed on the ride over. It shocked her when he asked, "Do you believe in ghosts?"

She froze, startled by the sudden question. She picked up her glass of wine and took a gulp before answering. "Do you?"

He took a sip of his drink as his eyes met hers squarely, "I think the world is full of unanswered questions, but if there is life after death – I'm not sure. But I wonder if perhaps the stories around town were having you jump at shadows lately. You had a startled look about you earlier, and even when I asked you about ghosts you had a look of fear in your eyes."

"I believe in the possibility of ghosts. I do believe there are energies all around us and sometimes that energy leaves an imprint."

"So I take it you haven't seen any ghosts at the plantation then?"

"I'm not sure what I have seen at the plantation to be honest with you. There have been some unexplained disturbances lately, as if the house is trying to tell me something."

"Perhaps the death of your husband has made you more susceptible to seeing ghosts."

Shrugging her shoulders, "I'm not sure. Perhaps the house has been waiting for the right person to come along and tell its story to."

"Maybe, but what kind of story does it have to tell."

Nicki shuddered at the thought, "I'm not sure I'm ready to find out, to be honest with you. The discovery of those photos still has me disturbed."

"Those photos would give most people nightmares."

As the server placed their food in front of them, they changed the conversation to their childhood. Over dessert he talked about why he joined the police force.

As they left the restaurant, James gently reminded Nicki, "There is a chance that Mrs. Fontaine won't be able to tell us anything."

Nicki gently shook her head, "I realize that, but it can't hurt to talk to her."

They pulled into the nursing home's parking lot, and Nicki found herself anxious. Entering the building, Nicki was excited to meet the lady who owned the home. A part of her wanted to ask if she had witnessed any ghosts herself, but Nicki decided now was not the time for that. She wanted James to take this visit seriously, and the mention of ghosts may not help.

At the front desk, the attractive receptionist asked, "Can I help you?"

James gave her a warm smile, "We are here to speak with Mrs. Fontaine."

The receptionist gave them a surprised look, "It is so nice to see Mrs. Fontaine receive visitors."

Nicki's heart broke at that news, "She doesn't get any visitors?"

Shaking her head, "No, ma'am. She has a gentleman who comes to check on her a few times a week, but other than him her visitors are few and far between."

James asked, "Where would we find Mrs. Fontaine?"

"She spends most of her time out on the breezeway sir. It's quiet right now. I can take you to see her."

Nicki replied, "We would appreciate that."

When they stepped out onto the breezeway, the receptionist pointed to an elderly woman sitting at the far corner. She was rocking and staring out over the flower gardens. Before leaving the receptionist stated, "You chose a good night to come visit, she has had a good day." Looking over at the patient compassionately, she informed them, "But please don't stay too long. Mrs. Fontaine likes to be in bed by eight p.m."

Mrs. Fontaine was a tiny woman with a deeply wrinkled face. She had short, silver hair that looked as if it had been recently permed.

Moving closer to where Mrs. Fontaine was sitting, she turned towards them and smiled. "Hello. I'm sorry, but my memory is failing. Do I know you?"

Nicki shook her head, "No, ma'am, you don't. I bought Rosewood Plantation from you."

Nicki was amazed at how the elderly woman's demeanor changed right before them. She knew something, but what?

With trembling hands, Mrs. Fontaine patted the seat of the rocker next to her, "Come, my dear and sit next to me. There is so much we must talk about. So you are the one who bought my house?

"Yes, ma'am, I did."

As Nicki sat next to her, the elderly woman took Nicki's hand in hers. "I am so sorry, cher. I had hoped by selling the house that I would break the curse that hung over that place."

"What curse?" Nicki asked.

Tears filled the woman's eyes, "Such terrible things happened there. Things that I can never forget – or forgive."

Nicki squeezed her hand, "Mrs. Fontaine, please tell me what happened there?"

Shaking her head, the tears rolled down her cheeks, "No, I can't. Please, you don't understand, it was awful. But my husband is gone now, and it will no longer happen." She sat there for a second, and then looked at Nicki with true sorrow. "I thought that with my husband gone, the house could find peace. Only his death upset the house. It must have known what I did."

James looked over at Nicki, stupefied by the woman's statement, "Mrs. Fontaine, what happened to your husband?"

"I killed him," she said with perfect clarity.

James shook his head in disbelief, "I'm sorry, but did you say that you killed him?"

"I had no other choice. I couldn't allow him to hurt any more girls." Crying, "What he did was awful. At first I couldn't believe that my Gerald would even do something like that. That poor girl, he cut her into pieces."

Nicki watched the intrigue flit across James's face as he asked, "Where did you see your husband hurt the woman Mrs. Fontaine?"

"In his workshop."

"Mrs. Fontaine, this is important. Where was his workshop?" Nicki asked.

"Why in the bunker, my dear." Looking into Nicki's eyes, she asked, "Do you hear the footsteps at night too? When I was first married, I thought I was going crazy. My husband never heard the footsteps. When I asked him about it several months after we were married, he said that I was dreaming. But I know I wasn't. Even after his death, I would hear the footsteps.

Nicki nodded her head, "I have heard the footsteps."

"Oh dear. I hoped when I moved away the ghosts would find peace. I'm so sorry my dear."

Before they could ask her any more questions, a nurse appeared. "It is time to get Mrs. Fontaine ready for bed. You can come visit her another day though. I'm sure that Mrs. Fontaine would enjoy that."

Clasping both of their hands, she agreed. "Oh yes, please do come back."

On the drive home, Nicki asked, "Where do you suppose the bunker is?"

"I don't know, but I would like to find out."

As they drove up to the house, Nicki was shocked to see that she had left several lights on. Looking at the house, she was amazed how the windows reminded her of eyes glowing in the dark. Perhaps they were the ghosts of lost souls gazing at the world they left behind.

Later that night, as Nicki fell asleep, she found herself in an unknown part of the house. She looked around, but nothing seemed familiar. A mist began to rise up from the floor as women began to take shape. They were all speaking at once, and she couldn't understand them. A look of horror crossed their faces and they pointed behind her.

She could feel a cold breath on her neck. Someone was standing behind her. She bolted awake, swallowing back a scream. Oscar was sound asleep at her side, the rise and fall of his chest even and rhythmic. She ran her fingers through his silky fur and wished that she had a real human lying beside her. She wanted to feel a strong pair of arms wrapped around her. What she really wanted was to have someone to chase her fears away.

Should she tell Detective Cook about the ghosts? Or perhaps she should talk to Frank Ingalls. He seemed to be more receptive to the possibility that the plantation might be haunted.

But what would either man do if she flat out told him that ghosts were actually talking to her.

***

The sound of the alarm clock woke Nicki. She stepped out of bed, dressed, and walked downstairs. She was stunned to find James already in the kitchen, "You know you make it very hard for a person to be a perfect hostess when you are already downstairs brewing coffee."

He smiled and poured her a cup of coffee, "Seeing your beautiful face is enough thanks for me."

Nicki blushed at the compliment, "Will you at least let me cook you breakfast?"

He poured some coffee into a thermos and stated, "No need. Besides, I need to get to the office. There is still the matter of a killer on the loose. I want to catch this SOB."

"I know and I hate that you feel obligated to spend the night out here."

"Tell yourself that you are doing your civic duty by allowing me to stay here?"

Laughing, she asked, "And how did you come to that conclusion."

"If I am here and the killer does make an appearance, I will be able to arrest him."

Nicki shuddered at that chilling thought, "Well, then who am I to argue."

As James prepared to leave Nicki informed him, "I will be in town most of the day. I have to pick up some appliances."

"Have fun. I'm off to catch the bad guys."

After James left, Nicki toasted her a bagel for breakfast. She finished her coffee and bagel, fed Oscar, and waited for Darren. After Darren arrived, she left for town.

In town Nicki was able to get a lot accomplished. She found the cabinets she liked at the local hardware store and a kitchen sink that would fit in perfectly. She also found replacement ceiling tiles and fixtures that would not break her budget. Thankfully Darren had recommended a plumber that could install the sink and add a dishwasher in the kitchen.

Everything she chose fit with the house. Nothing screamed contemporary or 21st century.

When Nicki returned home, she let Oscar out and put away the small amount of groceries she had purchased in town. After letting Oscar back inside, Nicki started working on restoring a few more of the pieces she had found tucked away.

She had been busy with her current project, and didn't pay attention to the time. It had surprised her to hear James knocking on the door at 6 p.m. The smell the fried chicken greeted her when she opened the door.

James laughed at her disheveled appearance, "I may be your knight in shining armor tonight."

Opening the door wide for him to come in, she agreed, "You are so right." Then giving him a mischievous grin, she continued, "But then again any man carrying food may be considered my hero."

He placed a hand over his heart, "Ohhh! The woman knows how to cut down a man's ego quick."

Following him into the kitchen, she laughed, "Ha ha."

While he opened the take out boxes, Nicki placed some plates and silver on the bar. "It won't be too much longer before I can prepare us some gourmet meals."

"Oh yeah? I take it you had some luck in town today?"

"I did, and I stayed within budget."

Over supper, they continued their conversation. Afterwards, they cleaned up the dinner dishes and decided to go for a walk outside.

Chapter 61

Sheriff Thompson walked into his office and shut his door. This last murder had turned the town upside down. The phones had been ringing nonstop since yesterday morning.

Feeling restless about this case, he left his office and went over to the conference room where Detectives Cook and Veret were hard at work on this case. They had previously set up a murder board and laid out the cases to search for some little clue that they may have missed.

Adam looked up from the file, "Morning, sheriff."

"How is it going?"

Adam let out an exasperated sigh, "Mon dieu, we are going over everything with a fine tooth comb, but so far we have no suspects."

Sheriff Thompson scowled deeply as he stared at the boards. Still restless, he walked over to the window and stared outside. He watched as people came and went from the courthouse and the other various businesses that made up downtown. Several vendors were busy preparing for the lunch crowd. The killer was out there, and now they needed to find out which one of these people was the killer. He turned back to Adam, "We need to dig deeper into any newcomers.

There haven't been too many people who moved here in the last year or so."

Adam informed him, "We have already started looking into everyone's background."

Sheriff Thompson asked James, "What about witnesses? No one has noticed anything out of the ordinary?"

James admitted begrudgingly, "We haven't been able to find any witnesses to the murders. No one noticed anything out of the ordinary that day or the days leading up to the murders. Hell, no one even noticed anything when the bodies were disposed of. It's as if this guy is a ghost."

The sheriff's scowl deepened further, "I don't believe in ghosts and I don't like that this killer has us playing a waiting game. Right now the killer is the one in control and I want to switch roles with him. I don't like that we have to wait for the other shoe to drop. It is completely unnerving."

James continued to speculate, "Maybe we would be better off tracing the victims' movements over the last week or two before their deaths. There is a chance that they crossed paths with the killer."

Adam stated, "I'll organize some officers to track the victims' movements and see if maybe we find a common denominator that way." Looking over at the sheriff, "You know this will add up to even more overtime."

Sheriff Thompson nodded, "Just do it. I want this bastard behind bars where he belongs."

Sheriff Thompson noticed how tired James looked. Hell, they all looked as if they needed a good night's sleep, but that would have to wait for the case to close.

Chapter 62

As Nicki dozed off, a woman appeared at the foot of the bed. "Please, you have to stop him. He is a very bad man, worse than those before him."

"I don't understand, what do you mean he is worse than the others?"

"This man is a very bad man. I tried to warn the other lady, but she didn't see me. She couldn't hear me."

"I don't understand, what bad man?"

"He knows this house. He has been here before. He came here when the other lady lived here. I tried to tell her, but she couldn't see me."

The smell of rotting decay permeated the room. A shadowy vapor took form around the ghost. "Where is he?"

"Near where the fog rises."

Nicki shook her head, "I don't understand."

The woman never answered, though. Instead, she dissipated and floated away.

As Nicki went back to sleep, she wondered where the woman was talking about – where the fog rises. Perhaps somewhere near the bayou? Could there be a hidden room somewhere on the property?

And what if this place had been used to murder these women? She wasn't sure she could face the truth. This plantation was starting to feel like a home.   But how could she live in a place that harbored a deadly secret?

Chapter 63

Sheriff Thompson called Detectives Cook and Veret into his office. Adam could see him fuming from here. He told James, "This isn't going to be a pleasant conversation."

James ruefully shook his head, "Mais non. I still can't figure out how in the hell the press is finding out some of the more intimate details of the case. I have talked to the officers that were at the crime scene and everyone swears that they didn't breathe a word to the press."

Adam had been thinking about it too, "Frank Ingalls has been awfully quiet lately. He never seems to have too many questions about the recent murders. I am beginning to wonder if the killer is making contact with the press and they are not informing us."

"Mon dieu, I hope that is not the case."

As they entered Sheriff Thompson's office, they could feel the tension in the air, "I want to know how in the hell the media are getting wind of their information."

James looked at him, "We are trying to figure that out. I chewed some ass this morning and got no answers."

Sheriff Thompson slammed a fist down on his desk, "This whole damn case is going to blow up in our face."

Sheriff Thompson let out a long breath, "When I find out who is leaking information…" He trailed off before letting his temper get the best of him.

It wasn't often that he came close to losing his cajun temper, but when he did, he felt for those in his path. He may be stuck behind a desk now, but he was still a damn good cop. He had to keep reminding himself that a good cop didn't lose control. He shouldn't have gone off on the two detectives, they were good cops. They wouldn't be where they were if they were anything less than the best.

Adam told Sheriff Thompson, "The killer may be talking directly to the press."

"Mon dieu, the shit would really hit the fan then. Do you think that is how the information is getting released?"

James answered, "We aren't sure yet sir. If the killer was talking to the press, surely he would have mentioned the dismemberment."

Adam agreed, "That is what has me stumped. Somehow they know some pretty intimate details, but so far no one has reported how gruesome the murders really are."

This damn case was a jigsaw puzzle and they needed to turn each of the pieces until everything fell into place. "Go back and talk to the families one more time. Make sure we didn't miss anything in the timeline of these victims. Somehow they all came into contact with this killer."

Sheriff Thompson scanned the paper one more time. He was grateful they hadn't given their killer a name. "I don't like that he is getting all of this media coverage. This may be fueling whatever is driving him."

Adam agreed, "Yeah, but unfortunately we can't stop them from writing about him."

Adam and James headed back to their desks to continue searching for a connection between the victims and the killer. They also needed to see if they were missing any gaps in the timelines. Maybe they were overlooking a tiny detail.

Adam picked up his coffee to take a swallow, needing the caffeine rush. He scowled as the cold, bitter brew hit his throat and pushed the cup aside.

After reviewing the timelines, he pushed them aside. If only he had more details about their lives, it would be easier to notice any missing pieces.

His grandmother's warning about being careful what you wish for ran through his mind. Right now, he would be glad to get what he wished for, though.

His growling stomach reminded him that it had been a while since he last ate. As much as he wanted to find out who the leak was in the office, he needed to grab a quick bite and worry about finding this killer. That was his top priority.

Chapter 64

Nicki's eyes snapped open as the dark interior of her bedroom came into focus. She wasn't sure what woke her, but something did.

Then her heart caught in her throat. She felt a cold breath on her shoulder and turned to see no one there.

She turned on the lamp and looked around the room. The book she had been reading was still where she left it. Unaware that she had been holding her breath, she gently released it. She laughed at herself for being scared over nothing.

As she settled back in bed, another noise caught her attention. It was a low, ominous creaking sound. The closet door slowly opened. She was frozen in fear as the door continued to open. Somehow Nicki found her voice and screamed.

James came running into the room, gun drawn. She pointed to the closet door and stuttered, "The closet door opened."

Someone, or something, had recently been in there. They could see the muddy footprints. Horrible thoughts rushed through Nicki's mind.

"I'm going to sleep in here with you for tonight."

"I would rather sleep in your room."

Once in his room, Nicki was still uneasy. "Do you mind sleeping in the bed with me?"

James looked down at her, "I was going to sleep in a chair by the door, but if it would make you feel better I can lay here with you for a while."

She threw back the covers, "Please."

Once he was in bed with her, Nicki curled up into his warm embrace and fell sound asleep.

***

The next morning while James inspected the closet, Nicki went downstairs to brew a pot of coffee. She heard the front door open and called out, "I have a fresh pot of coffee made if you want a cup."

When no one answered her, she stepped into the entryway and the hair on the back of her neck rose. She heard Darren's saw outside. She knew the front door opened; she heard it.

"Nicki…" A voice called out. Her heart pounded in her ears. Stepping back into the foyer, the voice called out again, "Nicki…"

It sounded like it came from the dining room. Except when she entered the room, it was empty.

"Nicki…" She swallowed hard before looking back. This time, the voice came from the butler's pantry. Once again, the room was empty.

"Nicki…" This time the voice came from the kitchen. Once again, she followed the voice and found the room empty. Panic welled up deep inside of her; her heart skipped a beat.

As she calmed her racing heart, James walked down the stairs. "I didn't find any secret passages in your closet."

"Maybe Darren had gone into the closet for some reason. I will have to ask him."

After James left for work, Nicki decided to paint one of the smaller guest rooms on the second floor.

Once done, flecks of paint covered her. She headed to her bedroom and showered before cooking supper.

She lathered up and scrubbed at the specks of paint on her skin. As she rinsed off the soap, she inspected her arms to make sure she'd removed the paint. But what she saw horrified her. Her arm was covered in small bruises. *How did she manage to hurt herself?* She didn't even remember bumping into anything hard enough to cause such bruises.

Finishing her shower, a chill swept over her and goose bumps crawled up her skin.

She cautiously peered through the shower curtain to see a young woman staring at her. Curious if the woman wanted to show her something, Nicki stepped out of the tub. She wrapped her robe around her wet body and stepped out of the bathroom. The apparition walked into Nicki's room. Only, once there the woman disappeared.

Disappointed, Nicki fell onto the bed and stared at the ceiling. She had hoped the woman would lead Nicki somewhere, but she had not.

Chapter 65

Sheriff Thompson paced in his office while he contemplated this case. The media presence was increasing. He couldn't step outside of the sheriff's office without running into a news van, camera crew or a reporter trying to ask a question.

Then there were the curiosity seekers hanging out downtown. They milled about hoping to catch a rumor of something that was going on with the investigation. The vendors in front of the courthouse were extremely busy with all the people around. The PitStop, Sheriff Thompson's favorite, loved all the business. He couldn't keep up with the boudin and andouille corn dog sales. He also sold alligator on a stick and bowls of Pierre's gumbo. The enticing aromas made Thompson's mouth water as soon as he stepped outside.

To make matters worse, they still had no leads or a suspect. He walked over to the conference room to see if they had any updates. Detective Veret was looking over the board when he walked in the room, "Anything new to tell me?"

He ruefully shook his head, "No sir. I sure wish I did. Right now I am trying to track their movements. There has to be one place that they all went to, but I am not having any luck. With this being a small town you would think their paths would have crossed a few times, but trying to locate that point is turning out to be an impossible task."

Sheriff Thompson perused the crime scene photos, "What on earth could set off another human being to do something so cruel to another person?"

Adam shook his head, "I wish I knew, sir."

Sheriff Thompson exhaled deeply, "What bothers me is that he appears to be cool and calm while executing these murders."

Chapter 66

He watched as she entered the hotel room. He waited a few minutes before he moved in. It had been so easy to swipe her credit card when she wasn't looking. Knocking on the door, he called out, "Ms. Harrison, I'm sorry to bother you, but you left your credit card at the front desk."

When she opened the door, he acted quickly. As he handed her the card, he used the taser gun to subdue her.

***

Panic surged through her body. Animal instinct and the elemental will to survive took over. She pulled against the restraints as hard as she could, but her attempts were in vain, they were too tight. Fear ran in rivulets down her back. She knew she was in the presence of true evil. It was thick and heavy in the air, as thick as the fog that hung over the bayou in the early morning hours.

She watched as he raised the knife again. She tried to prepare herself for what was about to come, this was how he would kill her. Time seemed to stop as the knife made contact with her abdomen. The gag in her mouth muffled her guttural screams.

Never in her life had she ever endured such excruciating pain. She prayed the pain would become too much and she would drift off into unconsciousness, sparing her the agony she was suffering right now.

***

Looking down at her dead body, there was something strangely intimate about her cold and brutal death. Black pools of blood formed on the bed from where he had perfected her naked body.

***

The next morning the housekeeper found the body when she entered the room. She woke up the remaining guests with her incessant screaming. In the middle of the bed lay a woman bound and gagged, brutally dismembered and eviscerated. Her soulless eyes stared up at nothing.

Chapter 67

When James arrived at the hotel he greeted the young officer standing guard. He shook his head at the thought of another crime scene. He asked, "Has Adam made it here yet?"

"He's inside, sir."

From the doorway he could see technicians brushing the room for prints. This place was going to be a nightmare. He had no doubt that they would recover many prints, but would any belong to their killer, and if so how would they know. The only good thing that came from the murder taking place at the hotel room was that they had an actual crime scene to work with, and from the looks of it the killer didn't bother to clean up. Maybe, just maybe, they would get lucky and find something he left behind.

The smell of death hit James as soon as he walked into the hotel room. The metallic odor of blood was overpowering. He doubted housekeeping would ever get the smell out. They would need to collect the blood soaked mattress. It looked as if the blood had seeped all the way through. Grotesque blood splatter patterns marked the wall and ceiling.

James frowned down at the body. For a fleeting moment, he thought he would be sick as he looked at the carnage.

A police photographer was busy taking pictures of the crime scene. There were numerous blood splatter striations on the walls. "Did we get pictures of the body?"

Adam replied, "Yeah."

James yanked on a pair of latex gloves. "What kind of sick freak are we dealing with?"

"Aren't they all sick and twisted?"

Dr. Metcalf arrived and observed the body. Adam said, "There is so much mutilation."

Adam nodded his head in agreement, "He also came prepared. He tied her up and gagged her."

From the extent of the rope burns on her wrists and ankles, she did not give up easily. She was a fighter. Her eyes showed the terror she went through before she died. This fucking bastard put her through hell.

James instructed the crime scene techs, "I want y'all to cut the ropes off her carefully. Make sure we bag her hands. Maybe we will get lucky this time and find some DNA in the rope knots."

"Yes, sir." One of the techs began carefully removing the ropes.

James felt a headache starting at the base of his skull and his stomach was in knots. Their killer was definitely a psychotic exhibitionist. He was definitely staging the bodies for the most shock value.

One of the crime scene techs called from the bathroom, "Detectives, it looks as if your killer cleaned up in the bathroom before he left."

Adam watched as the crime scene techs collected evidence. It would most likely to be a waste of time. So far, all the results had been a big fat goose egg. All the blood had been from the victims. How could someone mutilate another individual and not at least nick themselves? This was one lucky bastard. The cotton fibers found at the scene came from any one of a thousand sources and no trace or any other forensic evidence was found on the bodies. It was as if a ghost performed these murders.

James looked over the body, "Our guy likes to slash and carry."

Frustration raged through him as he observed the crime scene, trying to look at it through the killer's eyes. He turned his eyes to the ceiling asking the Lord for help. This was going to be a long day indeed.

Chapter 68

When Nicki heard the knock at the door, she rushed to greet James. "I had assumed you would be working late."

James held up a pizza, "Hunger won out. I come bearing gifts."

Nicki smelled the delicious aroma of the hot pizza and opened the door all the way to let him in, "Pizza sounds great."

James informed her, "I suppose I should have called, but something deep inside of me told me to come check on you."

"You are more than welcome to come over, but something tells me that there is more to this visit."

Nodding his head, "The killer struck again, and I didn't feel right not checking on you tonight."

"I'm so sorry to hear that, but it has been quiet here. But if it would help put your mind at ease, you are more than welcome to check things out yourself."

"I appreciate that, but pizza first."

Laughing as she led him into the kitchen, "Okay."

As James placed the pizza on the kitchen counter, he noticed the changes in the room, "It looks like Darren is doing a great job with the renovations."

While Nicki took out the plates and glasses from the cabinet, she agreed with him, "Yes it is starting to feel like home. At first, I wasn't sure about my decision, but now I am glad that I did this. Tom would have loved this adventure."

After they finished their supper, James meticulously searched every square inch of the house. He checked every closet and dark corner to ensure that no one was lurking about. "There is no one here, but I still plan on staying the night."

"You don't have to spend the night. I will be fine."

James shook his head, "There is no way I can sleep knowing that you are out here by yourself with a murderer running loose."

"Well then I don't want it on my conscience that I was the reason you didn't get any sleep."

James followed Nicki upstairs and to the guest room he used on the previous occasions. She told him, "There are fresh sheets on the bed and clean towels hanging in the bathroom."

As James went into his room, he turned around and told Nicki, "Goodnight. If you need me for any reason, please don't hesitate to wake me."

Nicki stood on her tippy toes and kissed him on the cheek, "I am sure I will be fine, but thank you for being so kind."

Slapping her leg, Nicki called to Oscar, "Come on boy, let's go to bed."

Oscar, who had been studying the two at the end of the hall, jumped up and ran to her door. She chuckled and told James, "Besides, I have this terrifying dog to protect me."

James laughed as Oscar stood at the door to Nicki's room and growled into the vacant room, "Oh yeah, he's a great protector against shadows."

Nicki shook her head as she ushered Oscar into the room, "You tell that shadow who's boss, Oscar. Don't listen to Detective Cook. I know how brave of a dog you are."

Oscar's reply was a quick yelp as he jumped onto the bed and under the covers. Nicki couldn't understand what had gotten into this dog lately. James was correct in his assumption that Oscar had been jumping at shadows. Perhaps it was the new house.

Distorted images of ghostly figures invaded Nicki's sleep. She recognized the house, but not one of the rooms the images were in. It didn't resemble any of the rooms in the plantation.

The figures walked through her, as if she wasn't there. She heard discordant voices all around her. As one of the women let out a horrifying scream, the hairs on Nicki's arm rose. A cold chill snaked down her spine.

Nicki woke up in a cold sweat. She pulled Oscar, who was sleeping next to her, closer to her body. As she tried to calm her nerves, she heard footsteps in the attic. Although not heavy footsteps, they didn't belong to an animal.

She bolted out of her room and rushed into James's room – not taking the time to knock.

James, who must be a light sleeper, woke up as soon as she entered the room. "Nicki, what's wrong"

Breathing shakily, she said, "There's someone in the attic."

"Do you have a flashlight handy? Mine's in the car."

Nicki walked over to the nightstand, and explained, "When I moved in to Rosewood the electricity was fickle, so I made sure each room had candles and flashlights handy."

"That was smart thinking."

James took the flashlight from her and started walking towards the attic stairs. As they walked up the stairs, Nicki clung to his t-shirt.

James slowly opened the attic door and shined the flashlight into the room. "Someone has been in here. Dust is floating in the air."

As they looked closer, they could see muddy footprints on the floor. They appeared to be adult sized prints. James told Nicki, "I don't see a ghost leaving footprints behind."

Nicki shook her head, unable to form the words. The realization of what they were looking at made it difficult to breathe. Sheer terror washed over her. She was glad that James had insisted on sleeping here last night.

"Go lock yourself in, and don't open the door to anyone but me."

"But…"

James gave her a discerning look, "No buts Nicki. Do as I say." James pulled out a gun he had tucked in his pants and told Nicki, "Call 911. Tell the dispatcher I said to send backup immediately."

Nicki nodded her head and rushed back down the stairs. Once in her room, she locked the door and pulled Oscar close to her. She reached for her phone on her nightstand and called 911, "This is Nicki Brady at Rosewood Plantation. Detective Cook is here and he needs backup – immediately. There is someone in the attic."

"I'll dispatch backup right now. Please stay on the phone until they arrive." On the other end Nicki could hear him making the appropriate calls. Nicki's heart was pounding as she waited for James.

She could hear James walking around above her. His footsteps sounded heavier than those she had heard earlier.

Approximately fifteen minutes later, the backup police officers arrived. While she heard James go downstairs to let them in, she couldn't hear what he was saying. She could hear the officers moving through the house. She prayed they found whoever was in the attic.

Nicki watched the clock as the minutes slowly ticked by. Twenty minutes later, James knocked on her door, "Nicki, it's me. You can open the door now."

Nicki rushed into his arms, "Did you find the intruder?"

James shook his head, "No, I'm sorry – we didn't."

Nicki felt crushed. "I wonder who it could have been, and how they got in."

James put his arms around her, "Perhaps the footsteps were from earlier, and you didn't notice them."

"I don't know what to think anymore. I know I heard footsteps earlier."

"We searched the house and the grounds thoroughly and didn't find any signs of an intruder." He tilted her chin up to look at him. "We will get to the bottom of this mystery, promise." James turned her towards the bed, "Why don't you try to go back to sleep and I'm going to go see the officers off."

As Nicki climbed back in bed, Oscar jumped down from the bed and took after James. "Oscar come back here! Stop boy!"

Nicki went after Oscar. She didn't want him outside this late at night, especially if there was someone wandering the grounds. She stopped abruptly when she found Oscar in James's room. "Oscar, what are you doing? You know you aren't supposed to be in here."

As Nicki moved closer to Oscar she let out a gasp as a cold chill swept over her. Oscar had pulled a muddy shoe out from under James's bed.

Nicki felt her heart catch in her throat. She could hear James coming back up the stairs and quickly ushered Oscar out of the room as she nudged the shoe back under the bed. She pushed Oscar from the rear and rushed them into the room, softly shutting the door behind her.

Her mind had a hard time grasping the realization that James had a muddy pair of shoes under his bed. Why would he even be up in the attic at this time of the night? And if it was him up there, why not admit it? Why bother going through such an elaborate cover up?

While she listened for James's door to close, sleep reluctantly came to her. When the blare of the alarm woke her in the morning, she wanted to hit snooze for a few minutes more. Instead, she padded downstairs and started a pot of coffee.

She brewed it stronger than normal and started scrambling eggs for breakfast. Her weary mind was still reeling from last night's discovery.

When James walked into the kitchen, she pointed to an empty barstool. "Take a seat. I cooked us some breakfast and the coffee is done."

"You didn't have to go to all that trouble. I could have picked me up something on the way in."

"Nonsense, you were nice enough to stay the night. It's the least I can do for you."

After eating a quick breakfast, James told her, "I need to get to work. Again, thank you for breakfast."

"You are more than welcome. Have a good day at work, Detective Cook."

Nicki picked up her coffee cup and followed James out the door. After he left, she sat in a rocker and watched him drive away. While she drank her coffee, she pondered everything that had happened lately. There was no way the footsteps last night were made by a ghost. An actual person was up in the attic. But was it James? And if so, why?

Shaking herself out of her reverie, Nicki went inside and started to clean the house. She went into the laundry room and gathered her cleaning products. She wanted to work on restoring the baseboards and molding in the entryway. The stairs also needed a good polishing.

Before she started cleaning, she fixed Oscar his breakfast. "Oscar, come on. Let's get some nummies."

She waited to hear him come bounding down the stairs, but was greeted by silence. She walked upstairs and found Oscar nestled under her bed with an old blanket she had never seen before. "What's wrong? Aren't you hungry?"

He let out a low bark, but refused to budge. Nicki shrugged her shoulders and stood up. She walked back downstairs to the entryway and started dusting the woodwork. She could slowly see the beauty of the baseboards come to life. As she cleaned the door frames, she was amazed at the intricate detailing in the woodwork. A lot of love had gone into the finer details of the house. She was thankful that the previous owners had kept the original molding in the house. Next she would have to work on the ceiling medallions. After that, she wanted to remove some of the peeling wallpaper in the bedrooms. Darren had already suggested a local who worked on plaster repair. Unfortunately, she wouldn't know the extent of the damage until the wallpaper was removed. A few of the bedrooms also had carpeting installed and she wanted to pull that up as well. She hoped the original wood floors were still there.

As she scrubbed the wainscoting under the stairs, a faint noise caught her attention. It was so faint, she almost thought she had imagined it. She listened closer. It sounded like a soft scratching noise coming from behind the wainscoting. She hoped that they didn't have a mice infestation in the house. Although it wouldn't surprise her.

An array of voices sounded around her. The voices seemed to fade then increase in volume. The old house groaned under its weight as she said, "I can't understand what you are saying."

The voices slowly merged, their echoes and mutters evolved into one voice. "It is not safe here." "Go away." "He will kill you."

Then she felt someone breathing on her neck. The hairs on the back of her neck stood up. She slowly turned around and saw a bloody woman standing directly behind her. The blood was so heavy that it flowed to the floor. Deep, gory gashes plagued the body. The scent of blood tickled her nose as she jumped backwards.

The woman moaned and pointed to the spot where Nicki had been cleaning. Nicki began tapping on the wall, searching for a possible hidden door. As she polished the wood paneling that made up the wall under the stairs, a hairline crack in the wood caught her attention. Nicki began pushing on the paneling to see if it possibly needed to be nailed down again and was shocked when a hidden door opened. It was no wonder she had missed it before, the door was a wooden chameleon.

What astonished her even more was that as she swung the door open, it didn't squeak. The hinges appeared to still be well-oiled. She reached inside the hidden room, but didn't feel any light switches. She rushed back into the kitchen and found a flashlight. Shining the light into the tiny closet, she noticed a stairway at the end of the room. "Now why didn't anyone mention that this house had a basement?"

As she descended the stairs, the smothering blackness enveloped her. She walked slowly, keeping her eyes fixed to the floorboards so she wouldn't trip.

While the edges of the stairs were black as tar, the centers were a dark sandy shade. When was the last time someone had been down here?

Nicki counted the stairs as she went. Five… Ten… fifteen…

At last, after twenty-two steps the floor leveled out. There was no hardwood flooring here, only a dirt floor with dirt-covered brick walls. She raised her flashlight to inspect the area.

She had expected to find a room packed with hidden treasures like the attic, but, instead, she found what resembled something more like a workroom. To her right was a low, wide table with tarps thrown over it. Along the wall were antique tools that were hanging from nails. She counted at least thirty tools, and some were so medieval looking that she couldn't even imagine what they may have been used for.

Opposite her, at the other end of the room, was another table with a work light overhead. Beyond that table was another unusual piece with a large cloth covering it.

She surveyed her surroundings once again. She had expected most of the items in here to be covered in a thick grime, but other than the horrible odor – it seemed to be relatively dust free.

Nicki walked over to the largest table and slowly picked up the tarp that covered it. Nicki immediately recoiled at the sight in front of her. A human skull gazed up at her with empty eye sockets. Several other bones were scattered around the skull. The grotesque revelation had her hastily backing up.

Then a chilling reality settled over her. *Was this the room where those poor women had been killed?* Cold prickles ran up her back and down her arms. *Had they truly been murdered here in this house?*

She had to call James at once. He needed to know what she had found. Nicki rushed back up the stairs and bolted into the foyer.

Nicki was glad to be away from the gruesome find and oppressive darkness. She sent James a text message since she knew he was busy working the most recent murder. *I found the room where the murders may have taken place. A hidden room was under the stairs.*

Chapter 69

Adam saw the evidence clerk heading toward their desks, "Detectives we got the DNA reports back from the crime scene."

Adam perked up at that comment, "Please tell me we got something."

The evidence clerk nodded his head, "We got something. Unfortunately, there was no match in CODIS, but at least it is something solid."

James rubbed his hands together, "Finally, we are making headway. We need to nail this guy before he takes another life."

Adam didn't want to get his hopes up, "I want to catch this guy just as bad as you, but how do we do that when we don't have a match in CODIS."

James reviewed the report the evidence clerk recently brought to them. If they only had a suspect to go with the DNA. They needed something solid to bring someone in and, right now, they didn't have that. If it were up to him, he would make everyone in town line up for a DNA analysis. He knew that was wishful thinking.

He still couldn't believe that someone here was capable of committing these heinous murders.

Whenever he passed people, he wondered if they were the killer. What made it worse was the killer may be someone he knew. Could he possibly talk to this person every day and not know that he was capable of committing these murders?

He tried to picture what the killer may look like, but it was too difficult to picture a normal person committing these crimes. Evil should look like a malicious monster and not the person living right next door to you. Nevertheless, evil was deceptive. It wouldn't be ugly until it was ready to show its true self and by then it was too late. It wanted to make itself hard to recognize because that was what evil did best, deceive.

At first evil was charming and knew all the right words to say. It drew you in, made you trust it, and then when you least expected it, evil would show its soulless eyes. By then it was too late.

Their killer had to be physically fit in order to drive a large knife into the bodies and dispose of them after death. The mere thought of the pain the victims endured sent a shiver through his body.

Chapter 70

Sheriff Thompson called in Detectives Cook and Veret. When James saw Mayor Jenkins also sitting in the office, he knew this wasn't a normal pow wow.

Mayor Jenkins looked over at the detectives, "So detectives I need to know if you feel we are out of our element here?"

James rubbed his growing beard as he contemplated the best way to answer this question. He couldn't believe that Sheriff Thompson set them up, but one look at his face told James that even the sheriff had no idea the mayor was going to ask the question.

Upon further examination, James noticed how jittery the mayor was. He was normally calm and collected, this morning he was far from either.

Although the question aggravated James, he needed to answer this in a manner that would show their ability to handle this case. He refused to be pulled from the case when they were getting close to figuring this out.

He knew the mayor didn't like the obstacles he was currently faced with. These murders were gruesome and causing some uneasy feelings in the residents of Lost Bayou.

Sheriff Thompson stepped in, "Mayor Jenkins we have some of the town's finest detectives working on this case. They have been busy compiling evidence and they want to catch this guy just as bad as you, if not more. Trust me, if they felt they were out of their element and this case was too much for them, they would be the first to ask for assistance. Right now we don't have enough to bring the FBI in on and the state trooper's have their hands full."

Adam spoke up, "Mayor Jenkins you have nothing to worry about. We will track this killer down." He said it with as much conviction as he could muster. However, he feared he did not convince the good mayor.

Irritation flashed through Mayor Jenkins's eyes, "So tell me detective, what should I tell the concerned citizens that call me at all hours of the day and night? I don't think that informing the public we have the best detectives working the case will help put their minds at ease, do you? I don't want to hear excuses. I want you to catch this sick fucker. I want the criminal element in Lost Bayou shaking in their boots."

Sheriff Thompson wondered if Mayor Jenkins was causing this much of a headache for him because he wanted this motherfucker caught as bad as they did or if it was part of his political agenda.

James looked over at Sheriff Thompson before he divulged too much information. When Sheriff

Thompson nodded, James handed everyone a copy of the trace evidence reports from the crime scenes. "I believe we are making headway. Our killer left us some evidence that we can go on. Before leaving the crime scene, he took a shower in the hotel bathroom. The crime scene techs were able to procure several strands of pubic hair with a follicle attached."

Mayor Jenkins perked up, "So you are telling me that we may have this asshole's DNA?"

Adam nodded his head, "Yes sir. Unfortunately, he isn't in CODIS but it does give us enough to start pulling suspects in for matches. We are also doing background checks on all the newcomers in town, just to be on the safe side. I have a hard time believing that someone who has lived here all their life simply started killing, but we can't rule that prospect out. I believe we need to check into those that moved into town a little before the killings started as well. I have run checks through VICAP and so far we have had no hits, but that doesn't mean that some of the smaller towns haven't had unsolved murders like ours. I have sent out a request to all the law enforcement agencies and I am hoping that we get a response. If we do, then we can compare their possible suspects to ours. Or maybe we will get lucky and they have someone who moved away right after the killings stopped."

"I want this guy stopped before he kills again."

James knew this was easier said than done. They were getting closer to solving this puzzle. He hoped it would be before he killed again. The time in between the kills was getting shorter.

Adam let out a sigh of relief after Mayor Jenkins left. Adam looked over at James, "This guy is bound to get careless. I hate knowing that he is out there walking the streets of Lost Bayou."

James asked Sheriff Thompson, "Do you think the mayor will try to get the FBI involved?"

"I think we gave him enough information where he will hold off for now. Besides, the feds won't be interested in this case. It isn't high profile enough for them. If this killer starts escalating then we will have to look into it some more."

While Sheriff Thompson talked, James felt his phone vibrate. When he read Nicki's message, he couldn't believe the words he saw, "Sir, I hate to interrupt you, but it appears that Ms. Brady has found a secret room in her house. And it also sounds as if it is where the murders may have taken place."

Sheriff Thompson looked at him stunned, "Call her immediately. I will have forensics head over there asap."

As Sheriff Thompson made arrangements for the crime scene techs to head to Nicki's house, he gave her a call, "Nicki, are you certain that you found the room?"

Nicki sighed, "I am fairly certain. This room looks similar to the background in one of the photos. And there is a wall with tools that could be used for torture." Holding back the tears, she added, "And there are human bones."

"I will call the ME as well. Crime scene techs are on their way over. Adam and I will be there as soon as we can."

Nicki responded, "If you don't mind, I will wait outside. I need some fresh air."

***

Nicki and James were both disappointed that they didn't discover any clues to the killer's identity. But it did confirm James's suspicions, Rosewood Plantation was being used as the killer's playground.

Chapter 71

It was time to up the ante in the game. Leaving the bodies for Detective Cook to find had lost its appeal.

***

At first James wasn't going to answer the pealing ring of his cell phone. He didn't recognize the number. But then he got a bad feeling deep in his gut. "Detective Cook."

Silence. The bad feeling twisted in his gut.

Then he heard a hiss, followed by a scream – a woman's scream.

His stomach constricted when he heard the distinct swooshing of the knife as it was plunged into the woman's body, and the gurgle of blood as the knife was removed. The screams became horrific as James made out the sounds of a saw moving through her body.

He jumped out of bed and burst into Nicki's room exclaiming, "I need your cell phone. NOW!"

A groggy Nicki reached to the nightstand for her cell phone and handed it to him. An upset Oscar was barking madly at the interruption.

Without offering an explanation, James called the precinct and briskly informed the front desk, "I need a trace on my cell phone – immediately. I'm on the phone with the killer, and he has a victim as we speak."

His line went dead. He hit the call back button, but the line only rang, over and over again.

Nicki walked up behind him, "What's going on?"

Still clenching his phone, "The killer called me while he was with his latest victim." His jaw clenched as he revealed, "A woman was screaming."

Not giving Nicki a chance to continue the conversation, he called Adam, "The killer called me. He has another victim."

Groggily, Adam asked, "What? "Wait a minute. There's no way. He just killed."

"The woman was still screaming when the phone went dead. I'm having the call traced now. But there is a chance she is still alive. Get ready to move."

James knew that while the woman may still be alive, she wouldn't be for long. But if they could trace that call to her exact location, perhaps they could catch this killer. "He's escalating, Adam. And he's upping the game plan if he's making contact with us."

***

The killer looked down at his victim. "They won't save you in time, cher."

He watched as the life faded from her eyes. Blood soaked the bed, and dripped from the walls. It was a magnificent sight.

There was no time to linger or enjoy his work though. It wouldn't be too long before the cops were here. And this time he wanted to make sure he had a good seat. It would be a helluva show to watch.

***

As James was pulling up to Adam's house, his phone rang. It was the precinct, "Sir, we traced the phone call. It came back to one-twelve Sycamore Street."

James jotted down the address and instructed Adam, "Buckle up. We have an address."

Turning on his lights he took off into the darkness of the night. Sycamore wasn't far from here – maybe ten minutes if you obeyed the speed limit. Which, of course, he had no plans of doing tonight.

While James drove to the scene, Adam was on the phone and police radio barking orders.

Adam told everyone to go in silent. This was a tactical call. If they went in with the sirens screaming and lights blaring and the killer hadn't killed her yet, he could get spooked and kill her before they could move in.

Adam gave the orders, "Do NOT alert him. Go in and take him down."

Wearing bullet proof vests and guns drawn, they slipped into the house. The distinct aroma of spilt blood permeated their senses. If she wasn't dead, she was close to it.

"Be alive. Please be alive." James repeated to himself.

The remote house was small. They spread out to search the house. James's gaze swept over the bedroom. It was hard not to miss the woman sprawled out on the bed. Blood soaked the room and dripped from the ceiling. Her arms and legs were bound to the bed, but her body had clearly been dismembered.

"Son of a bitch." James hollered out loud to no one in particular.

This woman had been alive less than an hour ago, but now she was dead. Fury had his body tensing. He could not take his eyes off the woman's frozen features.

They had been too late. He shook his head at the broken sight of her body. *They didn't get there fast enough.*

James backed away from the bed and told one of the officers, "Call the ME. Get the forensics team out here. This will be a long night."

He ordered the rest of the officers, "We may not have been able to save her, but that bastard could still be nearby. I want every square inch of this place searched. Inside and out." Stepping back outside, he pointed to the surrounding woods, "There is a lot of ground to cover, and plenty of places for him to hide."

Over the course of the next several hours they took their time, doing their best not to destroy any evidence. They searched room by room inside. Outside, they gridded the area and searched intently.

As the morning sun rose, James noticed the police cars that lined the street. Uniforms had fanned out and were searching the nearby woods. But James knew they wouldn't find him. They had missed him.

The killer was screwing with them. The bastard actually wanted to jerk them around, because he could. Then it hit James, because the killer wanted to watch.

He commanded the officers, "You need to fan out more." His gaze drifted up to the trees, "Check high and low. He lured us here so he could watch us. He has to be here."

The killer wanted them to know he was in control of the game. A game in which he was the one having fun.

Only the killer didn't know James very well. James would show him in the end who the winner would be.

Chapter 72

Unable to go back to sleep after being woken so abruptly by James, Nicki walked downstairs to start her day. As she descended the stairs, a low, scraping noise came from underneath her. Nicki was still spooked from the phone call, and the noise seemed to grate on her nerves.

Perhaps a walk as the sun rose over the bayou would soothe her mood. She walked into the kitchen, put a pot of coffee on to brew, and went into the laundry room to change into something comfortable to walk in. When she returned to the kitchen, she poured her a cup of coffee and stepped onto the front porch to enjoy the early morning hour.

Nicki breathed in the crisp fall air. The leaves were beginning to shake free from their limbs. Some remained their original vibrant green, others were a beautiful yellow, while some were a fiery orange and some had already turned a bright red.

Fall was Nicki's favorite season. While most despised the cold, she welcomed it. At least in the cold weather you could bundle up more to stay warm, but when the heat of the summer strikes – it was almost impossible to keep cool.

Once the sun had risen, Nicki walked down the overgrown path in search of clues to a possible hidden shack, any place that these women might have been killed on the property. As she walked, she surveyed the area closely. She desperately wanted to find the bunker Mrs. Fontaine had talked about.

Besides, she had been so busy cleaning the house and getting settled that she hadn't taken the time to enjoy her enchanted surroundings.

With her mind swirling with all the "what ifs" and "whys", the fresh air helped calm her disjointed thoughts.

Leaves and broken branches crunched under her feet. She wasn't sure where this path would lead, but there was only one way to find out. Birds flew overhead as woodland creatures scurried about the further along the path she walked.

As the trees became denser, a chilling sensation snaked down her back. A *thump, thump, thump* resonated in the air. It reminded her of a slow heart beat, as if the trees were actually alive in this part of the woods.

She spun around, searching for any nearby creatures. She didn't see anything, but swore that someone was watching her. *Watching and waiting.*

"Is someone out there?"

A maniacal laugh echoed through the trees, followed by a garbled cry.

Crippled by fear, Nicki froze in place. When the sound came again, she ran back the way she had come as fast as her feet could take her. She didn't know what she was running from, or who, and she didn't care.

As she rushed down the overgrown trail, her feet tripped on an exposed root, sending her crashing to the ground. She fell hard, colliding with the damp earth.

The side of her cheek burned from where it hit the ground. She could feel the blood trickling down her face, but didn't take the time to look for other injuries. As she stood up, a realization washed over her. This had been the area where the ghost had stopped the other night.

But James had carefully inspected the area and didn't find anything – or so he said. Curious, Nicki felt for the exposed root she had tripped over. Only it wasn't an exposed root – it appeared to be a handle hidden in the leaves. Could this be the bunker Mrs. Fontaine had mentioned? But she was certain she had found the room they had used to kill the women. Or had she?

Eager to see what she had found, Nicki started brushing leaves out of the way, and slowly revealed the hidden door. Nicki had expected the door to be difficult to open, but instead it opened with complete ease.

Nicki took her phone out of her pocket and turned on the flashlight app. She directed it into the opening and was shocked to see a rickety ladder haphazardly attached to the door frame.

Nicki carefully made her way down the stairs, half afraid to discover what was hidden down there. Once her feet were on firm ground, she shined the makeshift flashlight around the room and shuddered in revulsion.

The deeper she moved into the room, she began to notice a foul odor. A sound from behind her caused her to stop and listen. There it was again, a footstep, then another. Someone else was in the room. She held her breath, waiting in fear.

It seemed as if an eternity passed with no further sounds. Then she heard laughter behind her and shined the flashlight towards the sound. She gasped when she saw the man in front of her, "What are you doing here?"

He reached for her and forcibly pushed her against the wall, "Don't you know that curiosity killed the cat? You couldn't simply move away when the ghosts appeared could you?" Sneering down at her, he continued, "Even after the ghosts warned you to leave, you stayed."

Letting her go, he began to pace the room, "I was glad when Jake suggested that I do the renovations. It allowed me the opportunity to keep a close watch on you, and to also make sure you never discovered the secrets of Rosewood." Sighing, "Only I didn't know that some of the journals were in the attic." He glared over at Nicki, "You see, I thought I had found all the journals when Mr. Fontaine had passed away, but I guess the old woman had found some too."

"You knew Mr. Fontaine?"

"Huh, I knew him better than his own wife. He was my mentor, my teacher. He was the only man who believed in me, saw something special in me." Looking down at the ground and shaking his head, "He made me who I am. If it hadn't been for him, I would have been miserable growing up. My mother cleaned house for Mrs. Fontaine, but would bring me with her when there was no school. At first, I had been so bored when I visited here. There was nothing for a scrawny boy who had no interest in the outdoors to do. That was until I met Mr. Fontaine. He taught me so much in the short time I knew him."

Nicki grimaced, "You mean he taught you how to kill. How not to have any respect for human life."

"No, he gave me the confidence I desperately needed at that tender age. He taught me there is more to life than just merely existing."

***

James looked at Veret, "I have a bad feeling. Something doesn't feel right."

Veret nodded his head in agreement, "We should have found some evidence that he had stayed around to watch us. But it is as if he killed her and left – not caring if we found a body."

James slammed a fist into the palm of his other hand, "Damn it! It was a diversion."

"A diversion?"

"To get me away from Nicki. She is out there by herself with me working a crime scene."

Without saying anything else, James took out his cell phone and called the dispatcher, "Get SWAT out to Rosewood Plantation. I have a nagging suspicion the killer is out there."

"Yes, sir, I will get them out there at once."

"Tell them not to leave any area untouched. There is a lot of property to search. Veret and I are headed that way now."

By the time James and Veret had arrived, no one had seen Nicki and Oscar was barking madly near the path where James had seen the ghost. Pointing to the dog, he asked Officer Thompson, "Did you send someone to check where the dog was barking?"

Shaking his head, "No, sir, we were focused mainly on the house. There really isn't any place to hide her in the open like that."

James took off at a run towards Oscar, "You fool! There are hidden tunnels all over the property. That is why I told you to search everywhere."

Without waiting for further instructions, Officer Thompson bellowed out, "Search the woods. Make sure you look for any evidence of a hidden bunker."

In unison, the men shouted out, "Yes, sir."

As James neared the area where Oscar was barking, he swore he heard people talking. He began searching for signs of a hidden trap door. When he saw the opening in the ground, he signaled for Officer Thompson, hand gesturing what he wanted done.

Officer Thompson dropped a smoke bomb down the shaft, and James hoped Nicki was down there and unharmed.

The men acted quickly and dropped down the shaft, hoping to catch whoever was down there by surprise. As the smoke cleared, James was shocked to find Darren Fontenot holding Nicki hostage with a knife to her throat.

He pointed his gun directly at Darren's head and stated, "It's over Darren. Let her go."

Waving the knife in the air, he exclaimed, "Don't take another step closer or I swear I'll kill her!"

"Put the knife down, now, Darren!"

"That's not going to happen and we both know it. You will have to shoot me first. The question is can you take the chance that I won't kill her before you get the chance to kill me?"

"I don't want to kill you. You are the only one who can identify the people you have murdered."

Darren pushed the knife close to Nicki's throat; a thin bead of blood drew from the contact with the tip of the knife. "Darren, you need to let her go now."

The time had come to act with no second thoughts or regret. Without hesitation, James fired his gun, hitting Darren directly in the right shoulder.

He dropped to the ground, howling in pain. Once free from his grip, Nicki ran to James.

James told Officer Thompson, "Tell the paramedics to get down here now."

As Officer Thompson helped Nicki out of the bunker, James took out his handcuffs and walked over to their killer, he made sure to kick the knife out of the way. "Darren Fontenot, you have the right to remain silent and refuse to answer questions. Anything you say may be used against you in a court of law. You have the right to consult an attorney before speaking to the police and to have an attorney present during questioning now or in the future. If you cannot afford an attorney, one will be appointed for you before any questioning if you wish. If you decide to answer questions now without an attorney present, you will still have the right to stop answering at any time until you talk to an attorney."

Epilogue

Madame Cormier, the traiteur that James had found to help cleanse the land, stated, "Merci cher. You are experiencing several phenomena here. Most houses are haunted by a spirit, but dere are some who haunt dis area dat can actually manifest itself into moving items. Dis take a lot of power, and den you have some who seem to be able to manipulate images as well. Dere is a very malevolent spirit here dat means to do harm."

Nicki agreed, "There was true evil that lived here. It committed awful acts of cruelty."

"Mais, dere are spirits here dat want to continue to torment the living and those dat are trapped here as well. Dere are some strong spirits here dat are want to hurt you, but some want to protect you and dis house, but I fear dat dey are failing."

Nicki asked, "Can you help us?"

Madame Cormier nodded her head, "I may, but des spirits will not be easy to make go away."

Using her long boney finger, she pointed to a clearing in the back, "We shall perform the ritual there." They followed Madame Cormier to the designated spot.

As she led the way, she sprinkled a powdery substance on the ground. She then took white candles and placed them in a wide circle, then lit each one.

She instructed the two, "Step inside the circle."

In the center of the circle, she placed an old wooden box, an antique looking wooden cross, and a statue of St. Gerard.

A loud moaning filled the night air. Nicki wasn't sure if it was from the wind or the ghosts inside voicing their complaints about the ritual to come.

As the moaning increased, the sound sent chills down Nicki's back.

She instructed Nicki and James, "No matter what dis spirits tries or does, do not talk to it."

Nicki nodded her head as Madame Cormier swayed side to side while chanting. The chanting became louder as the moaning grew louder. She stopped chanting and told her companions, "Mais, der will be a confrontation tonight. De evil spirits want to keep deir victims trapped here. Dese evil spirits are not ready to leave."

As Madame Cormier began her chanting once again, a gust of cold air blew through the area, carrying with it malevolence. A flash of lightning illuminated the night sky as a storm rolled in from the bayou.

Madame Cormier stated, "Lord, we pray dis night for de souls of dos taken by de evil dat dwells on dis land. Let us banish de evil away from dis land."

Madame Cormier instructed them, "Let us join hands while you pray with me." They all joined hands, "In de name of de father, I ask for de cleansing of dis land. I ask dat you call upon de angels to watch over dos who live here in dis house and protect dem from any evil dat may reside here."

Nicki felt the overpowering presence of evil all around her. A large black shadow began to rise from the ground. She gripped James's arm, "Please tell me that you see that?"

"Yes, I do."

Madame Cormier raised her finger to her lips commanding the two to be quiet as she continued her chanting. A horrible stench permeated the air, and Nicki gasped as more hazy apparitions materialized. Bones appeared from the darkness of the shadows and took form. Tendons connected to the bone that moved on their own accord as muscle and skin took on a human shape. The apparitions' skin glowed with a sickly green demonic color.

The apparitions moved towards the circle, reaching out to them. One apparition let out a deep groan and the night air filled with a putrid stench as black shadows reached out of the apparition's open mouth.

Madame Geroux instructed the apparitions, "I order ya to return to yar grave. Return to yar graves, all of ya."

The apparitions let out a loud howl that sounded guttural and unearthly. The largest of the apparitions reached for Nicki, "Not without her!" The lightning began to streak violently as thunder rumbled deep in the sky. It was as if they were trapped in an otherworldly place.

Madame Geroux stated once again, "NO! I send ya back to de dead. I order ya to release dese poor souls ya have trapped here. Back to yar graves ya debils."

A vortex of fire opened in the sky and reached out to capture the apparitions. The air was putrid with the stench of burning flesh. Lightning exploded through the sky. Hard, large drops of rain became torrents of water as the sins that occurred here were washed away.

A misty fog reached out from the center of the vortex and moved towards the remaining ghosts. A moment later, hundreds of wailing voices cried out as the mist took the form of a funnel cloud. Flesh torn souls of the damned morphed along the edges as their skeletal arms grabbed for those that remained. A mouth of razor sharp teeth appeared at the opening of the vortex and swallowed the apparitions whole.

As the evil spirits that haunted the grounds were banished, a magnificent light show took place. Tiny

orbs of light floated up into the sky, "Go my lovely
children. You may finally rest in peace. Dese men can
no longer hurt you."

As the vision in front of them vanished, a calming
peace fell across the land.